Harbor Village is a vivacious retirement paradise known for its beachy locale and active senior scene. But ever since murder moved in, the idyllic coastal community is becoming a little less lively . . .

With the first annual antique car show cruising into the tranquil bayside oasis of Fairhope, Alabama, there are bumpy roads ahead for Harbor Village director Cleo Mack. As an automobile-themed lecture series gets off to a rough start, she finds herself balancing one too many responsibilities— and dodging advances from a shady event sponsor. It's enough to make Cleo feel twice her age. But the festivities reach a real dead end when she discovers a body at the Royale Court shopping center . . .

When an innocent man lands in the hot seat for murder, Harbor Village residents look to Cleo to crack the case. Aided by an eclectic group of energetic seniors, Cleo races to identify the true culprit from a growing list of harmless Sunday drivers—before a killer revs up for another hit and run!

Books by GP Gardner

MURDER AT HARBOR VILLAGE
MURDER AT ROYALE COURT

Published by Kensington Publishing Corporation

Murder at Royale Court

GP Gardner

LYRICAL UNDERGROUND
Kensington Publishing Corp.
www.kensingtonbooks.com

LYRICAL UNDERGROUND BOOKS are published by

Kensington Publishing Corp.
119 West 40th Street
New York, NY 10018

All Kensington titles, imprints, and distributed lines are available at special quantity discounts for bulk purchases for sales promotion, premiums, fund-raising, educational, or institutional use.

Special book excerpts or customized printings can also be created to fit specific needs. For details, write or phone the office of the Kensington Sales Manager: Kensington Publishing Corp., 119 West 40th Street, New York, NY 10018. Attn. Sales Department. Phone: 1-800-221-2647.

Lyrical Underground and Lyrical Underground logo Reg. US Pat. & TM Off.

First Electronic Edition: June 2019
eISBN-13: 978-1-5161-0901-2
eISBN-10: 1-5161-0901-5

First Print Edition: June 2019
ISBN-13: 978-1-5161-0902-9
ISBN-10: 1-5161-0902-3

Printed in the United States of America

Acknowledgments

Many thanks to editor John Scognamiglio, to agent extraordinaire Dawn Dowdle, and to William Melvin "Bud" Gardner—first reader, plot advisor, and resident automobile expert.

Chapter 1

I had been at the office of the Henry George Utopian Tax Colony in downtown Fairhope for ninety minutes, and my head was spinning with terms like leases and flow-throughs and demonstration fees. All my questions were answered and I was ready to get out of there and back to the Harbor Village office a few blocks away, but Terry Wozniak, acting president of the Colony, as it was known, was still talking and I didn't want to be rude.

"You should take our class, Ms. Mack. Great opportunity to learn about our little town." Wozniak sat behind a battered desk, shirtsleeves rolled to the elbow, a gray wool vest unbuttoned. His short, dark hair looked freshly cut. "Henry George thought we would fail, you know. Never even came here."

He bent toward me as if he were about to tell a dirty secret. "Too busy running for mayor of New York. Beat out Teddy Roosevelt but still lost." He leaned back again and adopted a smug expression. "What would he think if he could see little Fairhope today?"

I leaped into the opening.

"That *is* an interesting question, isn't it?" I hopped out of my chair before he could start a new sentence, gave him a big smile, and stuck out my hand.

"I must let you get back to work, Mr. Wozniak. Thanks so much for taking time to explain the tax procedures to me."

Wozniak tried to delay me but I sensed freedom and kept moving. He followed me, a big man but moving nimbly through the tight space. We wound around the glass partition and into the sparsely furnished front office, where he stopped at the old beadboard counter.

"Always glad to meet newcomers, Cleo. Now, you'll want to take our class. You'll meet lots of Fairhopers. Eight weeks, one night a week. I can sign you up right now and save you a phone call later."

He rolled a pencil between big, fleshy fingers, just itching to add my name to the list on his clipboard.

I shook my head and smiled as I folded my notes and pushed them into the outside pocket of my shoulder bag.

I had no intention of signing up for any class. The history angle might be interesting but I was still learning a new job and, anyway, single tax theory? That was economics, I was pretty sure. Turn of the century economics at that, and I meant the nineteenth century.

"Let me think about it." Trying to be polite was my first mistake.

The second mistake came as I turned toward the exit. I paused to look at the photographs. The walls and partitions and windows were covered with big, bright posters announcing Fairhope's first Grand Concours, the antique automobile show only days away.

Behind me, Wozniak made a grunt of annoyance. "You sound like a student."

That didn't seem fair! "Well, I just learned about it a minute ago, Mr. Wozniak. I'll have to go back to the office and check my calendar."

He rested his elbows on the counter, leaned so that his face came close to mine, and gave me an evil grin. "And what day you gonna check, hon? What month?"

"Oh. Well." I smiled, embarrassed. "You're right. I did sound like some students I've known. Sorry. I'm going to check the day you're about to tell me."

He was an okay guy, in a curmudgeonly way, just bored to death here, all by himself. Eager to talk and flirt with anybody who stopped by, and today that happened to be me.

Curmudgeons were my specialty these days, but in my former life, as a professor of social work, I'd known lots of students, too. It'd been just four months since I took early retirement and moved to Fairhope, Alabama, the most charming little village on the Gulf Coast. I'd planned to enjoy life, travel a little, take up a new hobby like painting or quilting, maybe find a part-time job. But things had worked out differently and here I was, Executive Director of Harbor Village, a sprawling community for active retirees that happened to be built on property belonging to the Henry George Utopian Tax Colony, which explained why I came to be in this office in the first place. 'Twas the season for property tax, and the Harbor Village tax bill—or rent bill, as it happened—had arrived with a bang.

"Monday nights." Terry Wozniak plunked a bright yellow flyer on the linoleum countertop and slid it toward me. "Seven until nine, beginning the second week in January. The exam's in March."

"There's an *exam*?" *Ugh.* I picked up the flyer and glanced over the course description.

"Yes, ma'am, there's an exam. And you have to make at least seventy. Most people don't. Not the first time."

My heart sank with a crash. "Sounds fascinating." By which I meant a step above horrid. I tried not to grimace.

But Wozniak pressed on. "Why don't you invite me out to do a little talk for the Harbor Village folks? Like you're doing for this car show. You've got a lot of newcomers out there. Surely some of them want to learn about Fairhope history."

I was glad to hear something I could agree with. "Great idea. We try to have some type of educational program every week or two."

Visiting lecturers were a new project, one I got credit for even though Charlie Levine and the kitchen staff did all the work. I took another step toward the posters on the wall. One showed a gigantic black-and-gray automobile, with a uniformed driver standing beside the open-air chauffeur's compartment. I wondered if it would even fit into my garage. Another poster focused in on a voluptuous white fender with a single headlight recessed behind a curved chrome grille.

"Fifty-three Corvette." Wozniak was staring at the poster, a wistful expression on his face. "First year of production. Always wanted one of those."

He gave me a flirty smile, his dark eyes sparkling and busy. "I guess every kid did. What do you drive, Cleo?"

I laughed. "Nothing interesting, I'm afraid. A four-year-old Prius, inherited from my husband."

"He moved up to an SUV, I bet. Men don't like those little cars."

"I'm afraid he's no longer with us. The Prius was almost new when he died, and he liked it very much."

Wozniak smiled at me in a way that made me regret my candor.

"Sorry to hear that." He moved a step closer. "When does your lecture series begin?"

"Tomorrow night. Why don't you come?"

That wasn't going to help things. What was I thinking? I needed to get out of there without encouraging him. I tried again:

"Everyone's invited. And while you're there, you can talk with Mr. Levine about giving a lecture. His committee arranges for our speakers."

He took a business card off the counter and looked at it before passing it to me.

"You tell him we need to get it scheduled before the holidays. The class begins in January." He paused. "We could talk about it at dinner tomorrow, before the lecture. If you're not already spoken for." His brows went up in query.

I shook my head immediately. "No, not available. Sorry." Was that clear enough? I slid the card and the canary yellow flyer into my bag, alongside the notes from our discussion, and wiggled my fingers in good-bye. "I'd better run." That was the truth.

"I'll be looking for you in class," Wozniak called after me. "Come early, so you get a good seat."

A bell on the door tinkled as I let myself out. *Whew*!

The day was sunny, the temperature almost seventy, even though we were a week into November, and Fairhope Avenue was rumbling with activity. City crews had taken over the block, setting up barricades around their work trucks. One man in a cherry picker leaned out into the branches, coordinating with men on the ground to wrap strings of lights into a street tree. An engine whined as he maneuvered the bucket up and down.

On the ground nearby, a man in an orange jumpsuit took big red poinsettias off a truck and passed them to a coworker, who plunged them, pot and all, into the flower bed beside the crosswalk. Charming little towns didn't come easy.

I looked in each direction and jaywalked to the Prius, tossed my bag into the passenger seat, and drove down the hill for a quick peek at Mobile Bay before I headed back to the office. With the sun setting earlier now, I'd been missing my walks on the pier at sunset.

I circled around the fountain and rose garden and pulled into one of several vacant parking spaces. The bay was bright blue today, with just enough wind to set the surface sparkling in the midday sun. Lots of people were out walking, but there were no sailboats on the bay and no ships in the channel, so far as I could see. The bird condos looked forlorn with the purple martins gone south, but farther out, gulls and brown pelicans looked like lamp finials, standing atop every channel marker. The city of Mobile was just a pale bump on the horizon.

I sat there a couple of minutes, letting the serenity seep in the way it always did. Then I backed out and drove up the hill.

The town clock indicated lunchtime. I might've stopped at Andree's, my favorite of several little cafes and delis, but there was another bucket truck out front, bracketed by orange traffic cones, and the line of cars looking for a parking space wound back through the intersection. I drove on. If I went straight to the dining room at Harbor Village, I might still get some lunch.

A few more blocks and I turned onto Harbor Boulevard, its median dotted with flowers and palm trees. With the administration building looming ahead, I took in the pastel apartments, the five-globe lamps, and heard the gulls laughing in the parking lot. A soft glow of happiness spread over me as I swung into my assigned space in one of two community garages. From there it was a short walk back to the dining room, where Carla and Lizzie served just one meal a day, Monday through Friday. As I walked, I congratulated myself for coming here.

Charlie Levine's voice echoed down the hallway. I turned into the dining room and saw a dozen residents sitting around the long table.

"Most of these show cars are better than new," Levine droned, his back to the entrance. "Polished under the hood, slick leather upholstery. The judges go over them with white gloves, even use mirrors on poles to inspect the bottom side. Reg will tell us all about it."

Reg would be the visiting lecturer, I assumed. Nita Bergen, my first Fairhope friend, caught my eye and smiled. She sat beside Levine and across the table from her husband, the security-conscious naval officer who always sat facing the door.

"Cleo!" Jim boomed when he looked my way. "You're late!"

The Bergens were past eighty, Nita tiny and birdlike while Jim was well over six feet and rigidly erect. Both still had an abundance of silvery white hair, which Nita wore in a smooth, pageboy style. She indicated the vacant chair beside her and I nodded, walking on toward the steam table, greeting other diners along the way with smiles or comments or a pat on the back.

Dolly Webb was a retired mathematician from DC who'd known my husband Robert—technically, my *second* husband—professionally. That little connection, plus her friendship with the Bergens, had formed an immediate bond between us. At the moment, Dolly was boxing up the remains of her lunch.

I patted her shoulder and she gave me a little wave. "Delicious soup, Carla. What did you call it?"

"Minestrone." Carla, Harbor Village's young cook, ran a slotted spoon around the green beans and shook out some liquid before reaching for the empty plate I held out. Pendant lights above the steam table reflected off her small butterfly nose pin. "It's basically vegetable soup with pasta added."

She plopped the last of the green beans onto my plate, dropped the spoon into the pan, and passed it to Lizzie, her helper, who scurried off to the kitchen.

My neighbor Ann, in the seat next to Dolly, pushed back her chair, stood, and laid her knitting project on the seat. "Come sit down, Cleo. I'll scrape the food trays and serve you the dregs. Carla can get us drinks. Who else wants a refill?"

Carla took a quick inventory and darted away, and Ann continued the minestrone conversation while she served my plate. "It has to have some kind of beans. They give soup a nice body."

I'd never know. The soup pot was already empty. Lizzie unplugged it and took it to the kitchen.

"I could give you this." Dolly looked at me and tapped her to-go container. "I've eaten out of it, but I don't think I have any bugs."

I held up a hand and shook my head as I passed by.

Ann Slump, one of the few Fairhope natives living at Harbor Village, was small and thin and quick, with short, red hair. Not only did she teach knitting and crochet at our art and craft room, but she also went into town regularly to work at the knit shop she'd turned over to her niece a couple of years ago.

In addition to her other projects, Ann had adopted the Harbor Village dining room, earning the gratitude of all residents. It looked as if she might succeed in turning Carla into a good cook. I saw them together every day, hosting an endless kitchen party where they tested recipes, devised menus, and baked, always in a cloud of laughter. Even Jim Bergen dropped by occasionally, but only as a taster, I was sure.

I pulled out the chair beside Nita and she leaned toward me. "The dressing was delicious."

Jim, sitting across the table, scraped his chair back and got up clumsily. "You're right, Nita, it was. I think I'll get seconds."

"Too late," Ann crowed. "It's gone."

"Oh, divide it with Jim," I told her.

She grumbled, but when she delivered my plate she had a second one for him. There was cornbread dressing with gravy and roasted chicken, green beans, and a thick maroon sauce containing cranberries and little orange-colored wedges.

"The kumquats came from that bush by your porch," Ann told me. "Maybe you saw me picking them yesterday."

"No!" Nita barked abruptly.

I jumped and looked at her.

She sat rigid, staring across the table. "Jim! Cleo hasn't eaten. You had a big lunch already."

Jim gave her an embarrassed grin but hovered over the little plate and picked up his fork.

"It's fine," I assured Nita. "I'm not very hungry."

She shook her head, still glaring at her husband.

I whispered, "You're going to give him indigestion."

She relaxed and laughed a little. "Myself, maybe. Not Jim." She patted my knee. "Busy day?"

I nodded.

"You're not working Saturday, are you?"

I shook my head. "I hope not. Why?"

"I'll tell you later," she whispered back.

Mr. Levine was watching me, waiting to regain the attention of his audience. "I've been telling people about our speaker, Reg Handleman. We grew up together. He worked in automobiles his whole career. Still edits books and consults with museums, all over the country, I understand."

"And gives lectures," Jim said between bites.

I wasn't too excited about the upcoming automobile show, but I didn't broadcast the fact. I told Charlie, "I'm looking forward to his talks." And I was, in fact. I'd enjoyed every speaker we'd had so far. Maybe this one would measure up, too.

Carla handed me a glass of iced tea and waited until I took a sip. I nodded to her. Some days the unsweet got contaminated with sweet, but not today. Carla went back to work and I asked Charlie Levine, "The first lecture is tomorrow?"

He gave a series of slow nods. "Tuesday, Wednesday, and Thursday. Seven o'clock in the ballroom."

That reminded me of Terry Wozniak's business card. I got my bag off the chair back, fished the card out of the side pocket, and passed it down the table to Charlie. "He wants to give a talk about Fairhope history. Sometime soon."

Levine read the card, nodded, stuck it in his shirt pocket, and went back to cars. "This year's a trial run. The plan is to rival Amelia Island in five years and Pebble Beach in ten. Personally, I think we'll make it before that."

He was referring to the country's two big automobile shows.

It seemed that all of Fairhope was suddenly obsessed with automobiles, even the residents of Harbor Village. People were dragging out old photograph albums, telling stories about suicide doors, or describing how they'd learned to drive with a floor shift. Jim Bergen had made up a list

of every car he'd owned. Buicks and Cadillacs tied for first place. Charlie
Levine had told us how his father couldn't tell the front from the back
of Studebakers in the late forties. And inspired by all the car talk, Dolly
Webb had gone out and purchased a sporty little lime-green convertible.

"I've been at the Henry George Colony this morning," I said at the next
lull in conversation. "I see they're sponsoring the show."

Mr. Levine scowled, which made him look like Alfred Hitchcock.
"Along with the Grand Hotel and Airbus. And the Mercedes plant in
Tuscaloosa. Plus a few others I'm forgetting. This is a really big deal, you
know. Really big."

"Don't forget the polo club." Jim leaned back, his plate empty. "Out
there manicuring their grounds right now, I suppose."

"I never understood why everything has to be the biggest and best,"
Nita complained. "Why can't we have just a nice little car show, without
the shuttles and crowds and news helicopters? The polo ponies will
be scared silly."

Her husband laughed and shook his head.

Ann didn't share Nita's negativity, either. "Well, I, for one, can't wait.
They're expecting twenty thousand people, I hear. Imagine that. Twenty
thousand! Just think what that means to all our little businesses."

"My grandson's coming from California," Dolly said. "With a movie
crew for that TV man, what's his name?"

Jim was still shaking his head. "This show is not for our benefit,
people. It's a moneymaker. Tickets to get in, organizers and sponsors and
awards, entry fees for the cars. There's a banquet with prizes Saturday
night. Big bucks."

"They've hit up all the merchants for a silent auction." Ann was working
at her knitting again. She drew out a long strand of yarn. "But it's to benefit
the hospital, so I don't really mind."

"No," Nita relented. "I hope the weather's good."

I caught Carla's eye and gave her the yummy tummy signal about lunch.
She flashed a big smile.

The car show would be held at the polo field, but I had no idea where
that was. I asked.

"Near the pecan place." Mr. Levine gave a vague sweep with his big head.

"Two miles south on Ninety-Eight." Jim pointed with his fork toward
the highway that passed in front of Harbor Village. "But don't drive, Cleo.
You won't be able to park if you do. Use the shuttle service. Harbor Village
is one of the stops."

I'd forgotten about that.

"Does that mean our parking lots will be full all weekend?" Nita sighed.

"That's why we have a garage, honey. The parking lot won't affect us." Jim grinned at me and took a sip of coffee.

"Cleo?" Mr. Levine leaned around Nita. "I left you a message this morning. Is the guest suite available? Reggie can quote specs of any automobile you name, but he can't make a reservation. And now he expects *me* to do something."

Harbor Village kept a furnished two-bedroom apartment for visitors, usually family members of residents. It was available for a modest fee on a first-come basis but I didn't know its status for the week. I'd never even seen the suite, but it was near the front of the complex.

"I'll check on it when I get back to the office," I told him. "It's in one of the front buildings, right?"

"Where Stewart is working on the porches," Nita said. "They're going to be so nice."

"I think we're calling it One South now," Jim said. "First building, south side of the boulevard. Upstairs." Jim was always precise. I attributed it to his military training. "That numbering system is an improvement over nothing, but I still think bird names were better."

Nita smiled at me. We'd taken a poll to determine how Harbor Village buildings should be identified. Jim had campaigned hard but bird names lost out.

Mr. Levine was grumbling, too, and adjusting his collar. "Eloise thinks he should stay with us, but I'm not up to that. Anyway, the kids may come."

"Who is this fellow?" Dolly asked. "Our next speaker? Why does he need a place to stay? I thought he lived here."

"No, no," Mr. Levine grumbled some more. "I just told you, Dolly, he's Reg Handleman, an old classmate of mine. High school and college. We even worked at the same place for a while, but we lost touch. He was in engineering and I was in management, you know."

"And you invited him to visit us." I thought it was obvious.

"No." Levine had Wozniak's card out, looking at it again. "Invited himself, actually. Like this fellow."

"Automotive engineering? No wonder he knows details. He must've done well." Jim rubbed thumb and forefingers together in the universal money sign and looked at Levine for confirmation.

Levine nodded. "Oh, yes. Yes, we both did. Couldn't do better than Detroit, back in the day."

I drained the last of my tea and pushed my chair back. "You want to walk to the office with me now, Charlie? We'll see if the guest suite's available."

Levine shook his head. "Call me later. I'm going to have a little shut-eye right now." He rocked forward and back and rolled up onto his feet, grabbing the edge of the table to steady himself.

Carla was circling the table, unobtrusively removing coffee cups and saucers and the remaining dishes, then passing the stacks to Lizzie.

Jim signaled for her attention. "Charlie says the motels are full. What would you think about opening the dining room this weekend? Every restaurant south of I-10 will have a line."

She shook her head and took his plate and cup. "You know we're closed Saturday and Sunday." She headed for the kitchen and he called after her.

"That's what I'm saying, Carla. Maybe you should make an exception."

She glanced over her shoulder, gave him a sassy grin, and disappeared.

Charlie Levine had started for the exit. "I'll bet the yachts are already down at the hotel marina. Maybe I'll go have a look after my nap. Is Jay Leno really coming? He's a big car collector, you know." He looked at me.

I shrugged and stood, brushing crumbs off my black pants. "This is all new to me, Charlie."

"New to all of us," Nita muttered.

"Well, it won't be next year. Just imagine what it'll be like in ten years." Levine looked up, spread his hands apart, and announced in a loud voice, as if he were reading a banner, "The Grand Concours of Fairhope and Point Clear."

"I won't be here to see it." Nita's voice was saturated with finality. She caught my hand. "Cleo, do you have a minute?"

I perched back on the edge of my chair. Nita was still a pretty woman and took pains with her appearance. Today she was wearing nice trousers in a fluid, menswear fabric and a high-necked, bright blue sweater that matched her eyes.

She patted my arm. "I wanted to tell you, I'm keeping Ann's shop Saturday morning so she and her niece can go to a meeting. Would you like to go with me? It's a beautiful shop and you've never even seen it." Her voice sounded accusing.

I had knitted years ago but not recently. Ann and Nita wanted me to take it up again, and I'd promised I would as soon as I felt comfortable with my job. I hadn't quite reached that point yet, but a visit to the knit shop sounded like fun.

"I'd love to go."

"That's wonderful. Saturday's the main day of the car show, but you'll probably want to go Friday, before the crowds come. Or you can still go in the afternoon, if you really prefer Saturday. I told Ann we'll be at the shop by eight forty-five."

We agreed I'd pick her up at eight thirty Saturday and I moved to depart, but Carla intercepted me before I reached the door. She turned her back to block Jim's view and thrust a takeout box into my hands.

"Here's your dessert. He's had his already. And I didn't mean we *can't* prepare lunches this weekend. Not if you want us to."

I gave the box a gentle shake and heard something slide inside. "Sounds like pie."

She nodded but looked concerned. "We need to decide soon if we're going to do it. I have to get the order in by Wednesday."

I agreed. "We wanted to check out weekend demand, and this is a good opportunity. But let's think about it overnight."

Carla nodded, and I took my dessert and headed for the office.

Chapter 2

From the outside, the administration building at Harbor Village was a frothy confection of dormers and porches, with rocking chairs and ferns and red shutters gathered under a curvy black roof. It looked like a fairy tale come to life, but everyone called it the big house, which infuriated Nita.

"That sounds like a prison," she often complained.

The two upper floors held twenty-four rental apartments and I seldom went up there. The main floor was divided into three sections housing administrative functions and services. One end contained the physical therapy clinic, a barbershop/hair salon, our dining room and kitchen, and elevators.

The middle section was a big lobby with tile floors and a soaring ceiling, where a web of beams supported a chandelier that, turned on, was probably visible from the space station.

As I walked through the lobby, heading for the office, I glanced toward the back window wall. The vegetable and ornamental gardens were still green, thanks to our near tropical climate. A few people sat on benches in the sunshine, and a man with a little boy tossed food pellets into the koi pond.

I dodged around an easel displaying an announcement for the lecture series and shifted my attention to the rugs we'd just purchased to anchor the lobby's tables and couches. They provided spots of color and certainly softened the acoustics in the big space.

The third and smallest portion of the big house, accessed through a wide doorway, held a dozen or so offices, including mine. Outside of work hours, it was essential that this part of the building, holding personal and sensitive records, be secure. We used a metal gate for that purpose. It had fit in perfectly with the prison image until a month ago, when Stewart, our multi-talented, multi-tattooed handyman, fabricated a nine-foot giraffe to look down over the bars.

When I arrived after lunch, one of Nita's neighbors was standing near the gate, showing the giraffe to her grandchildren. Or maybe they were great-grands.

"They think we should have a contest to give him a name," the woman told me.

"And I know the best name." The little girl's voice was shrill. "Stilts!"

"Oh, good choice! And have you thought of a name?" I looked at the boy.

He frowned and stuck a finger up his nose.

"Let's give him time to think about it," I proposed. "But I do like the idea of a contest."

I had originally joined the Harbor Village staff as part-time Director of Resident Services, but Patti Snyder had assumed that position when I was named Executive Director. Patti still worked from the reception desk but was nowhere to be seen at the moment. Instead, a young man stood beside her desk. His back was turned toward me.

I saw him hook a finger into the drawer pull and open the top drawer. Then he glanced around and saw me.

"Can I help you?"

He leaned against the desk, crossing his arms and trying to bump the drawer closed with his hip.

"Naw, I'm just looking for Patti."

He was still a kid, twenty or so, tall and slim with a forelock of blond hair combed into a swirl. Thin lips, narrowed eyes, and a shadow of whiskers said wannabe tough guy. He gestured toward the still-open desk drawer.

"I was looking for some paper. To leave her a note."

"Of course," I said, with a smile I didn't feel. "Or I'll be glad to give her a message. What name shall I say?"

He shifted his weight and moved away. "Tell her Todd's looking for her. She'll know."

He slowed his pace when he reached the lobby and I gave a sigh as he sauntered out the main door. I hoped Patti wasn't involved with him. I'd liked her immediately, partly because she was so much like my daughter. They were the same age but Stephanie was married and had a two-year-old. Even as a kid, she'd been too lighthearted for a character like Todd. Maybe Patti would be, too. All that frivolity should have some advantages.

A note was propped against the vase of flowers on her desk. I bent closer to read it. *Be right back.* At the bottom was Patti's trademark, a smiley face with a squiggle of curls. I smiled back at it.

There was another curiosity on her desk, too. A flat piece of driftwood held three little ceramic turtles, sitting in a row.

I walked down the side hall, shoes clunking on the tile floor. The door to the conference room stood open, and cans of paint and a raft of painting equipment had materialized in the time I'd been out. That would be Stewart's next project, I supposed, when the screened porches were finished.

The next door was mine. Cleo Mack, the nameplate said, followed by a string of letters indicating my credentials. A second plaque identified me as Executive Director. This afternoon there was a third attachment, a note from Charlie Levine taped above the doorknob. I pulled it off and unlocked the door, and the blinking message light on the phone claimed my attention.

"Three new messages," robo-voice said when I pressed the button.

Two calls from Travis McKenzie and one from the daughter we shared. Maybe it was something genetic. I took out my cell phone and punched in Stephanie's number. There was a lot of chatter in the background when she answered.

"Hi, Mom. I'm teaching. Can I call you back later?"

"I'm returning your call."

"Oh, Patti answered my question. I should've told her there was no need for you to call. Let's talk tonight." She clicked off.

Stephanie, along with her son, Barry, were the lights of my life now that Robert was gone. She was part owner of a quilting shop in Birmingham and taught classes at this time of year. Right now, with the holidays approaching, the shop would be a madhouse of sewing students working overtime to complete table runners and handmade gifts. Stephanie had wanted me to move to Birmingham when I'd retired, and if I'd done that, I'd probably be in the class right now, stitching away. I shook off that image and felt like I'd avoided a small disaster.

Travis McKenzie, Harbor Village CEO and my ex-husband from long ago—Stephanie's father—had persuaded me to take the Fairhope job. His two phone calls were probably follow-ups from our earlier discussion about the invoice from Henry George Colony. I'd known nothing about it when he called, irritated and complaining, but I'd hung up and arranged an emergency meeting with Terry Wozniak. Maybe he'd called to apologize? Probably not. I got out my notes and glanced over them as I hit redial on the office phone.

After a few rings, Travis's assistant Yolanda answered at Houston headquarters.

"Harbor Health Services, Mr. McKenzie's office. Good afternoon, Cleo."

"Sorry to bother you," I told her. "I'm returning a call from Travis."

I'd gotten to know Yolanda on my two trips to Houston and liked her mellow, musical voice with its faint trace of England.

"He must have gone already, if he's switched his phone to me." She sounded cheery. Maybe because Travis was out of the office?

I was a little relieved myself, to miss him. "There's no rush. Just say I called."

"He's going to be away for a few days. I think you'll see him before I do."

So much for my feeling of relief. "He's coming here?"

"Well, eventually. Haven't you invited him to some event?"

Oh, crap! Travis is coming for the car show?

"This is Monday. The show doesn't begin until Friday." My voice sounded whiny, but Yolanda, the perfect professional, ignored it.

"I hope his visit wasn't supposed to be a surprise. You did know he's coming?"

I took a breath. "Not really. I didn't know he had any interest in old cars, I only mentioned it when he asked what's going on here."

Yolanda gave a little bubble of laughter. "Yes, that was it, an automobile exhibition." She switched to an amused, confidential tone. "He's following up on a hot tip from his investment advisor, I understand. But he's not going directly to Fairhope. He's visiting other facilities along the way. I'm sure he'll phone you later."

I was sure he would, too. I told Yolanda good-bye and hung up. Travis had been a big help when I first took this job, but that seemed only fair since it had all been his idea.

I looked around my desk and settled back into the routines of work. Numbers would never be my favorite part of any job, but I needed to do a little digging into the budget soon, in preparation for the new fiscal year. And there were sample decals to evaluate with security. We'd decided to order them for all the cars belonging to residents and staff, and there were lots of decisions: how large, what color, inside or outside adhesive.

I jotted a note to myself about opening the dining room for the weekend. I'd need to let Carla know about that right away.

But first, I decided, reading over Charlie Levine's note, I'd walk to the front of the complex and inspect the screening project Stewart was working on. And while there, I could take a look at the guest suite.

Patti was back at her desk when I walked out. She swiveled around with a surprised look on her face.

"Oh! I didn't know you were back."

Patti was tall and slender with a halo of shiny curls, and today she was wearing red glasses, little round ones that reminded me of John Lennon and matched her shark-bite tunic.

"Cute," I said. "They look good on you."

Everything did. She had a rainbow collection of eyeglasses and matched them to her outfits and nail polish like flavors of the day. Patti tilted her head, making her curls bounce, and batted her lashes.

"Stephanie called. Is she really thinking about moving down here? That would be so fun!"

"Stephanie? Moving? She's got a business to run in Birmingham. Why do you ask that?"

Patti shrugged. "I just wondered. She asked about Royale Court."

I drew a blank. "Which is...?"

"You know. That cute little shopping area Ann owns."

I shook my head. "Is that where the knit shop is? I guess I'm about to see it. Who handles reservations for the guest suite?"

"That would be *moi*." She placed spread fingers against her chest and I got a glimpse of barber pole nail polish before she opened a desk drawer and pulled out a red notebook. "When do you want it?"

"Right now, if it's available. For the rest of the week."

She showed me a calendar that was mostly empty. "One night at the beginning of the month and now nothing until Thanksgiving week," she griped. "Then everybody wants it, naturally. And December is totally booked. Shall I put your name down?"

"No, Mr. Levine wants it for the speaker. What's his name?"

She reached for a flyer on the corner of her desk and read aloud. "Reg Handleman. From Indiana but I don't have the address. Are we comping him?"

"I guess. We're giving him an honorarium but it's a pittance. Let's charge both to the publicity account. Travis wants us to make a big splash in the community and this can be a start."

Community visibility was another bone he'd picked with me on the phone, along with my ignorance of the property tax bill. I still smarted when I thought about it. I looked at Patti.

"What do you think about a contest to name the giraffe? Might be fun, get the grandkids involved. Great-grands, I mean. And these car lectures ought to draw some community people in. Have you sent out notices?"

She nodded. "I fired the hot blast." That was Patti-speak for contacting all the social media, radio, TV, and newspapers. She would've hung posters in the usual spots and distributed flyers to the Chamber and the Welcome Center, too, as well as to all Harbor Village residents.

"I'll do a follow-up before I leave today and email our residents again in the morning."

I thanked her, even if I wasn't optimistic about attendance. "We'll see if anybody wants to hear from a car expert. Are you coming?"

She wrinkled her nose and gave her curls a shake.

I told her where I was heading and turned to go.

"Can I go, too? Emily can answer the phone for a few minutes."

She buzzed the business manager and told her how long we'd be out, then hopped up and rolled her chair under the desk.

"You had a visitor earlier," I said as we walked to the door. "Todd. He said you'd know."

"Todd Barnwell? What did he want?"

I shook my head. "Apparently something out of your desk. I saw him open a drawer."

She looked startled and glanced back over her shoulder. "Do you think I should lock up while we're out?"

"I think you should always lock up when you're not here."

It was a topic we'd covered before, when Stewart put up the iron security gate. Somehow, making security fun had removed any awareness of its true purpose.

Patti grimaced but went back, took a set of keys from her purse in the bottom drawer, and locked the desk. Then we headed for the exit again.

"He said he was looking for paper to leave you a note."

"I don't think he'd steal anything." She giggled. "Not since he just inherited four million dollars."

I raised my eyebrows. "Four million? And I thought he looked like a vagrant." I led the way through the automatic door.

"Well, he tries. Stewart and I saw him Saturday night. He's staying at his grandfather's house on Andrews Street, back behind you, and hanging out with the bikers at L'Etoile."

Its full name was L'Etoile Bistro and it was located on Fairhope Avenue, at the center of town. I drove right past it whenever I went to the bay, but it was a nightspot and I was a lunch customer.

We crossed the driveway and took the wide sidewalk that ran behind my apartment building.

"You and Stewart go to a biker bar?"

"Bike as in bicycles. Most of them are health nuts. A bunch of trustifarians trying to figure out how to get their hands on money their grandparents

left. I should have such problems." She giggled again. "You don't think
Stewart's too old for me, do you?"

I looked into my lovely little screened porch at the corner of the apartment
building and wished I were there on the wicker lounge, dozing in the
sunshine with a cup of vanilla chai steaming on the corner table. I looked
at the heron lamp with its square shade and thought about the pelicans at
the pier. Was it possible to find a pelican finial?

"Do you?" Patti demanded when I didn't answer promptly.
"Think he's too old?"

I grinned. "I don't know how old Stewart is."

Too mature to be interested, I would've thought, but people surprised
me all the time.

From a resident's perspective, Harbor Village consisted of sixty-some
privately owned houses and condos, plus two hundred and twenty-four
rental apartments offering an array of prices and luxury features, and an
Assisted Living program that could accommodate twenty-six individuals.

Prior to my arrival some of the apartments had fallen into disrepair
and remained vacant. Others had been rented to inappropriate tenants
who didn't fit the community profile. But we had a good team now, and
everyone was focused on correcting those problems. Stewart and his crew
were renovating vacant apartments, our new rental agent had several
prospective tenants lined up, and Patti and the other staff treated every
resident like a favorite aunt or uncle or grandparent. No doubt this was
the way back to profitability, but it wasn't going to happen overnight, no
matter how hard Travis pushed me.

It had been Patti's idea to turn the second-floor walkways into nicely
furnished screened porches, one running down each wing of the L-shaped
building, tying upstairs apartments together with a shared outdoor living
area. The building known as One South had the highest vacancy rate and
we'd selected it as our test case.

We waved to Drew, who worked from the grassy lawn, passing batten
strips up to Stewart, who reached down from the top of a ladder. Patti and
I stopped to watch for a minute. The new screen panels were in place and
Stewart was using a battery-powered drill, attaching thin wooden strips
to cover their edges.

"Look at that," Patti whispered.

I looked at her instead. "I assume you mean the screens."

She giggled.

Stewart saw us, finally, and took a few screws out of his mouth before
calling down, "Hello there. Y'all come on up."

"We'll use the elevator." I turned toward it.

He came clanking down the ladder and followed us. "Patti's got some furniture to arrange."

Patti squealed and pivoted, curls bouncing, to look in all directions. "It came? *Stu-wart*! Why didn't you call me? Where is it?"

Stewart was a wiry man in his early thirties, wearing a wide-brimmed hat to work in the sun. Tattoos peeked out under his rolled-up sleeves. He jerked a thumb upward. "The driver helped us get everything upstairs. I didn't figure you wanted to get involved with the lifting."

Patti gave him a starstruck look as we entered the little lobby and took the world's slowest elevator to the second floor. We stepped out and I saw the light-filtering effect of the screens for the first time.

"It's dark!"

"Just think how much cooler it'll be next summer," Stewart said confidently. "No sun, no heat."

I took a closer look. "I guess it's a good trade-off. Now that my eyes are adjusting."

"Now, remember." Patti was looking up at square, recessed lights, centered flush with the ceiling, one in front of each apartment door. "These lights will be gone and we'll have some bling instead."

Stewart put hands on hips and looked up, frowning. "I still prefer wicker. It's outside, Patti."

They quibbled. Maybe it was a new form of courtship.

Rattan love seats and chairs and tables were stacked against the apartment wall, legs wound with protective strips of brown paper for shipping. A little farther down the porch, I noticed a stack of big boxes.

Stewart whipped a utility knife out of his tool belt. "Better let me take that paper off the legs."

"What's in the boxes?" Patti asked. "Open them first."

He stabbed through the tape and slit the flaps loose. The first box was packed tight with colorful cushions that plumped up as Patti pulled them out.

She didn't need help from me. "Where's the guest suite?"

"That way," they answered simultaneously, pointing toward the other wing of the building.

"The last unit," Stewart said. "Watch your step around there."

I walked back past the elevator. The opposite walkway was also newly screened and held another stack of furniture, plus several rolls of carpet in blue and green patterns.

I picked my way through the congestion, stopped at the last door, and knocked before using my passkey.

The guest suite was a furnished two-bedroom, two-bath apartment, clean but totally without charm. The walls weren't quite yellow and the carpet not quite white. Mini blinds on all the windows were angled downward, casting patches of sunlight across the floor. I readjusted the blinds to throw light to the white ceiling, but faded streaks remained on the carpet, probably from years ago.

I did a quick walk-through, checking everything.

Yellow-and-white striped kitchen towels lay on the counter, and the holder had half a roll of paper towels. There was yellow Fiestaware in the upper cabinets and a starter set of cookware and some standard cleaning supplies in the base cabinets. The fridge was empty but cold. In the bathrooms, pairs of white towels were laid out beside the sinks, topped with a new bar of soap still in its box. The beds had inexpensive floral spreads.

The only eye-catcher in the whole place was a paperback book of Sudoku puzzles on the nightstand. I was addicted to Sudoku in the difficult versions, but this was a drugstore purchase, easy to solve and printed on heavy newsprint. I picked it up and flipped through. Someone had worked a couple of puzzles at the front and started a few more that weren't finished. Most of the book was unused.

"There you are!" Patti flounced into the bedroom. "Did you see the carpets for the porches? We got two big ones for each side and some little round ones, to go with the round tables. People are going to be eating outside all the time. I can't wait to get everything set up. What've you got?" She looked over my shoulder.

"Sudoku. Ever try it?"

"No. Where're the clues?"

I folded the book and ripped out the used pages, then dropped the book back beside the lamp. "There aren't any clues. You use the numbers one through nine. No repeats in rows or columns or inside the nine small boxes."

"That sounds simple enough." She gestured to the soiled pages. "There's a trash can downstairs by the elevator. Did you notice how dreary this place is? I thought maybe you could put something in the new budget for a little makeover next year. Think about it, okay? I came to tell you not to wait for me. I'm going to stay here and put the new furniture in place, while Stewart can help. Come back later and see it set up. It's going to be awesome."

"Okay." I checked the thermostat before locking the door.

I called Mr. Levine when I got back to the office and told him the guest suite was ready for Reg Handleman. "Patti will have the key."

"He just called Eloise. Says he'll be here by lunchtime tomorrow. I guess we have to feed him, too."

"I'm looking forward to meeting him, Charlie. I know you two will have a nice visit."

"Hmph."

Apparently, Emily had gotten involved in some project and forgotten she was supposed to be filling in for Patti. The phone kept interrupting my efforts to look up costs and assess the financial side of opening the dining room for the weekend.

It was always hard to predict how many residents would eat there on any given day. People had visitors and appointments and travels. Adding in the car show confounded things more than usual—some people would want to hit the local restaurants in spite of crowds. In fact, waiting in lines might be part of the fun.

And even if the numbers were the same as on a normal weekday, with the additional staff costs, we'd do well to break even. But there was another important factor. Change was good at a retirement community. Opening the dining room on Saturday and Sunday was a minor thing, but it brought a bit of excitement to Harbor Village, and that was always valuable.

I tried to call Carla to give her the go-ahead, but no one answered in the kitchen. When I looked at the time, I understood. Emily and Carla had left long ago. I got my purse, turned off the lights, locked the door, and saw Patti swooping down the hall.

"Can you come see it now? It's gorgeous! Beautiful! If I say so myself." She spun about in a circle, arms angled out like a ballerina taking a bow. "Everyone's so excited. Now the first floor wants theirs done, too. But I think it should be a little different, don't you? Not cookie-cutter."

Another hour passed before I finally got to my apartment. I had admired Patti's arrangements of furniture, rugs, and potted plants, and talked to all the residents who'd come out to see the changes. People from other buildings walked over as the word spread, and the poor little elevator got quite a workout. Finally I took the stairs and walked home.

Tinkerbelle was waiting inside my door.

"Did you think you'd been abandoned again?" I scratched her chin and rubbed both ears. "Have you been sleeping on the bed all day?"

She looked smug and rubbed against my legs, leaving a swath of calico fur on black fabric. I went to the bedroom closet for a sticky roller and cleaned the pants before I hung them in the section reserved for clothing that got another wearing before it was laundered. I put on jeans, a long-sleeved sweater, and the suede moccasins I wore indoors. There was leftover vegetarian chili in the fridge and I stuck it in the microwave and washed up for dinner.

The phone rang as soon as I put my bowl on the table. It was Travis, and he was in a talkative mood. "Sorry it's so late. You wanted me?"

"You left me a couple of messages. And I've learned all about the Henry George Utopian Tax Colony."

"Shoot," he said.

Papers rustled. He was probably multitasking. For some reason it irritated me but I gave him a rundown of the facts I'd collected.

"The Henry George Utopian Tax Colony is a nineteenth-century relic and Harbor Village is built on property that belongs to it. We pay an annual rental fee, which is what the current invoice covers, and they pay the property tax. The bill is high because we pay for all the houses and condos, not just the apartments. And we recover the costs through rents and monthly fees."

"Boy, Alabama's got some weird ideas."

"No argument there, but the Colony follows Henry George principles and he lived in New York. Never even came here."

"Really? Tell me more."

"Don't tempt me. I listened to ninety minutes of economic theory and now they expect me to take a class." I relayed a few details I'd gotten from Terry Wozniak and worked my way around to the Harbor Village perspective again.

"The Colony's rental rates didn't go up this year, so if the association fees were properly set last year, they should still be okay. I'll check that when I can, but I didn't have a chance today. The Colony also collects a demonstration fee and uses it to benefit Fairhope. It amounts to a lot of money, in the aggregate, but it shows what good government can accomplish. The Colony gave all that waterfront property to the city, plus parks and sidewalks. They support the projects that make the town so attractive."

I heard the sneer in his voice. "Sounds like a cross between Santa Claus and nineteenth-century socialism."

"You're showing your age, Travis. Socialism's not a bad word now. The Colony gives the schools some much-needed funds. It's a sponsor for this car show we're about to have."

"Speaking of which, I think I'll come. Save me a ticket for the Saturday night banquet. Better make it two tickets. I may bring a friend."

I didn't have any tickets for Saturday night and didn't know where to get them.

"I'll try." I transported back twenty-five years and remembered one of the reasons why I'd become the *ex*-Mrs. McKenzie. "It may be sold out already, from what I hear."

"Didn't you reserve a table for Harbor Village? Jeez, Cleo."

I ended the call ASAP and went back to the kitchen, where I set the chili to reheat. Where was I going to get banquet tickets at this late date? Nita might have an idea, but she'd be in bed by now. And Riley Meddors, another of my go-to guys, was still out of town. I supposed I'd be visiting Terry Wozniak again in the morning.

I watched CNN while I ate and then cleaned up the kitchen.

Stephanie called right after I finished my shower but sounded as tired as I was, so we didn't talk long. I forgot to ask her why she wanted to know about the courtyard in town.

When I got in bed, I tried to work a Sudoku. It went hopelessly wrong right away, and instead of erasing and starting over, I turned the light off and fell asleep immediately.

Chapter 3

On Tuesday I went to the gym early. The usual four men were there and I kidded them about wanting me to leave so they could switch the TV back to FOX. Not that it was a joke.

I waved at Dolly, just leaving the pool when I walked back to my apartment for a quick breakfast, a piece of toast and some fruit. Then I changed into one of the dozen pairs of black pants in my closet, put on a tan sweater set and what Stephanie called an "important" necklace, and walked to the office. It was early and still quiet there and I got some budget work done before other people started showing up.

At nine I called the Colony office and talked to a nice woman who said she'd check on a table and call me back when she learned more.

When I walked to the dining room later for a cup of coffee, Carla came out to sit with me for a minute. We talked about weekend lunches.

She was excited about the idea and already had plans. "I thought we'd do sandwiches and a salad for lunch on Saturday. Maybe soup if the weather's not too warm."

"Sounds good."

"And on Sunday a chicken and rice casserole with a nice salad and another vegetable. Do you like glazed acorn squash? If we do that, everything's cooked in the oven. What do you think?"

Carla's casseroles were so popular that she made them up for residents to cook at home. I approved all her plans for the weekend and offered to get residents to sign up if they wanted meals on the extra days.

Carla nodded. "But whatever the number, I'll prepare for a few extra, just in case. People always forget to put their names on the list."

"Yes. I'll try to do better," I promised.

I took my coffee and went by the rental agent's office, thinking I'd say hi to Wilma. I hadn't seen her in a couple of days, but like the invisible man, she wasn't there again. I had been back in my office maybe ten minutes when Patti burst in, closed the door, and plastered her back against it.

"Oh my god! Did you see that man?"

Her eyes were wide with horror or fear or another of her dramatic emotions, but a little tingle of alarm shot through me.

"Who? What's wrong?"

She darted across the office and threw herself into a chair in front of my desk, talking so rapidly she was gasping. I could barely understand her and the hair on my neck prickled.

"Remember that program about Neanderthals on *National Geographic*? The one that said they interbred with humans? That's all I could think about."

I was halfway to the door by this point. "Where is he?"

"Gone. Did you see it? That's exactly what he looks like. Great big eyes, all scary and serious and boring right into me. And big, shaggy brows. Eww!" She shivered convulsively.

I was alarmed and grabbed her shoulder. "Patti, who are we talking about? Did he touch you?"

"Oh, no. *No!*" She was almost shouting. "I would've *died*, right there. It wasn't—he's the most—the most *intense* person I've ever seen."

"Do you know who he was?"

She half collapsed against the chair but calmed down and looked at me like I was dense. "The speaker, Cleo. Reg Handleman! Oh my god!" She flopped again, rubbed her arms, and shivered.

I couldn't help it; I fell into the chair beside her, laughing with relief. "Forgive me." I stifled a giggle. "I thought you'd been attacked."

"That's *exactly* how I felt! Attacked! Just wait until you see him."

"You gave him the key to the guest suite?"

Her shoulders slumped. "He asked about the gym, too. How long is he staying, all week? Do I have any vacation days left?" Her lower lip actually trembled.

I patted her arm. "Patti, we can't help how we look."

"Oh, Cleo." She gave me a limp smile and a shrug but thumped the desktop with her palm. "If he comes back, you're dealing with him."

An hour later, Patti insisted we go into town for lunch. It was something we did occasionally, and she didn't admit that this time was anything out of the ordinary, but I was pretty sure she was avoiding the dining room and another encounter with our visitor.

We went early, parked in front of Andree's, and walked to the Colony office so I could follow up on getting a table for the car show banquet. Patti window-shopped along the way and went into the art gallery to pet the cat.

"We're calling it a gala," the Colony office manager told me, "not a banquet. Supposed to sound more festive."

"Is there a difference?"

She laughed and nodded. "About a hundred dollars a ticket. Galas are expensive."

Local supporters had signed up for tables a year ago, but I'd given her a sob story about being in town only three months. "Our CEO wants to come from Houston."

She was writing up an invoice for an astonishing sum of money. "We can always add another table, even if we have to pack people in." She warned me it wouldn't be the best seats in the house. "Those were gone months ago."

On the walk back to Andree's, we met Mary Montgomery, the Fairhope police officer who was recently promoted to lieutenant.

"Come have lunch with us," I invited her.

Mary was six feet tall and always made me think of a pumpkin with long, skinny legs, but she was tough. She'd been difficult to get to know but we'd lunched together a couple of times and always found something to talk about. I thought she probably didn't have many friends. Maybe that was a hazard of the cop's job?

Mary looked at the menu posted outside Andree's. "What do they have, little froufrou salads?" Turned out, she meant that was what she wanted. There were several to choose among and Patti and I recommended our favorites.

"I need to lose a few pounds before the holidays." She tugged at her jacket. "Too much desk work now that I've moved up in the world."

Patti ordered a hummus-and-veggie wrap, and Mary and I chose froufrou salads with tart apple slices, cranberries, candied pecans, and feta.

"Are you working the car show this weekend?" I asked her as we ate.

She speared a slice of apple. "Yeah. Everybody works this weekend. Are you going?"

"No way," Patti answered immediately. "I don't want anything to do with the car show if that man's involved."

"Who?" Mary Montgomery squinted.

I told her about Patti's fright and Montgomery was uncharacteristically sympathetic.

"Women should pay attention to their intuitions. Your subconscious can keep you out of a whole lotta trouble." She looked at me. "Don't you agree?"

"We're in Fairhope." I picked up a glazed pecan with my fingers. "Probably the safest place in the state."

Mary shook her head and lowered her voice. "You'd be surprised how much stuff goes on here. You don't hear about it because it might scare the tourists away, but people aren't nearly careful enough."

I wasn't convinced. "This is a professional man who's here to give a series of lectures."

She gestured with a wheat cracker. "Well, keep an eye on him until you know him better."

Patti gave me an *I-told-you-so* smirk and seemed much more confident with Montgomery on her side. Travis called while we were eating and I went out to the sidewalk to avoid disturbing others.

"Any luck on the banquet tickets?"

"The table's near the kitchen and you may need opera glasses to see the speakers, but it's all arranged." I didn't mention the cost.

"Are you playing Mexican Trains Friday night?"

"Of course. Every Friday."

"You wouldn't want to skip it and have dinner with me?"

I chuckled. "Sorry. They count on me." I dodged a baby stroller coming out of Andree's.

"Then I'll ask Jim."

The domino game was always at Jim and Nita's apartment, and while Jim never played, he was always on hand for the sandwiches. I didn't think he'd abandon us for dinner with Travis, but I didn't say so.

"What time's the lecture tomorrow? And what's his topic?"

I told Travis the time but didn't know the topic. "Something about old cars. The first one's tonight. Maybe I'll know more after it."

The afternoon passed quickly once we got back to the office. I got a lot of work done and went home soon after five. I brushed the cat and scooped the litter box, walked garbage to the containers beside the garage, then took a hot shower and shampooed my hair. While a thin slice of cheddar melted on a piece of bread, I ran the vacuum over the carpet and Tinkerbelle's favorite cat nests. Then I had to eat fast to make it to the ballroom before the lecture began. As I locked my apartment, I was hoping attendance wouldn't be embarrassingly low. I'd hate to discourage Charlie Levine and his committee.

But I rounded the end of the garage and saw the parking lot full, with more people walking from the lot at the opposite end of the building, near the swimming pool. And the ballroom, when I got there, was already packed, with Harbor Village residents accounting for only about half the crowd.

Carla dashed by wearing a long skirt and a flustered expression.

"I had no idea there'd be so many people. We don't have enough cookies or punch. Lizzie's gone for soda and Ann's defrosting all the pastries in the freezer."

"I'm bringing chairs out of the lobby." Stewart passed by with a wicker chair under each arm. "We'll open the garden doors and let people sit out there if we have to."

I went into the ballroom and looked around at a sea of humanity.

Reg Handleman was easy to spot. He was at the front, surrounded by people, and didn't look nearly so intimidating as I had imagined from Patti's description. He'd probably been six feet tall at his prime but he had a bit of a stoop now. His hair was dark and long, worn in sort of a Tarzan cut, and his brows were shaggy with deep creases between them. I slipped between two men and introduced myself.

When Handleman turned his full attention to me, I realized what had affected Patti so deeply. His eyes were dark blue and absolutely riveting. A natural hypnotist. Instead of shaking hands, he took my hand between his. Would he bend over and kiss it?

"Thank you, my dear. Charlie says you're the one who found me a roost."

"I'm glad the guest suite was available." I smiled and pulled my hand back. "And I'm looking forward to your talks."

"So am I," a voice close beside me said. It was Terry Wozniak from the Colony office.

"Hello, Cleo." He clapped his hand down on my shoulder and gave me a familiar, one-armed hug, like we were old friends who hadn't seen each other in a while. "Is this our speaker?" He stuck out his right hand and locked into a vigorous shake with Reg Handleman.

I turned away as Charlie Levine tapped on a microphone, signaling for the crowd to be seated. There was an empty spot in a row of wicker chairs Stewart had placed along the back wall, and I headed for it.

Usually, when the lights went off for a slideshow, Harbor Village residents fell asleep. Not with Reg Handleman. He went right into his performance, flashing slides rapidly and getting the audience involved in a guessing game. He even seemed to keep score in a rough way and encouraged a rivalry among a few men who shouted out the names of cars or early automobile makers or mechanical milestones like electric starters and automatic transmissions.

"Windshield wipers!" the man beside me shouted.

The crowd was laughing as pictures flashed onto the big screen, another of our recent acquisitions. It rolled down at the touch of a button.

Handleman pointed toward the voice that was quickest to give the answer he wanted.

"That's three for you." He pointed. "This side of the room is falling behind now."

Finally, the slideshow was over and the lights came on. He ran through a quick review of what we'd seen.

"There's a common belief that Henry Ford invented the assembly line, but that's wrong. His contribution was setting the line in motion, bringing the car to the parts. And to keep the line moving, those parts had to be standardized, avoiding the common but expensive practice of custom fitting. Now, who knows why Model Ts were black?"

"Paint!" Terry Wozniak shouted.

Handleman pointed to him with a flourish. "What about it?"

"Quick drying!"

"Right! Black paint dried faster, so cars could move faster through the painting room. Okay, what year did the Model A appear?"

The answer came from everywhere. "Nineteen twenty-eight!"

"And who was the stylist?"

"Edsel!" people shouted.

"Edsel Ford, Henry's son. Remember that, because he never gets the credit he deserves. And now that we've got all that straight, I want to tell you some big events that preceded Ford." He looked at his watch. "But I think we'll take a little break first. Ten minutes, how about that."

"How about refreshments?" Jim Bergen called out.

Reg glanced around the ballroom. "Refreshments? Okay. Help yourselves, but we'll start again in ten minutes. Take your time—make it twelve, since there's a crowd."

People rushed toward the refreshment table, to the bathrooms, or to Reg Handleman's side.

Nita appeared beside me, wearing a frown. She put a hand on my arm and I bent down to hear her. "I've got bad news, Cleo. Ann's meeting was changed to Thursday morning. I don't suppose you can go then."

I looked around the ballroom and thought about three nights of lectures, plus a Saturday night banquet.

"Yes, I think I can, if you still want me. I need to get away from here occasionally."

She beamed. "That's wonderful. I know you're working too hard. I've been so worried you'll burn out. Shall we say eight thirty? And have you heard from Riley?"

"No. And I've missed him. Is he back?"

She shook her head and a little crease appeared between her brows. "I thought he was coming for the lectures. I hope everything's okay. I should've called him but I didn't want to intrude on his family time. And it's too late to call tonight."

I got out my phone to change the reminder for our trip to the yarn shop. "I'll pick you up Thursday morning, eight thirty, at your apartment, right? Did you try the punch?"

* * * *

The next day Ivy, the nurse who ran the Assisted Living program, called to ask if we could have a working lunch. "I want your thoughts about several little things. Maybe Patti can come, too? We're going to need her help with a resident coming out of the hospital."

I told Patti. "We can eat in the dining room or go to the Assisted Living dining room and avoid Reg Handleman."

She put her hands over her ears. "Don't even say his name."

The turtles were lined up on her desk again, but today there were only two. "What's the deal with the turtles?"

Patti shook her head. "Turtles are psychic, you know."

"O-kay," I drew the word out. No point in eliciting TMI.

My neighbor Ann Slump came rushing out of the main dining room as Patti and I walked toward the exit. "We're making extra cookies and lemon bars this afternoon, so we'll have plenty for tonight and tomorrow. And we're restocking the freezer, too."

I hugged her. "Thank you for helping, Ann. I'm looking forward to seeing your shop tomorrow."

She leaned against the handrail that ran along both sides of the main hallway. "I appreciate it so much. Prissy and I are meeting with the Grand Hotel people about a knitting retreat in February. Thirty people and three days. It's the first time we've done anything like that, and I'm already a wreck, just thinking about it. But it's all small potatoes to the hotel people."

Patti and I went down the ramp beside the PT department and walked in the middle of the street, talking about publicity for the lectures and the upcoming weekend lunches. We passed the recycling shed and the maintenance barn. Assisted Living was a single-level, yellow building dripping with white gingerbread trim and an open porch across the front.

I always enjoyed meals with the Assisted Living residents. They had their own cook, got three meals a day, seven days a week, and the food was reliably good. The staff was funny and affectionate, too, so it was like eating with a big, happy family.

The four kittens they'd adopted in the summer were half grown by November but still doted on by the residents. Patti and I stopped in the sitting room to pet them before we followed the crowd to the dining room.

While we ate, Ivy told us what was going on in the program. I approved her plans, giving myself a mental pat on the back for hiring her.

And Patti promised to give a little extra attention to Mr. Hocutt until his wife got home from the hospital. "I'll drive him over there later and take her a little flower."

Travis called after lunch. "I'm leaving Tuscaloosa. Should be there by seven. Are you free for breakfast in the morning? I thought I'd ask if Stephanie and Barry want to ride down with me. I assume you'd like a couple of houseguests." Travis always stayed at the motel a few blocks away.

"Sure." I answered before I thought what day it was. "No, I can't do breakfast. The houseguests are fine, but I've got an early appointment in town."

"Then let's have lunch. Somewhere nice. We can go over your budget."

I agreed, knowing we wouldn't get much work done with Barry along.

Twenty minutes later, Stephanie called, complaining about her father. "He doesn't realize I've got responsibilities. Barry got up with the sniffles and I'm snowed under at the shop." She wasn't coming.

I got some real work done in the afternoon. I looked over applications for CNA positions—certified nursing assistants—for Assisted Living and passed several options along to Ivy. Stewart stopped by the office and said he preferred to wait about finding an additional helper for maintenance and grounds. With grass-cutting season over, he could be picky and find just the right person. "We're in people's private space. And old folks are so trusting."

I liked Stewart.

The community gardens group had sent a thank-you for Harbor Village's cooperation with their program and wondered if they might increase the number of raised beds behind the big house next year. I thought it was a great idea and called the number they'd listed. We talked through the details and set the project into motion.

Later, I glanced over the latest financial report from Emily, our business manager. The cost of electricity was up from the previous year, and there were all the additional costs of Patti's porch furnishings, a project I hoped would pay for itself soon by reducing vacancies. Overall, we looked okay, due largely to personnel changes and some fraud-elimination steps I'd instituted. I went home for a quick dinner by myself and listened to CNN for a minute. All the news was about the election.

The lecture audience was just as large on the second night, but we were better prepared this time. Extra chairs that had been against the back wall were gone, incorporated into the other rows. I sat in the last row and did a rough head count, then hoped the fire marshal wasn't there.

I didn't know the fire marshal, I realized, and made a note to invite him to lunch sometime.

Reg Handleman opened lecture two with a twist—a vintage music video featuring Duke Ellington playing "Take the 'A' Train" on a grand piano. The sound was good but lighting was poor. The camera focused on Ellington's hands and the keyboard, then gradually moved up to reveal reflections on the glossy wood where Steinway & Sons was printed in gold leaf.

Handleman froze the video. "What's the connection to cars?"

There were no answers, and I had no ideas.

Handleman clicked and the image changed to something that resembled a four-wheeled bicycle. "What's this?"

There were answers but not the one he wanted. "Ever hear of a horseless carriage? Well, this is what it looked like."

He flipped back to the piano keyboard and put the two images side-by-side on a split screen. "Figured it out yet?"

He had our attention but no one seemed to know the answer.

"Here's a hint, for any New Yorkers in the room. What Long Island factory manufactured a Daimler engine like the ones used in horseless carriages?" He paused and waited. "No ideas?"

A photo appeared of a long, low shop with a big sign.

"What's the name of the factory?"

Steinway & Sons, I read on a sign. The piano company made engines?

While Handleman told the story, the glass door to the lobby swung open silently and Travis McKenzie slipped into the ballroom. Heads swiveled, and for a minute or so, Reg Handleman lost the feminine portion of his audience. Travis had always been a handsome devil but maturity and success had worked some serious magic. I looked back to the screen.

After fifty minutes of early automobiles, our speaker looked at his watch. "Now, you'd probably like to stretch your legs, and I need water. Ten minutes, okay?"

A dozen rows in front of me, Terry Wozniak stood up and looked around. I felt him spot me and start in my direction. Without looking directly at him, I zipped out to the opposite aisle and headed for the punch bowl, but he caught up with me there.

"You haven't signed up for my class yet." He smiled and moved in too close, shoulder to shoulder.

I smiled but took a step back and turned to face him. "I'm probably not going to make it this time, Terry. Still settling in here. When will you offer it again?"

Wozniak narrowed his dark eyes. "Not for a whole year. Give it another thought, hon. Where's this Mr. Levine I'm supposed to talk to?"

I stood on my toes to look around and felt Wozniak's hand touching my elbow, as if he were steadying me. "Over there," I said when I spotted Levine. I stepped away from Wozniak. "Come. I'll introduce you."

As soon as they were talking, I slipped away for a cup of foamy green punch, drank it down quickly, dropped the paper container into the trash, and started back to my seat. Travis was at the front of the room, deeply absorbed in conversation with Handleman, who was shaking his head stubbornly. It wouldn't be a big stretch to say they were arguing, which was odd, considering they'd met only a couple of minutes before. I slipped past Jim Bergen and three or four other men who appeared to be paying close attention to Handleman's discussion.

I got to my chair, and after another minute or two, Handleman took center stage, wearing a tiny microphone on a headset. The last stragglers headed for their seats.

Someone leaned over my right shoulder and planted a soft, tickling kiss on my cheek. I turned, expecting to see Travis.

"I'm baa-ack." Riley Meddors's eyes twinkled.

"Riley!" I hopped up to give him a hug.

Instead of the clean-cut banker who'd left less than three weeks ago, Riley looked like a sailor, or a psychology professor who'd lost his razor. A short beard explained the tickle. I automatically reached to touch it, but caught myself at the last minute.

"Go ahead." He offered his cheek.

I brushed the back of my fingers across dark hair, already past the prickly stage. "There must be a story behind this. Did you have a good trip?"

He nodded. "Great trip. We got Joel married off. I saw the grandkids and had a nice reunion with Diane."

Diane was his ex-wife. She'd been a coworker of Nita's years ago, and I'd heard Riley's relationship with her described as cool or cordial or something of that sort. But he certainly looked happy after visiting her.

Audience members were settling down. A few chairs scraped into better positions. I jumped to a conclusion and whispered, "Don't tell me! You're getting married again."

"No!"

He recoiled, the smile startled off his face. Then he chuckled and whispered back, "Well, maybe. But not to Diane. I'll tell you all about it. Can you go for coffee when this is over? Or dessert?"

I shook my head, thinking about my morning plans and how I'd need to get to bed as early as possible. The speaker rapped for order.

"I'll talk with you tomorrow."

I looked around to see Travis watching me. I gave him a wave and a smile, which he returned, and he sat down in the front row near the Bergens.

Vacant seats were more numerous than an hour earlier, but not necessarily because of any lack of interest in the lecture. Eight o'clock was bedtime for many Harbor Villagers.

"I'm getting some questions about the value of certain vehicles," Handleman began. "Save those for tomorrow night, when our topics will include some investment options in collectible and classic automobiles. There are major pitfalls there, so don't sign anything between now and then."

His audience laughed.

We seemed to be laughing at anything he said, as though he'd conditioned us. Which might be true. I should pay closer attention to his techniques, in case I ever returned to teaching.

"And I've got a little added bonus for you," Handleman said. "Tomorrow afternoon at three, I want you to bring your family photos to this room. I'll be here for an hour or so and I'll identify and date any cars in the photographs and tell you a little about them."

There were whispers and rustles and comments in the audience. I remembered seeing such photographs in my family. Harbor Village residents must have albums full of them, going back generations.

"Genealogists find that type of information very useful," Handleman was saying. "So, if you're doing a family tree, you'll want to come. We can tell a lot about people from the cars they drive. Now, I'm just assuming this room will be available tomorrow. Is the little lady from the reservation desk here? Patti?" He scanned the crowd.

I joined with other voices in answering. "No!"

Handleman shrugged. "Well, I'll check with her first thing in the morning to be sure this room is available, and I'll put a note outside if we have to go elsewhere. Now. Ready to jump back in?"

A few people in my vicinity gave me inquiring looks, but I didn't know what was scheduled for the ballroom this week. Music groups practiced there, clubs held meetings, there was an occasional wedding or reunion. So Handleman's announcement caused me some distraction in the second half of the lecture. Patti would be by herself in the morning, while I went off with Nita. I didn't know how she'd cope with a visit from Handleman.

When the lecture ended, I spoke to Travis briefly, confirmed our Thursday lunch date, and thanked the speaker for a good presentation. "Do you have everything you need in the guest suite?"

"It's perfect." His navy-blue eyes seemed to examine the thoughts rattling around inside my cranium. I turned away, wondering if he was really as good a speaker as I thought or if we'd all been mesmerized.

Most of the audience left right away, chatting as they filed out of the ballroom, primarily through the parking lot exit. A few went through the lobby or out into the garden on their way around to the PT end of the big house.

Carla and Ann were stripping away empty serving dishes and the punch bowl, stacking kitchen things on a cart. I didn't see any leftover food. Lizzie pulled the filled trash bags out of containers, replaced them with fresh bags, then tied the full ones and hauled them out. They'd have the dishwasher going when they left for home.

A few people, Travis and Jim and Terry Wozniak included, still milled around at the front, peppering Handleman with questions that seemed more and more contentious. What in the world were they discussing? Nita was watching from a chair on the front row, handbag on her lap.

I gave her a wave.

"Eight thirty?" she called.

I nodded and looked around for Stewart just as he came in from the lobby and stopped, hands on hips, looking around.

I took a few steps toward him and he spotted me. "I'll lock up," he volunteered without being asked.

I thanked him and went home. It'd been a good day. And a long one.

Stephanie called while I was in the closet, locating the turquoise sweater I wanted to wear the next day. I'd bought it from Etsy, but someone had knitted it by hand and I thought the knitters at Ann's shop would enjoy examining it. Nita had said we could count on seeing six or eight knitters, women who came in every Thursday morning for what they called their knit fix.

"What's the temperature there?" Stephanie asked.

While we talked, I untangled a silver and turquoise necklace from the jumble on the jewelry carousel. "I just walked home from the ballroom and it was pleasant out. Sixty, maybe sixty-five."

I found the shoes I wanted and set them out, along with thin, diamond-patterned trouser socks. Then I sat cross-legged on the bed. The cat jumped up and insinuated herself into my lap.

"It's forty-four degrees here and may freeze tonight." Stephanie was at home in Birmingham.

"Is that why you asked Patti about retail space in Fairhope?"

"She didn't need to tell you that. Can't a girl even dream? Is Dad there?"

"Not here, but I saw him at a lecture tonight." I stroked the cat and she rolled over, exposing her tummy.

"Wouldn't it be funny if all of us wound up living in Fairhope?"

My hand dropped onto Tinkerbelle and she grabbed with all four feet, claws out. I flinched but didn't scream.

"Stephanie, your father lives in Houston."

I eased my hand out of the cat's grasp. Hadn't Stephanie been spared the reunion delusion? After all, she'd been a baby when Travis and I divorced.

"But he's in Fairhope an awful lot lately." She almost sang the final words.

"I've noticed that. But not for much longer, I hope. I'm feeling pretty confident with the job now."

I changed the subject and asked about my grandson, Barry, and Stephanie asked about some of my neighbors she'd gotten to know on previous visits. After a few more minutes of conversation, we told each other good night.

* * * *

Before eight Thursday morning, I had crossed the street to the office and was standing beside Patti's desk, figuring out which key unlocked it. The piece of driftwood was in its usual place, but the psychic turtles were missing.

I found the red reservation book in the top drawer. The only item scheduled for the ballroom was Handleman's presentation at seven that night. I drew a diagonal across the afternoon hours and wrote *Handleman* above it, then looked up the phone number for Charlie and Eloise Levine and dialed it from Patti's desk phone.

No one answered. Probably in the shower. Or still asleep. I waited for voice mail and left a message that the ballroom was reserved for Handleman all afternoon. "I don't have his phone number and I'm going to be out of the office this morning, so I'd appreciate it if you'd notify him."

If that didn't work, Patti would just have to deal with him. I wrote her a note of explanation, stuck it to the desktop, and replaced the reservation book. As I was closing the drawer, my attention was drawn to a small monkeypod bowl inside. It held six or eight ceramic turtles in various sizes. I locked the desk.

Nita was waiting on the sidewalk in front of her apartment. She wore a black jacket with a houndstooth scarf and red leather gloves, and carried a small canvas bag with knitting needles sticking out at the top. I looped around the median and stopped beside her.

She greeted me cheerily as she got in and buckled her seat belt. "Ann always parks in the public lot behind Royale Court. Do you know about it?"

I didn't, but she pointed out the appropriate turns when we got into town.

The lot was large and, since most stores wouldn't open for another hour, almost empty. But Ann was already there, standing beside a silver SUV. She directed us to the next space. "Perfect timing." She swung Nita's door wide and held it. "Great program last night, wasn't it? I do believe that man could sell ice to Eskimos."

Nita brought up a different cliché. "But we're burning the candle at both ends, Ann. Staying out late and getting up early. I guess you do that every day, though."

"Don't know how anybody sleeps late. Now, Prissy and I shouldn't be more than an hour. We're just signing the agreement with the hotel and giving them a deposit. You have the key, right?"

Nita dangled a key for Ann to see, attached to a fat red pom-pom. "There's no need for you to hurry. We're going to enjoy looking at all the pretty yarns. I do hope some of the knitting ladies come in."

"Don't worry. They'll be here. And you know where to find the coffee and filters?"

"I do." Nita nodded.

"Take your time," I encouraged Ann. "I've been looking forward to this."

"You don't have to leave when I get back. You can stay all day. I'd better go. I have my phone if you need me."

"We won't," Nita said confidently.

Ann hiked herself into the SUV and slammed the door, and Nita took my arm to walk across an unpaved, uneven, graveled area.

"They call this Skinny Alley." She pointed me into a narrow walkway between the end of a building and a weathered fence. "You don't want to meet someone going the other way."

"I see why it got that name."

The path was ten or twelve feet long and less than three feet wide. With Nita still holding my arm, we had to walk single file. At the end, we stepped out into a large, charming courtyard and the aroma of onions and garlic and spices. There were benches, a few crape myrtles that had lost most of their leaves, pots with red and white impatiens, and a splashing fountain. Dixieland jazz played softly.

I walked out on dark concrete pavers and turned slowly, looking around.

The wooden fence continued, with a tracing of vines here and there, and made up one long wall of the triangular courtyard. Beside us, the low gray building housed a doll shop, a candy shop, a nail salon, and a shop with a big mullioned window and a sign that said Lilliput. The adjacent wing of the L-shaped building was an art gallery, with more of the square windows, and a little shop that specialized in used paperbacks. A separate building, across the covered walkway, housed Boudreau's Gumbo and a T-shirt shop. Chairs and umbrella tables, flags, benches, and fat, frog-shaped pots decorated the courtyard. I could see a little sliver of de la Mare Street through a filigreed archway opposite Skinny Alley.

"Good morning, Nita," a woman wielding a broom called from the entrance to Lilliput. She kept sweeping.

"Evie, come meet my friend Cleo."

When Evie turned toward me, I realized she looked extraordinarily familiar. Not Ann, but close enough to mistake for her.

"This is Ann's sister," Nita said. "She has this wonderful little shop full of dollhouses." She rested a thin hand on Evie's arm. "I know you don't call them that, Evie. But I have to stop and think of their real name. Miniatures? Is that it?"

"Right, but lots of people say dollhouse. It doesn't bother me a bit."

"You look so much like Ann," I said. "Especially your hair."

Evie preened, fingering her short, reddish hair. "It ought to look the same. Came out of the same bottle." She laughed.

"We'll come look around in your shop before we leave," Nita promised her. "It always puts me in a good mood to see your little treasures. Are you still making the needlepoint rugs? Cleo needs to see them."

"They sell fast but I've probably got one or two." Evie picked up a doormat and swept under it.

The knit shop was in the corner, angled between the building's two wings, with display windows flanking the glass door. Nita pointed to the name, Royale Knit Shop, written across the windows in purple and green script with gold highlights. "Do you recognize the colors of Mardi Gras?"

I wouldn't have thought of the connection, but I'd already learned Fairhope had a tradition of celebrating Mardi Gras. Any holiday, in fact.

Nita tried the doorknob without using the key. To our surprise, it opened. She hesitated and looked at me.

"Jim says always check the knob first, to be sure it's locked and no one's lurking inside. But I'm sure Ann just left it open for us." She looked at me.

I nodded agreement and we entered the shop, exercising no particular caution. I wondered what life must be like for her, always conceding to Jim's hypervigilance. Nita clicked the lights on and the knit shop sprang to life.

A pink floral carpet covered much of the dark floor. The boxed-out display windows were decorated with stacks of luscious, jewel-toned yarns and mannequins outfitted in knitted garments. A wide purple stripe ran above the windows, around the walls and all the way to the high tin ceiling. On the side walls, bins of colorful yarns were topped with hat stands and plaster body parts displaying more knitted creations.

There was a shorter row of shelving in the middle of the room, ending at a glass checkout counter that sparkled under pendant lights. In the back, a big wooden table and chairs reminded me of a college library. I could imagine it lined with chatty knitters sipping coffee or tea as they twisted cables and counted stitches. The lighting must've been some special bulb, chosen because it so perfectly mimicked daylight.

At the very back of the shop, a pair of black Cracker Barrel rocking chairs held blue-and-white needlepoint pillows, and between the chairs, a mahogany table held a porcelain lamp glazed in the same colors.

"Isn't it an inviting place? Ann's a real artist, you know." Nita folded her gloves together and went to turn the lamp on. "The knitting group will be here soon. I'll put the coffee on and you can look around."

I stopped to inspect an infinity scarf twirled with Mardi Gras beads and displayed on one of several mannequins. I was a tactile shopper who had to feel everything, and the infinity scarf was like a softer, fluffier Tinkerbelle.

Evie came in the door. "Somebody's locked me out of the bathroom. Mind if I go through and unlock the door?"

"Of course not. I've done it myself." Nita was at the coffee bar measuring out dark grounds, but she could explain the Royale Court layout to me while she worked. "The shops share bathrooms. This one is for the knit shop and Lilliput."

Evie approached the door beside the coffee bar. "This one is shared three ways, actually. Ann and me, plus the back office. And somebody's forever leaving the door locked. I've got a key somewhere but it's easier to run over here." She opened the bathroom door, disappeared from view, and screamed.

Nita and I bolted as Evie burst out of the bathroom, clutching her throat. "There's a man!"

She took a few more steps before turning to stare at us, horrified, hands clasped against her chest. "I think he's dead."

"Call 911," Nita ordered, and reached out to console Evie.

My bag still hung from my shoulder. I pulled out my phone and punched in the number.

But I needed to know what I was reporting, didn't I? I opened the bathroom door.

Nita was right behind me. "I want to see, too."

Chapter 4

The dank, windowless bathroom had two doors, one from the knit shop and another directly across from it. A ceiling fixture high above cast a yellowish light on a white tile floor, a small vanity, and a toilet. I took in the entire scene in a single, quick glance. The seat was closed, but the man on the floor was the primary focus of my attention.

I stepped closer. "Sir! Sir?"

He was angled across the little bathroom on his back, one arm up like he was waving at somebody, knees bent slightly, feet against the vanity. Lying there, he looked like he'd fallen. He appeared to be about thirty and was wearing tight black shorts, running shoes, and a knit shirt. A bit of white fabric stuck out beneath his shoulder.

"Who is he?" Nita asked from the doorway.

I shook my head and the emergency dispatcher answered my call. I gave my name and squatted beside the man's head. "I'm at the knit shop in Royale Court. There's an injured man here."

As she passed the message to someone, I touched his neck, intending to feel for a pulse. But it wasn't necessary. He was cold to the touch.

"Deceased, I think."

I got to my feet, and in a flash of suspended animation, one of those moments that stick in your memory forever, I noticed the drone of an overhead exhaust fan.

"Police and EMT responding." The dispatcher snapped me back to the moment. A live person, speaking with a mechanical, unemotional voice, seemed oddly reassuring, a signal that the system was working.

"Stay on the line."

I stepped away from the body and the dispatcher recited a coded message to someone.

"Can you see him from where you are?"

"Yes. He's cold."

"Don't touch anything," she ordered, too late. "Is he breathing?"

"No. He's dead."

"Is this Ann Slump's shop? Is Ann there?"

"Yes, it's Ann's shop. She's not here."

There were more voices on the phone. I backed toward Nita. *How would Jim Bergen act in this situation?* He noticed things and, by this point, would probably have a guess about the autopsy results. So, I looked around the bathroom once more. A shelf above the toilet tank was decorated with artificial flowers and an air freshener. There was a box of tissues on the tank top. The knob lock across the narrow room was locked, and the light switch beside it was in the up position. There was nothing else to see, and I was hearing voices in the knit shop.

"Is it Usher?" dispatch asked.

"Usher?" I looked for Nita.

She still held the bathroom door open but had moved back into the shop, looking away from me. A cop appeared beside her.

I thanked dispatch and hung up.

The next five minutes were a blur of activity. The officer ran us away from the bathroom and directed emergency responders, including a man and a woman in scrubs, who arrived with a gurney. They left it just inside the knit shop and sauntered to the bathroom.

There were people outside, too, cordoning off the courtyard, talking into radios, holding people at bay. The emergency response felt active and organized and prompt, but there was no rushing about. There must be some code that told responders there was no life to be saved here.

After the initial spurt of activity, Nita and Evie and I were led outside. The original cop went to one of the umbrella tables, pulled out a chair for Nita, and took our names.

"Who is he?" he asked.

"He's dead, isn't he?" Nita had a worried look.

The officer looked at me.

I shrugged. "Never saw him before."

"Devon Wheat." Evie's voice was shaky.

"You're going to stay right here until I get back. Okay?" The officer went back inside.

Nita turned to Evie. "Who is he?" She reached out a hand.

"Devon Wheat." Evie pointed toward the miniature shop, then took Nita's hand. "He has the office behind my shop."

Nita seemed to recognize the name and shot me a worried look.

"The financial planner." Evie glanced over her shoulder, toward Skinny Alley.

I looked, too, hoping Ann would appear. Had anyone called her?

We'd been outside for a few chilly minutes when Lieutenant Mary Montgomery strode into the courtyard, entering by the walkway from Section Street. She stopped at the edge of the courtyard, planted both fists on her hips, and stared at me with narrowed eyes for several seconds before she turned and walked into the knit shop.

Just when we were getting to be friends.

"Are you warm enough?" Nita asked.

"Warm enough," I lied.

She took red leather gloves out of her knitting bag. "Take these, Cleo."

"No, I'd stretch them. You wear them."

The chairs were metal and cold and maybe a little damp with morning dew.

"I've got something." Evie pushed her chair back and got up. "If they ask, tell them I'll be right back." She went into the miniature shop.

Music still played from the courtyard speakers, one of which was mounted right above us in a leafless crape myrtle. Dr. John was singing about sweet confusion. I crossed my arms and balled my hands up in my armpits. Jazz and a dead man. Nothing sweet about it.

Evie came back with fleece jackets, one for herself and one for me. I put it on and stuck my hands into the pockets.

"Can we call Ann?" Nita asked.

I didn't see why not. "Do you know her number?"

Evie called out her sister's phone number. I entered the digits into my phone, then passed it to Nita and moved to the fourth chair at the table.

I hitched it closer to Evie. "What happened to him?"

Her gaze moved from the knit shop to Skinny Alley and back. "An aneurysm, do you think?"

I had assumed cardiac, but Evie knew him. "Did he have any health problems?"

She shook her head. "Nothing I know about. Always exercising, riding his bicycle."

That explained his clothing. I looked around the courtyard.

"Where's his bike?"

Evie glanced around before she shook her head. "Around back, I guess. Sometimes he puts it in the storeroom, but it's not there. That's where I got the jackets."

A man wearing a white apron walked out of the gumbo house and looked around the courtyard, where twenty or thirty people milled about, many of them in uniform. "Who is it?" he called to Evie.

"Devon," she told him.

The man looked around again and went back inside and Nita passed the phone back to me.

"Ann's already on the way."

We sat quietly for a few minutes, but my thoughts were flying. An aneurysm? Okay. Maybe he took an early bike ride and got to Royale Court before Evie arrived. I envisioned him entering the bathroom from the Lilliput side, turning the light on, and locking the door. But he didn't lift the toilet seat? Fell with his feet against the vanity? No, that couldn't be. Fell and writhed on the floor, then died with his feet against the vanity, knees bent? That didn't quite work, either.

I was glad to leave the investigation to the authorities and glad to have some observations to report when Jim Bergen began his inevitable grilling.

A few minutes later, a young woman from the restaurant brought us coffee and a plate of beignets. "Adrian thought you could use something."

"Thank him for us, honey," Evie told her.

I tried to avoid caffeine, but this was the time to make an exception. The coffee was hot and the beignets still warm and sweet. Delicious, and the powdered sugar would wash out of my turquoise sweater. I did try to keep it off Evie's jacket.

Lieutenant Montgomery walked out of the knit shop giving directions. "Get some tape across these walkways." She pointed. "And get statements from these ladies so they can go home. I'll take Ms. Mack."

I put the last beignet on a napkin and handed it to her. We moved to the next table and I answered questions: why were we there, what time had we arrived, exactly what had we done in the interval before discovering the body?

Other officers asked Nita and Evie questions.

There was a little disturbance when Ann arrived. I was sitting with a view of Skinny Alley and saw her duck under a strand of yellow crime scene tape and charge across the courtyard with a cop following after her.

"Evie!" Ann snapped. "What happened?"

Evie hopped up and went to meet her.

Montgomery got up, too, but I signaled to call her back. "The shop was supposed to be locked when we got here, but it wasn't."

She gave me one of her famous scowls. "You said Ms. Slump was here when you arrived."

I pointed toward Skinny Alley. "She was in the parking lot back there. She asked if Nita had the key, and Nita showed it to her. But when we got to the door, it was unlocked. I'm certain. Nita's husband is Jim Bergen. He has a—"

"Oh, yes. Jim Bergen." She nodded and glanced at Nita. "Yes, I know the Bergens. So, she tried the knob first?"

I nodded. "We even talked about it when we saw it was unlocked. She said Jim taught her to always check."

She nodded again, somewhat wearily, then turned. "Ms. Slump, I'd like a word with you." She pointed to a vacant table but glanced back and tapped my table.

"You wait here."

Ann was too antsy to sit. She and Montgomery stood in front of the knit shop. I could hear Montgomery clearly, ten feet away, since conversation in the courtyard had dropped to almost nothing. Everyone was eavesdropping.

"What time did you arrive this morning, and what did you do?"

"Eight o'clock," Ann answered quickly. "What happened?"

"Did you see Mr. Wheat?"

"No." She pointed to the courtyard. "I blew the leaves off the pavers and watered the poinsettias. Straightened up the chairs and tables, too. Lot of good that did." She scowled and pointed to the gumbo shop. "Boudreau was here but nobody else. What's happened to Devon? Is he all right?"

"And where've you been?"

Ann looked annoyed and glanced at her sister. "Prissy and I had an appointment at the hotel at nine. We just got back. Devon wasn't here, I can tell you that. He comes in at ten."

"Did you enter the bathroom?"

"The bathroom? Don't tell me he was in the bathroom. Is he dead?" She frowned. "One of my customers could've walked in there." She looked at Nita. "Did the knitters come?"

Nita shook her head.

Montgomery stepped between Ann and Nita. "I'll ask the questions, ladies."

We really didn't know if the knitters had come or not. They didn't get into the knit shop, but they might be standing behind the barriers right now. I glanced toward Skinny Alley and saw a young woman stoop and come under the yellow tape.

"Here's Prissy," Ann said.

Prissy was thirtysomething and resembled Ann in size and energy, but with a mass of reddish hair, shoulder length. She must've been waiting for the first cool day to break out high-heeled boots, which she wore with a narrow skirt and oversized jacket. She looked at Evie and pointed a finger as she went by, like she was giving the Pillsbury Doughboy a belly button.

"Auntie Ann, what's happened? Are you okay?"

Ann turned back to Montgomery. "I guess the shop has to be closed for a while? What about the restaurant? He's cooked already, and the servers count on tips."

Montgomery glanced toward the sidewalk on de la Mare, where a few people, perhaps the missing knitters, stood watching. Or perhaps they were customers arriving for an early lunch of gumbo.

"Thursday and Friday are their big days." Ann piled it on.

Montgomery summoned a uniformed cop and gestured as she gave directions. "Move the tape this way so customers can get to the gumbo shop. Give them access to a few tables over there. But only if they're actually eating. We don't need more gawkers."

She turned her attention back to Ann. "They're about to have a record day. Now, where were we? You went to the knit shop next?"

"Well, let me think." Ann watched the relocation of the crime scene tape. "I got to the courtyard before eight. Cleaned up out here, went around back, and put the leaf blower and hose in the toolshed. And kept going to the parking lot to meet my friends. That was at eight forty-five, wasn't it, Nita?" She glanced at Nita, then back at Montgomery. "Is that what you asked, Mary? I'm a little distracted, naturally."

"No, Ms. Slump. I'm asking about your shop. What time did you get to the knit shop?"

Ann turned to look at the shop and stood up straighter. "I haven't been in the shop today."

When I looked toward de la Mare again, twenty or thirty people crowded each other for a view into the courtyard. Only a couple had come in to the restaurant.

Ann was telling Montgomery about retirement. "The knit shop's not mine, you know. It belongs to my niece now. I just help her out sometimes."

"So Prissy was here earlier?"

Prissy, a few feet behind Ann, shook her head.

"Of course not," Ann answered. "We were at the hotel. She opens at ten."

Chief Ray Boozer of the FPD showed up with another officer. Montgomery directed us all back to our original table and told Ann to take the fourth chair. Then she went into the knit shop with Boozer.

Prissy spoke to everyone, then flitted around the courtyard, talking with cops and bystanders and popping into the restaurant for a few minutes. I saw Jim Bergen in the crowd, watching from de la Mare. I waved and pointed him out to Nita.

"I wonder who called him." She gave him a wave. "You know he's dying of envy that we're in here and he's not."

The next time I looked in that direction, there were even more people, and Travis was standing beside Jim. I waved again.

The EMTs came out of the knit shop with an empty gurney and pushed it through the breezeway and up the walk toward Section Street.

Chief Boozer was next to come out. He looked around and, when his gaze fell on me, walked over. We'd gotten to know each other in my first couple of weeks in Fairhope, but I hadn't seen him recently.

"Chief." I stood to shake his hand.

Boozer removed his hat and went around the table, greeting Nita and the Slump family members. When he got back to me, he pulled up another chair for himself.

"I hear you and Ms. Bergen found Mr. Wheat. I'm sorry that had to happen."

He had a lovely voice, deep and calming, and would've made a fantastic announcer for a late-night radio program.

"It was Evie more than us." I told him about seeing Ann in the parking lot and Evie coming into the shop to unlock the bathroom door. "She discovered the body. I went in and felt for a pulse while I was on the phone with the dispatcher."

He nodded, listening while he kept an eye on the comings and goings at the knit shop, nodding when one of his men shouted something.

"He looked like he might've fallen," I ventured. "But that seems unlikely in such a little bathroom."

Boozer sighed and rubbed a palm across his dark-brown, shiny head. It was a habit many bald men maintained, arranging hair that was no longer there.

"The coroner's man is here now. But I don't think he fell." He put his hat back on and gave it a tug. "I've got to talk to his wife. I understand there are children." I could see he was troubled by the prospect.

"I'm a social worker, you know. If you want me to go along…"

Finally, he shook his head. "I usually take my lieutenant. But thank you."

I spoke to Montgomery as she was preparing to leave with Boozer. "Are we free to go? You know where to find us."

"You gave a statement?"

I nodded. "You took it."

She looked me over. "You aren't taking anything except what you brought in?"

I had a shoulder bag, nothing else. Nita had a knitting bag and held it out as if for inspection.

Montgomery rolled her eyes and dismissed us.

Nita and I said good-bye to Ann and Evie before we walked to the archway, where Jim and Travis waited. Travis raised the yellow tape for us and Jim took Nita's bag and gave her a big, clumsy hug, which didn't suit her. She wriggled out of his clutches and straightened her jacket.

"Who was it?" a bystander asked. The group of onlookers spilled out into the narrow street.

Nita said the name and Jim repeated it in a loud voice. "Devon Wheat."

I recognized Patti's friend nearby and said hello. Todd Barnwell was just a few feet away, craning his neck and peering into the courtyard. He gave me a startled look. No swagger today.

"Where's your car, Cleo?" Jim held his arm out for Nita to take and leaned on the cane in his other hand. "Give Travis the key and let him drive it home. You come ride with Nita and me. My car's just down at the corner."

I looked again but Todd Barnwell had already disappeared into the crowd.

There were two factors at work here. Jim was always ready to take charge. We needed people like that. And being security conscious, he was also eager to get a detailed report of the morning's events. I thought I needed a little time to reflect on the solemnity of death.

"I'd better drive," I said. "Travis doesn't know where my car is."

"Then I'll ride with you," Travis said with authority. "We'll see you at home, Jim." He took my elbow and got us moving. "Which way do we go?"

Getting back to the parking lot required some walking, since we couldn't go directly through Royale Court. We walked down de la Mare and turned left on Church Street, then wound our way through the big parking lot. When we finally reached the car, Travis offered again to drive.

I said no. "I'm back to normal now. How'd you get here?"

"Rode with Jim." He made a fuss of holding the door for me, and then I closed my eyes and leaned against the headrest, inhaling slowly, while he walked around to the passenger side.

"You okay?"

"I'm okay." I straightened up. "Just not the best way to start the day. Poor guy." I buckled the seatbelt and started the car.

I should've exited the parking lot by another route, but I was a creature of habit and went out the same way Nita and I had gone in. At Section Street, where I needed to turn left, I encountered a knot of people on the sidewalk and a number of emergency vehicles parked erratically—ambulance, fire truck, multiple police cars.

I waited, watching for an opening in traffic, and my phone rang. "Dang it." I reached into my purse, between the seats.

It was Stephanie.

"Hi, honey. I'm in traffic. Talk to your father."

I straight-armed the phone to Travis and turned my attention back to oncoming traffic. She hated when I called him that, rather than using his actual name, but old habits died slowly.

"Your mother just discovered a body," Travis announced, right off the bat. "No, I'm not kidding. I don't know." He looked at me. "What did you say his name was?"

I told him and he repeated it to Stephanie. "No, I didn't say that." He looked at me again. "He wasn't murdered, was he?"

I had spotted an opening. I shook my head and gunned the engine, crossing one lane as some whacko in a pickup sped up and came right at me. "No. He fell off a toilet."

The pickup horn blared.

"Good lord! What?" Travis gaped at me.

I could hear Stephanie guffawing.

"She'll call you later," he snapped into the phone and disconnected. "Really, Cleo. You should let me drive. How did this guy die? Was he...?" His hands jiggled a hula. "Was he dressed?"

"Do *not* repeat what I said." I stopped at the corner and giggled from nerves. "I'm glad Jim didn't hear it. He'd want details."

"So do I."

I glanced to the left, saw nobody was coming, and turned right on red, heading for Harbor Village. The speed limit was twenty-five and I ignored it.

"He was spread eagled on the bathroom floor, fully dressed, if you count biking shorts. He looked peaceful, like he'd fallen backward. No blood, no twisted limbs. But his feet..."

"No weapon?"

I pictured the bathroom. "No weapon. Somebody mentioned an aneurysm. Maybe he has a family history or something."

I turned down Harbor Boulevard a minute later and saw Jim already at home, standing on the curb in front of their apartment. He waved his arms as we approached.

I gave a signal and pulled over, and Travis lowered the window.

"It's lunchtime." Jim bent over so he could see me. "Let's go to the steak house and you and Nita can tell us exactly what happened, before you forget."

"I'll drive," Travis said firmly. "My car's right there."

I hesitated. "I'll need to check in with the office. That'll take a few minutes. You want to get out, Travis?"

"Nita's freshening up. You can use my bathroom," Jim said.

Travis glanced at me and raised the window before he got out, and I drove around the corner and into the garage. I entered the big house through the parking lot end of the building and stopped at the bathroom first. When I looked in the mirror, I realized I was still wearing Evie's fleece jacket. I pulled it off, thinking I'd leave it in the office, but it was cool in the bathroom and I put it back on. I'd give it to Ann later and ask her to return it.

Patti was at her desk and gave me a cheery greeting. "And how was your morning? Are you knitting something for me?" She batted her eyes. "How about one of those silky infinity scarves? In blues and purples. I've already got the glasses to match."

I lowered myself into a chair and told her about the dead man in the knit shop, about meeting Ann's sister, Evie, about Lieutenant Montgomery and Chief Boozer, and about those nice beignets from the gumbo house.

At some point, Emily, Harbor Village's red-haired business manager, joined us. "How horrible," they exclaimed in turn, and made a proper fuss over me.

Pretty soon I was feeling normal again.

"How did he die?" Emily asked.

I shrugged. "They weren't sure when we left. Maybe an aneurysm. Are you by any chance related to Ann?"

Emily was surprised. "First cousins once removed. Did she tell you?"

"No. I just met Evie and Prissy. Lots of redheads in that family." I looked at my watch and got up. "Travis and the Bergens are waiting to take me to lunch. I'd better go."

"Maybe he had a heart attack," Patti said. "How old was he?"

Emily asked, "And who was he, do you know?"

"Too young. A financial advisor with an office in Royale Court. Devon Wheat."

"Devon?" Patti gasped, her eyes going round in astonishment.

"Oh, no!" Emily moaned.

I hadn't considered the small-town factor. Both of them knew him, of course. From L'Etoile Bistro, I gathered from their conversation.

"Part of the biker group?" I was guessing, based on his attire.

They nodded and hugged each other.

Patti was tearing up as she grabbed for her phone. "I've got to call Stewart."

"And he had a wife?" I asked Emily.

It took her a moment to answer. "Ex-wife, I guess. I've heard him talk about child support."

I left them consoling each other with the usual tautologies about it being his time and walked back toward the Bergen apartment. When I stepped into the open, a horn tooted from the parking lot. Everyone was already in Travis's car, waiting for me.

I got into the backseat with Nita and we went to the steak house in Daphne.

We had passed Publix when Jim twisted around so he could see me. "Cleo, with your professional background, I'll bet you have an idea what he died from."

I shook my head. "Someone said aneurysm. I don't suppose that has any overt indicators."

"You know Jim." Nita's voice held a touch of pride. "He hears hoofbeats and thinks zebras. I already told him there was no weapon, but he didn't accept it. Did you see one?"

"No."

"Nita, I can't hear you. Let's hold the discussion until we get there." He faced forward again and politely directed Travis's attention to a changing traffic light.

Nita and I smiled at each other and rode along in silence. So now I knew Jim suspected foul play. But wouldn't he always? The question was, what would the cops think? For that matter, what did I really think? That curious position of the body still troubled me.

The restaurant was dark and quiet. Jim knew the hostess and asked for a particular booth, one that offered a view of the entrance. He and Nita took the bench seat that put their backs against the kitchen wall, and Travis and I had individual chairs in what the hostess called a half-booth arrangement. We placed our orders and got drinks and then a loaf of hot bread to tide us over until the real food arrived.

Jim smeared soft butter on a thick slice of bread before he looked at me expectantly. Then, amid a flood of questions, Nita and I reported every minute detail of our morning.

Nita told about trying the shop door before using her key. "Just the way you do. And the door was *not* locked, whatever Mary Montgomery says."

"I thought about you, too," I told Jim. "I tried to think what you'd do if you were there." I told about the locked door, the light switch, the position of the body. "And the toilet seat was definitely down. Do you make anything of that, or the way he was lying?"

Nita frowned at the mention of a toilet, but Jim flipped his place mat over, removed a pen from his pocket, and sketched out the floor plan, approximately to scale. "Was he six feet tall?"

Nita shook her head.

I agreed. "Oh, no. He wasn't a big guy. Five eight, maybe less. And on the thin side."

He sketched in a body. "Carpeted floor?"

That I knew. "No. White tile."

"Drag marks?"

I shrugged. "On tile?"

"Any dirt or debris under the body? I guess you didn't check that." He asked a few more questions, trying to draw out insights we might not realize we had, and seemed to be fitting each detail into a master design.

"How did you know anything had happened?" Nita asked him eventually, after our meals arrived and we were eating. "You didn't just drive down to Royale Court to see what was going on in the knit shop."

He chewed and chuckled. "These things get complicated, you know."

"Tell me," Nita insisted.

Jim looked sheepishly at Travis. "You know Dolly? Dolly's neighbor Ada has a son who drives the ambulance. And Ada called to invite him to breakfast. He said he had to pick up a body, and Ada thought he meant at Harbor Village. She called Dolly to ask who died."

Travis nodded, no doubt wondering how complicated this could get.

Nita said, "Dolly had been to swim, I guess."

"And nobody there said anything about a death. But Dolly said she'd call around, and Ada invited her to breakfast in place of her son. Then the son showed up after all and said there'd been a delay before he could pick up the body at Royale Court, not Harbor Village. And Dolly knew that was where Nita was and called me." He nodded to Travis. "We've got our communication networks, you see."

I looked at Travis. "And how did you find out?"

He shrugged, blasé. "Jim told me."

I smiled at the contrast and remembered a question I'd meant to ask Nita. "Who is Usher?"

"Ann's only brother." She patted Jim's arm to draw his attention from Travis. "Jim, Cleo asked about Ann's brother."

"What's to tell? His name's Usher and he owns some little shops in town." He took a sip of black coffee.

"No, he doesn't." She looked at me and rolled her eyes. "Let me tell it then. Ann's the oldest, and Evie came next. You know them. Those two names were just coincidence, I believe, but at some point, the Slump parents realized there was a pattern, so the next two girls were Irene and Olivia, and finally there was a boy. Their mother wanted to make him a junior but the girls said no, they had to stick with the vowels, and the only male name they could come up with that started with U was Usher."

Jim wasn't amused. "Not much of a name, if you ask me. Usher Slump? Sounds like a sneeze."

"But I'll never forget it now," I said.

Nita looked puzzled. "Usher wasn't there this morning, was he, Cleo? I didn't see him. Did you hear something?"

I told them about the dispatcher asking if the dead man was Usher.

"Well, where was he?" Jim asked. "He's supposed to be managing the place. He ought to be there when the rescue squad and half the police force come."

"No, the dead man wasn't Usher, and I don't know where he was." Nita frowned. "I believe he's still the manager, but I haven't heard anything recently."

Heard something? She didn't elaborate, but I had a feeling there was more to the story.

We had a good lunch. As usual, Jim ate his food and a portion of Nita's. She and I had chicken salad with grapes and almonds, served on toasted croissants, and it was all quite good. The men had steaks. Jim proposed dessert, which I skipped in favor of a nice hot cup of decaf.

What I really wanted was a nap but there was no chance of that today. This week was wearing me out, and the knit shop visit, which was supposed to be fun, had turned into a major tragedy instead.

Harbor Health Services treated us to lunch. Travis pulled out a credit card and flashed a dazzling smile with even, white teeth. Stephanie had inherited those. I hoped Barry had, too, but it was too early to say. Orthodontia is so costly.

When we finally got up to depart, Travis held my chair and then Evie's jacket, which I'd removed during lunch. Nita watched and frowned, even though I knew she valued such courtly gestures.

Jim looked at his watch. "Folks, we've got to get home and prepare for the afternoon performance. Remember, Reg Handleman's going to be authenticating photographs. And I've got some old ones for him."

"My father's first car, in England," Nita elaborated with a smile.

"Think he'll know British cars?" Travis asked Jim.

"I should get back to work. I don't want Patti dealing with him by herself."

Travis looked at me. "Why not?"

I shook my head. "Nothing. Just silliness."

"There's nothing silly about that man," Nita said. "That's the problem. He's so deadly serious. Here, Jim. Take this." She handed him her bag and slid across the bench.

Travis was giving me a puzzled look. "There's something wrong with Handleman? He seems well informed on automobiles and investments."

"Well informed, yes," Nita answered. "He came for tea and he's a gentleman."

But Jim knew. "It's his eyes. Good man for interrogation work. We would've made a good team."

It gave me a little chill to hear him say things like that. Sometimes I thought I wouldn't have wanted to know Jim Bergen in his prime.

On the drive back to Fairhope, Nita previewed their plans. "We're going to the concours in the morning, then staying home the rest of the weekend. What about you, Travis?"

"I'm going down there right now. Want to go see some old cars, Jim?"

Jim shook his head. "I've got paperwork waiting and Handleman's photo session at three. I'll miss the poker group today. Do you play poker, Travis?"

"Not for a long time. I've moved on to other forms of gambling."

I wondered what he referred to but didn't ask.

Nita and Jim did ask about his family, including the sister-in-law they'd known when she worked at Fairhope. I'd heard all that already and let my thoughts drift away. The budget for the coming year was requiring me to prioritize appliance upgrades, roofing, and raises for staff. The coming year would be a critical one for our facility. I glanced at Travis, thinking of questions I should ask while he was there.

Travis stopped in front of the Bergens' apartment and walked around to assist Nita and Jim. I hopped out, too.

"Thanks for lunch," I told him. "I'm feeling much better now."

"We'll see you at the lecture tonight," Nita said.

I nodded. "Are the show cars here already?"

Travis answered. "Some of them, I understand. Want to go see?"

"Lord, no. Have fun, though."

I waved to everyone and walked to the big house.

Chapter 5

Stewart was in the lobby when I went in, assessing the number of chairs. "How many people do we expect tonight?"

I glanced around to see who was listening before I answered in a soft voice. "I can't believe there's been so much interest in these lectures. Can it go on another night? We could wait until the last minute and see if the ballroom chairs are sufficient. That assumes you'll be here to bring in more chairs if there's another overflow crowd."

"I'm enjoying his talks. I'll be here. I heard you were the one who found Devon Wheat's body."

"Yes, with Nita Bergen." I sighed. "Poor man."

Stewart was wearing jeans and a denim shirt, worn work boots, and his tool belt. He shook his head sadly and got a faraway look in his eyes. "Tough."

"He was a friend of yours, I heard. I'm sorry."

His gaze swung to the koi pond. A butterfly flittered across the walkway and landed on a dill plant.

"We were in Afghanistan together. Lately he's been at the Bistro pretty much every time I go in there. Not the nicest guy. A smart-ass."

"Stewart, I didn't know you went to Afghanistan. Army?"

He nodded. "Lot of guys couldn't take it. Devon covered up at first, but he was messed up."

"Drugs? Alcohol?"

He shrugged. "He never came to meetings. Maybe he was always messed up. The little man complex, you know. A know-it-all compensating with money. Or trying to."

I nodded, trying to understand what he meant. Devon Wheat had been a small person in the physical sense, but there were other measures. Maybe Stewart meant dishonest?

"His wife left him."

"I heard. Will there be a service here?"

He shrugged. "The body hasn't been released yet. And may not be for a while, depending on what they find. And I'm not sure who's calling the shots, as far as family. The wife, I guess, since she's got the kids."

He paused before slapping the back of a chair. The noise was surprisingly loud in the cavernous lobby. "Well, off to the salt mines. The ballroom's set up the way Handleman wanted for this photo thing. I'll rearrange it for tonight as soon as they finish up in there."

"Wait a minute. What do you mean, 'depending on what they find' with Wheat? Do you know something?"

He glanced at me and shrugged. "I know he wasn't the nicest guy in town. I'm always suspicious when somebody like that just happens to croak. You know what I mean?" He touched the brim of his cap in a slouchy salute and headed down the hall, tool belt clanking.

Maybe Stewart was another person who thought hoofbeats meant zebras.

* * * *

Marmalade is lost!

That's what the note on my office door said, in big, black letters.

I assumed it explained why Patti's desk was vacant, which was just as well, because through the window behind my desk, I could see Reg Handleman walking with big strides across the driveway, heading for the main entrance. It was early for the photo session, but perhaps he had preparations to make. I locked the office again and headed for Assisted Living to check on the orange kitten. If one of them disappeared, the residents would be frantic. Some of the staff, too.

Handleman was coming across the lobby, aiming for Patti's desk.

"Everything going well?" I asked him.

"Very. I was wondering as I walked down here, what do you get for these apartments?" He gestured toward Harbor Boulevard.

I told him the rental rate. "That's what I pay for two bedrooms with a screened porch and a space in the community garage. There are less expensive options if you want a smaller apartment, or no screened porch, or if you don't mind being on the second floor. Would you like to meet Wilma, our rental agent?"

"If it's convenient, sure."

"Are you thinking about moving south?" I led him down the hall but when I could see the rental office, it was closed. "Apparently she's out. She may be showing an apartment now."

We walked slowly back to the lobby.

"What's there to do here, normally? I mean, when there's no auto show going on." In spite of his eyes, he had a nice smile.

"Everybody seems to find something that suits them. What do you like? Art, community theater, shopping?"

"Well, I'd like to see an apartment while I'm here, if it's not too much trouble. I'm familiar with the guest suite but I'd need one of the upscale models. I should've asked earlier, I know."

"I can show you mine right now, if you just want an idea of what they look like. Do you have time?" I looked at my watch and wondered if he hadn't visited with his old friend Charlie Levine since he arrived. "I'm in the first building here."

He accepted immediately. "I've got some time before the photo revue."

I took out my key and headed for the door. "It's not professionally decorated or anything. Not even cleaned up for company."

"Even better," he said jovially and followed me. "I'm glad I didn't have to ask your assistant."

I was glad, too, but didn't admit it. "Patti's a master at helping people."

We left the big house and I pointed to the sidewalk we'd be taking. "These two buildings, the ones nearest the administration building, have garages. The other buildings have assigned parking and there are plenty of spaces for guests. Parking's never a problem here, although it may be tomorrow."

He was interested in the shuttle service that would run Friday and Saturday, making loops from the car show to Harbor Village every thirty minutes.

"The public will park in our lots or at the shopping center and ride down to the polo club. I think the charge is a dollar each direction. They've got buses running from the parking deck in town, too."

"There's a parking deck in town? I missed that somehow, but I've tried several of your restaurants. Fairhope is a nice little community. I mentioned your assistant Patti. I wonder if it's just me, or does she have a problem with black people? Do you have any black residents here?"

"At Harbor Village? Well, I can't think of any offhand." His train of thought addled me, jumping from Patti to black residents. "I've only been here since August and I'm still meeting people who live here, and we don't keep any records about race. Of course, you don't always know—I don't, at least. We do have several black staff members."

"Housekeepers and dishwashers, you mean?"

"Well…housekeepers, yes. And some of the CNAs and a driver. We'd welcome black residents, though, if you know anyone interested."

He gave me one of his penetrating looks. "I'm black, Cleo. I thought Southerners could always tell." He laughed, and I did, too. "May I still see your apartment?"

"Here we are."

We entered through the screened porch and I gave him a tour of the apartment—living/dining combo, kitchen, two bedrooms, and two baths.

Tinkerbelle was on the corner of my bed and Handleman stopped to pet her. "I see pets are allowed."

"Under thirty pounds. And there's a pet fee."

"That's good. People give up enough to move to a place like this. They shouldn't have to give up their pets, too."

"I don't see it that way at all." I risked another of his probing looks. "Of course, I'm still working, but a retirement community is just a new phase, not necessarily a demotion or a winding down. Happier, maybe. Tinkerbelle lived here before I moved in."

He leaped to a conclusion. "You mean her owner died."

"No, moved off and left her. Tinkerbelle survived on her own, outside, for a month or two, but she was quite happy to return to domesticity."

He frowned while he gave Tinkerbelle a few more strokes. "We don't have many strays in South Bend. Our winters are too severe, I guess. Fairhope cats have it easy."

Tinkerbelle was still purring but she narrowed her yellow eyes down to slits, and I rushed to defend her. "Fairhope cats are plenty tough. If they're outside, they have to deal with hawks and eagles and coyotes and all the little vermin like fleas and ticks and internal parasites."

"Really? Well, Tinkerbelle, you're a survivor. And you've got it easy now."

He seemed in no hurry to depart, but I didn't really like men standing around in my bedroom. "Do you have time for a cup of tea?"

He looked at his watch. "If it's a quick one. You won't be offended if I drink and run?"

We went to the kitchen and I told him more about Harbor Village and answered a few questions. While the tea brewed, we went on a quick tour of the public parts of the building. I pointed out the mailboxes, the gas fireplace, and a table with a jigsaw puzzle in process.

"This building and the one across the street have interior courtyards. All the apartment buildings have nice lounges with a kitchen, and residents get together there for bridge or potlucks or parties with their families."

Georgina came out of her apartment beside the entrance.

"Mr. Handleman." She recognized him from the lectures. "Don't tell me you've decided to move to Harbor Village?"

He told her he was thinking about it and she asked the critical question, "Are you a single man?"

"Not for the last forty-five years." He laughed.

Usually, the second question asked about a new man was whether he could still drive at night, but I hurried him back while the tea was hot and Georgina never got to that.

We had tea and lemon thins on the screened porch and Handleman told me about his black mother, from Mississippi, and the white father he'd never known.

"I suppose you wonder why, when I could live as a white person, I choose to say I'm black."

"Yes, I did wonder."

"I think about what black people have accomplished in the last hundred and fifty years, going from slavery to the presidency, attorney general, chairman of the joint chiefs of staff, successful work in chemistry and space science and medicine. The University of Alabama quarterback is black, can you believe that? I just can't deny that part of myself. Or my mother, who worked so hard to give me a start in life."

Finally, he mentioned his wife. "She's black, and she's reluctant to move South. I thought you might give me some ammunition for persuading her."

I understood. "It's more of an issue than people acknowledge, but most overt segregation is along economic lines, not color. I like to think that younger people won't even know about racial divisions."

"Ha! I like to think about time travel but that doesn't make it happen."

I shrugged. "What can I say? I'm an idealist."

"To tell you the truth, I'd like to be involved on the ground floor with this car show. It's going to be big, you know. And Charlie Levine's sitting here twiddling his thumbs, the lucky jerk. Have you been out to the polo field? Perfect setting. If only it won't rain."

I looked at my watch, and he remembered his photo session. I took our dishes to the kitchen and locked up and we chatted as we walked back to the big house.

"You know Mobile's the rainiest place in the country most years," I told him. "Rainier than Seattle, even. But this is the dry season, or what passes for dry. And the weather looks good right now."

There were at least twenty people waiting in the ballroom, clutching scrapbooks and photo albums or individual snapshots. I turned on the lights while Reg Handleman directed participants to one side of the long row of tables Stewart had arranged down the center of the room.

"We'll let you keep one table," he told Lizzie, who was setting up a container of coffee and arranging cups and spoons and the usual additives for the afternoon session. "But we'll need all the others. Now people, take a seat and stake out the table space you need to lay out your photographs in front of you. Everyone on the other side of the tables, please, facing me. I need a long runway here."

He opened his briefcase and removed a white disc, about the size of a thick bagel. He gave it a twist and it popped open, turning into a bright light, with no cord necessary. Then he laid out a variety of magnifying devices.

"We'll move right down the table. You can follow me if you like, but leave your photos in place so there are no delays. I may have to pay a return visit to the difficult ones. And maybe we'll make a little display for tonight's lecture, depending on what we find."

I went to stand with Mr. Levine beside the garden doors. "Everything under control?"

He nodded morosely. "He's staying until Sunday at least."

"Well, you've done a marvelous job. Everyone has enjoyed his talks."

"Hmph," he said.

"I thought you were friends."

Levine gave me a look of distaste bordering on pain.

"He just told me you're a lucky man."

Levine's head snapped up. "Was he talking about Eloise?"

What had I stepped into? "No, he didn't mention Eloise. He just said you're a lucky guy."

Levine looked toward Handleman, raised his eyebrows, and stood a little straighter.

I smiled and looked back at our visitor. "I wonder how he learned about our lecture series. You must've mentioned it."

He shook his head. "No. Not me."

That left Eloise. I patted his shoulder and went out, around the koi pond, and across the drive to the Assisted Living building. The porch was empty and the automatic door slid open with a *swoosh*.

There was a crowd in the sitting room, gathered around Patti. She was wearing green glasses today, and had Marmalade, the orange kitten, snuggled up against her cheek.

Crisis averted.

The kitten had grown since I last saw him and, at about six months of age, was in that gawky, teenage phase of cat life.

"Here's Cleo. Say hello to Auntie Cleo." Patti waved his little white paw at me. "You'll never guess where he was."

"Sleeping in my bed," Joanie Ross crowed. "Just a big lump under the covers! Thinks he owns this whole building."

I rubbed his fuzzy, orange-striped head and he sniffed my fingers. "Where are your buddies?" I asked the kitten.

Patti gestured around the room. "They're all here."

I made a circuit of the sitting room, stroking the other three kittens and talking with residents. Ivy watched from the back hall. I ended my circuit beside her and asked how things were going.

"Busy. We're officially full. Got a couple of respites for a week, and Mrs. Hocutt for a few days, before she goes home. Come speak to her." Ivy nodded toward a woman sitting in a wingback chair, a wheelchair beside her and the tuxedo kitten in her lap. She introduced me. "Mrs. Hocutt and her husband, Tom, live in the private houses on Andrews Street. She just had a hip replaced this week."

"And you can leave the hospital so soon?" I wouldn't have thought so.

"That's what they say." Mrs. Hocutt didn't look like a convalescent. She wore gray sweatpants with a red tunic that matched her lipstick. She must've spent the morning having her hair done. "The therapists are coming here so I can be near Tom."

"Hips are easy compared to knees," Ivy explained. "And she's got a sweet husband at home who can help her. Isn't that right, Mrs. Hocutt? You'll be back with him in no time."

I headed toward the door and Ivy tagged along.

"Does Emily still come every week to clip the kittens' claws?"

Ivy grinned and nodded. "She comes most days and does something. The cats were a great idea. We get a lot of visitors because of them, Cleo, which is wonderful for our residents. Dolly Webb is allergic, but she brings us a new cat toy every week."

"Really?" I didn't think of Dolly as a cat lover.

"We've got their vet visits scheduled for next week, for spaying and neutering," Ivy said. "Come see the recovery unit I've set up."

The nurse's office in Assisted Living had been a disaster when Ivy arrived, but Stewart had made some major improvements. The new paint was pale pink, and new fluorescent lights had wood trim, so they no longer looked like a garage. But there was something else, and suddenly it hit me.

"Ivy! You put in a skylight!"

That struck me as a big job, and an expensive one that had definitely not been approved, but Ivy was smiling and shaking her head.

"It was always there," she said.

"A skylight? No. I remember this room. It was dark as a pit. There was absolutely no natural light."

"They'd covered it up. Can you believe that?"

I looked up at a square shaft, eight or ten feet tall and painted bright white. "But why in the world would they cover it?"

She lowered her voice. "Some drugs increase your sensitivity to light." She raised her eyebrows and waited for the information to sink in.

"Oh. Yes, I see."

I thought back to the previous occupants of the office, the ones who'd been there when I arrived. There'd even been a drug theft from this unit the weekend before Ivy joined the staff. It seemed like a long time ago and wasn't something I liked to remember.

She showed me how she and Stewart had rearranged the two small offices. The second one, with another skylight, had been converted to storage room and cat spa, with food and water, four individual crates, carpeted ledges for climbing, wooly igloos for sleeping, and a row of litter boxes. "We'll take them to the vet one at a time, so people won't miss them too much. When they come home, they can stay in their crate for a day or two, until they fully recover from the anesthesia."

Both offices had transparent pet flaps. Unless they were closed in a crate, the cats still had the run of the building.

"Good work," I told Ivy.

As I walked back to the big house, I passed the pink building that housed the indoor pool. Music was playing and the windows were fogged. I couldn't see how many people were in the water exercise class. The outdoor pool was covered with a blue tarp that had collected a few puddles on top.

I walked up the ramp and entered the big house near the dining room, already closed by this time of the afternoon. There was a table just outside the entrance, where people could get fresh coffee or tea all afternoon. It held mugs and glasses, an ice bucket, napkins, and a jar of cookies.

Ann Slump burst out of the dining room, calling my name.

"Cleo! Oh, Cleo, can you *ev-ah* forgive me? I had no idea of getting you into something like that. And Nita, too. I am so, *so* sorry." She hugged me.

"You didn't know." I put my arms around her. To my surprise, she didn't feel like the powerhouse I always saw. Instead, she was thin and small. "Nita and I didn't know Devon Wheat, so it wasn't a terrible shock for us, like it would've been for you. Evie got the worst of it."

She dug in the pocket of her trousers for a tissue and blotted her eyes as we stood in the hallway talking. "Nobody deserves to die like that, in a public bathroom. I don't care what he did."

"And what did he do?"

Ann rolled her eyes and shook her head. "That girl should've left him long ago. But if she had, she wouldn't have those two precious children." She shrugged. "That's life, isn't it?"

"How is Evie? She actually found him, you know. But she seemed to take it well."

Ann didn't seem concerned about Evie. "Evie's like me. Just takes things as they come. The rest of our family—I'm beginning to think Evie and I must've been adopted."

I told her I still had Evie's fleece jacket and that I'd return it to her, if that was okay.

"Just keep it." She waved a hand. "She won't miss it."

I had no intention of that.

Cassidy Gee came by, escorting a man in a wheelchair to the PT office. Ann and I talked with them briefly and they left with a couple of cookies.

I leaned against the handrail near the dining room. "Is the knit shop still closed?"

She shook her head. "They told Prissy she could open but she's just sitting out in the courtyard, not doing any business. Let me tell you, if I'd ever had a murder to work with, I would've put on a sale like you wouldn't believe. I'd be a wealthy woman today." She laughed and stuffed the tissue back in her pocket.

I was pretty sure she *was* a wealthy woman.

"Prissy's customers just gawk and gossip, so they might as well enjoy the sunshine. I shouldn't criticize. But if my customers had any money, I managed to get some of it before they left." She laughed before lowering her voice. "Prissy's letting the business run down. And it'll get worse now that somebody's died on the premises."

She gave a little shake and looked at me. "But what's there to do. You smell the cookies?"

I did. "I'm surprised Jim Bergen isn't here." I started to leave.

"He hits the cookie jar every afternoon. But he's not the only one."

As I looked down the hallway, a man entered the lobby. It was Terry Wozniak, and he saw me, too. He stopped and waited, and I waved at him.

"I'd better go." I walked on.

Chapter 6

"Ms. Mack!"

I waved again. As I got closer, I saw Wozniak was juggling some framed photographs and favoring one arm. Heavy photographs, from the looks of things. He seemed overdressed for the weather, wearing a canvas windbreaker.

"I'll bet you're looking for Reg Handleman." I hoped he was. I pointed across the lobby. "They're already in the ballroom."

Wozniak took a couple of steps in my direction and I noticed beads of perspiration dotting his upper lip. He really was too warm. "I'd rather find you. Any chance we can get a cup of coffee somewhere? I'd like to talk with you."

I noticed Riley Meddors only when he stood up from the nearby couch, watching us. I thought fast and made a little gesture toward him, hoping Wozniak would take it was an indication someone was waiting for me.

"I'm so sorry," I told Wozniak. "I can't manage it today, I'm afraid. But they have coffee waiting for you in the ballroom."

He gave Riley a grim glance. "Then I'll just get these looked at by the expert. Don't forget our date, now." He readjusted the photographs and gave Riley another nod as he went by.

I walked over to the couch.

"I hope you didn't mind being implicated, Riley. I'm just not up for Wozniak today."

He frowned. "You have a date with him?"

His starter beard had some streaks of gray I hadn't noticed last night. I shook my head.

"He was talking about his Henry George class, which begins in January. He's trying to get me to sign up. The beard's looking very distinguished." I leaned around for a side view.

"I wonder why they let Wozniak teach that class." He frowned. "I know a dozen people who'd do a better job."

"You, for instance."

He disagreed. "I don't think much of single tax. It's only as good as the people involved."

"And are all the participants like Wozniak?"

"No. They're mostly pretty good. He's more of a hanger-on."

"I thought he was president."

Riley looked surprised but laughed. "I'll bet he told you that." He gave me a smile. "Would I fare any better than he did if I ask you to go for coffee?"

I winced. "I'd like to, but I haven't spent a total of sixty minutes in the office all day. You heard about our visit to the knit shop?"

He nodded. "Nita called, worried about you. I came by to be sure you're okay. I'm sorry it happened."

"That's very sweet." I squeezed his arm and took a step toward my office. "Don't forget, I'm looking forward to a report on your trip."

"How about sandwiches at my apartment before tonight's lecture? Just the two of us."

Riley and I went out together frequently, but always with Jim and Nita or occasionally with my daughter and grandson. This would be a first, but a girl had to eat, didn't she?

"Sure," I said, calculating. I'd need to stop at my apartment first, to check on Tinkerbelle and freshen up and then walk to his building. And we'd need to get back here by seven, when Handleman's talk would begin.

I looked at my watch. "Five forty-five? That'll give us about an hour."

He nodded and leaned over the back of the couch to grab a Greek fisherman's cap.

That left me a nice block of time right now to work on today's messages and mail and maybe next year's budget. But Lieutenant Mary Montgomery had other ideas. She pecked on my open office door a few minutes later.

"Got a minute?"

"For you, sure." I pushed the printouts away, dropped my pencil on the desk, and shoved my chair back. An unannounced visit from Montgomery was unusual.

She closed the door and I moved to the sitting area in the middle of the office.

"Chief's talking with Mrs. Bergen and told me to come tell you. Devon Wheat was strangled."

"Oh no." I sighed. A bad situation had just gotten worse. "That means murder?"

She snorted. "Unless you know something I don't. People very seldom go around strangling themselves."

"Well, there *is* that autoerotic thing."

She blinked a couple of times. "You saw a white towel under the body?"

I remembered seeing a bit of fabric but hadn't identified it as a towel. "That's the, umm—can you call a towel a weapon?"

"The implement." She shrugged. "Garrote, to be technical."

"The towel wasn't around his neck."

"You need to brush up on your crime scene analysis. Watch more TV."

"I didn't actually examine him, you know. Who'd want to kill him? Did he have any bad habits? I mean drugs?"

She shrugged. "We're checking on that and some other things. Preliminary estimate is he died between eight and midnight. He served in the military, came back and finished college across the bay, and moved over here six years ago. Joined Rotary and First Methodist but didn't stick with either one. Seems like everybody in town knew him, but we haven't found any close friends. That seem odd to you?"

I didn't think so. "It's the way young people are now. They strike out on their own and make professional friends, but they never stay at home to get to know the neighbors. And it wouldn't matter if they did. The neighbors aren't at home, either."

That was another point in favor of retirement communities, where everybody was always home and knew all about their neighbors.

"Where did he live?"

She stretched out long, skinny legs and crossed them at the ankles. "Rented a little house in the Fruits and Nuts. Stayed there when his wife took the kids and left eighteen months ago. We've had a hard time running her down, but she's in Huntsville, it seems, with her parents."

Fruits and Nuts was the expensive part of town, named for the streets, like Orange and Pecan. The area was close to the bay, where everybody wanted to be, and the houses were cute. I'd looked there initially but couldn't afford anything livable.

Patti knocked and stuck her head in.

She drew back automatically when she saw I had a guest. "I'm sorry. I was just going to tell you people are already coming in for tonight's lecture and it's still over two hours away. Looks like there'll be a big crowd. Stewart said he's going ahead with the extra chairs."

I held up a finger to hold her and looked at Montgomery. "Patti knew Devon Wheat."

The lieutenant looked over her shoulder. "Come in a minute, will you?"

"I heard something about Devon's wife leaving him," I prompted.

Patti hoisted herself onto the edge of the worktable and sat, swinging her feet. "She was here for the witches' ride a couple weeks ago. Had to meet with the attorneys so she came without the kids. The divorce is about to be final." Brief pause. "Was, I mean."

"What's her name?" I asked.

"Bria. Bria Wheat. Sounds like some kind of crop, doesn't it?"

The witches' ride was a pre-Halloween event involving bicycles and women wearing black cloaks and pointy hats. I'd heard it was popular because so few riders could safely pedal while they tossed treats and the crowd enjoyed the anticipation of spills.

Montgomery asked Patti, "Did she stay with him while she was here? Were they on that kind of terms?"

Patti gave her curls a quick shake. "No. She was with friends when I saw her, so we didn't really talk. But she's moved on. Still making excuses for him, though. Says he was always stressed out. She was being nice, which anybody might do until they get the money thing worked out. He was being difficult about that. But no, she wouldn't have stayed with him. Already got a new boyfriend."

"She's been gone awhile. Did he have a new girlfriend? Or a boyfriend, for that matter?" Montgomery asked.

Patti twisted her mouth to one side, pantomiming deep thought, then shook her head. "Not that I know of. He just worked and rode bikes and went to the L'Etoile. Participated in some races, Pensacola and Birmingham, I think. I remember him talking about steep hills. And he talked about investments and money. That's about it."

"Who'd he hang out with?"

She shrugged. "I only saw him at the Bistro. He ate with Todd sometimes but they weren't exactly friends. Todd's younger and was always going on at him, acting like it's his personal money Devon's managing. Which, in a way, it was, I guess, but Devon had to do what the judge said, didn't he?"

She kept glancing at me like she was seeking support, but I had only a bare idea what she was talking about and couldn't help.

Mary Montgomery nodded like she understood. "Todd, you said? Now remind me which one he is. One of the bikers?"

It was a good way to put a witness at ease and I'd seen Montgomery use it in other situations. Just imply you already knew the facts and the witness wasn't really telling anything, just helping you recall. Or maybe she really did know Todd.

Patti laughed and looked at me. "You know Todd. Not into fitness or anything. More like a freshman, or a dropout. Not serious about anything."

"I know him." I also knew he'd been prowling around her desk the first time I met him.

Patti chatted away, telling Montgomery a few gossipy facts. "He drives a Cadillac that belonged to his grandfather. You'd know it. Expired tag—you probably know that, too. His granddad died—when was it, Cleo? Christmas? No, Valentine's Day. Right?"

"I wasn't here then," I reminded her.

"Right. I forgot. But it was Valentine's Day, I'm pretty sure. Some holiday, anyway. He had one of the houses and lived here—oh, forever." She flapped one hand. "Todd's staying there now."

She glanced at me. "Just until the estate gets settled, he says. Maybe he's not supposed to, but you can't tell Todd anything. He's not supposed to drive without insurance, but he doesn't have an income so how's he going to get any? He's got four million dollars in a trust fund he can't touch until he's twenty-five, but he wouldn't believe that, either. Thought he could just talk Devon Wheat out of it, or at least tell him how to invest it. He threatened to sue if Devon didn't double his money by the time he gets it."

"Maybe I need to talk with Todd," Montgomery said. "Where do I find him?"

"Andrews Street," I said, basing it on Patti's remarks. "I'll get you the number." I reached for the Harbor Village directory and looked up Barnwell.

Patti closed her eyes and shook like a wet dog. "If I had to work with a bunch of clients like Todd Barnwell, I'd probably spring a leak, too."

Spring a leak? Was that new terminology for an aneurysm?

I wrote Todd's name and address on a sticky note, passed it to Montgomery, and said to Patti, "I didn't quite catch what Todd wanted Devon to do with four million dollars. Besides give it to him."

She rolled her eyes. "You know I don't know anything about stocks and stuff. He had a number. Forty, maybe? I don't remember."

"A four-oh-one k? A retirement account?"

"I guess. Does Bria get it now?"

I shrugged and looked at Montgomery. "Are you going to tell Patti your news? How he died?"

Patti stopped swinging her feet and looked at me. She tapped her temple. "Blood vessel, you said. Right?"

I wouldn't look at Patti. Montgomery's brows lowered and her mouth curved downward even more than usual.

"What?" Patti sounded scared.

"We're treating it as a homicide now."

Her eyes popped wide. "A homicide? You mean murder?" She looked from Montgomery to me. "A murder in Royale Court? That can't be, I'm there all the time. What does Ann say? Oh, Cleo! You don't think that man...Did you tell her?"

"What are we talking about?" Montgomery looked at me. "You know someone who strangles people?"

Patti cringed.

"Tell me what?" Montgomery insisted.

I waited and pointed to Patti. Montgomery gave her one of the stares.

"Well, there's this man staying here." Patti clamped her elbows against her sides and cowered. "There's just something scary about him. Cleo refuses to see it."

I shook my head. "No, Patti. He's a perfectly nice man." I looked at Montgomery. "She's talking about our speaker, Reg Handleman. He's from Indiana and doesn't know anybody in town unless they're connected with the car show."

"And Mr. Levine," Patti reminded me.

I agreed. "Well, yes. He knows Charlie Levine. They've been friends since high school." I didn't mention that the friendship seemed to have frayed a bit this week. "Handleman's thinking about moving here."

Patti gave a little gasp and stared at me. "Here? Tell me you're joking."

Montgomery must see a lot of foolishness in her line of work. She didn't react to the drama. "Thank you, Patti. We'll talk with everybody connected to Wheat in the next few days. You remember how long we spent last summer investigating a suspicious death. We'll look at everybody." She signaled an end to the conversation by sitting up straight, as if she were about to depart. "You're not going to the car show?"

Patti look puzzled. "Not going? Because of that man, you mean? I can avoid him if Cleo will just give us the morning off." She gave me her brightest, most wheedling smile and slid off the table.

"Why don't you drive the bus and take a group?"

She laughed. "And park where, here?"

"The shuttle service is going to pick up here," I said.

The lieutenant snickered at the idea of leaving from here and parking here. "Makes me think of the Atlanta airport, for some reason."

After Patti left, Montgomery had a question. "She's still freaking out about that speaker guy?"

"It's partly your fault," I pointed out.

Montgomery grinned. "Why's that? What'd I do?"

"She took an instant dislike to him when he arrived and you told her to pay attention to her intuition. Patti's a drama queen but I'm going to talk with her in case there's more to it than that."

"Like what?"

"Like a subconscious racial animus. Handleman looks white but thinks of himself as black. He thinks because Patti's Southern, she senses his ethnic background and dislikes him. Foolishness on both sides."

"She never says anything about race to me."

"You wouldn't notice if she did."

"Oh, I'd notice all right. I just wouldn't say anything. I need to ask you about this morning. You're sure the knit shop was unlocked when you got there? Ms. Bergen says it was."

"Ms. Bergen's right, no doubt about it. Did the murderer go out that way? Nobody was there to see, I guess."

"Don't jump to conclusions. Do you have anything else to tell me?"

"You said Wheat died about eight last night? Ann was here at the lecture then. Where was Usher Slump?"

She snorted. "Says he was at home. What else you got?"

I reminded Montgomery I'd never been to the knit shop before. "I wouldn't know if something was unusual. I didn't really notice the towel. Did it belong in the bathroom? Or did the murderer bring it with him?"

"Wheat's, probably. Lots of bike riders wear towels around their necks. To wipe up perspiration."

"If someone walked into the bathroom, why didn't he fight? Or run? Maybe it was a romantic meeting. And how do *you* explain his position on the floor, like he'd fallen over backward?"

Her mouth turned down even more. "Ask me something I can answer. Help me practice for the press."

"So…" I took her literally, but composing a direct question wasn't easy. "Where was he killed, Lieutenant?"

She answered in television interview mode. "The crime scene includes the financial planner's office, a storage room, and the room where the body was discovered. The rest of Royale Court has been reopened for business." She switched back to her normal voice. "I've got to go. I have an interview in a few minutes." She didn't get up.

"Where was the victim's bicycle, Officer Montgomery?"

"It's Lieutenant. And we haven't found it."

"You mean the murderer left on a bicycle? Only in Fairhope."

"We had a bank robber on a bicycle once." She bent her knees and rested her hands on the chair arms, about to push up.

"You're kidding."

"Before my day, but it happened. Anything else you want to tell me? No one in the courtyard when you arrived?"

"Not that I remember. The body was cold and you said he'd been dead for—what? Eight or ten hours? Whoever did it was long gone."

She stood and gazed out the window. I did the same. The eastern sky was already dusky and Harbor Village's five-globed street lamps had switched on automatically, creating a pleasant scene. It was late and I needed to get going.

Montgomery was still chatty. "We may know more after the autopsy. You going to the car show?"

"I guess so. And to tell you the truth, I'm just about sick of cars."

"You and me both."

Patti was still at her desk after I'd gathered up my stuff and locked the office. Probably hanging around because Stewart was there. I stopped and leaned against her desk, even though I had no time to spare. I got right to the point. "Handleman thinks you dislike him because he's black."

She was gathering up her things to leave but stopped and gave me a blank look. "I didn't say he's black. I said he looks like a caveman."

"You said Neanderthal. But that's not likely, since black people aren't related to Neanderthals."

"Are you kidding me? That man is really black?"

"Says he is. Says he'd like to move down here, but he's worried about his wife being accepted."

She twisted her eyebrows and got a fierce frown on her face. "Really? Well, that's just sad. She must be darker than he is. Do they have children?" She stood and reached for the little turtles, lifting them off the driftwood and dropping them carefully into the desk drawer.

I shook my head. "I didn't ask about children. They'd be grown by now, anyway."

"I hope so. Can you imagine a baby with eyes like his? Poor thing. So, who *is* related to Neanderthals? And how do you know?"

"DNA. What do the turtles say about tomorrow?"

"They won't say until tomorrow."

"That doesn't sound very psychic, Patti. Anybody can predict once the future gets here."

* * * *

Riley's apartment was on the ground floor of the building next to mine. I was five minutes late and he was standing outside, leaning against a post looking like some unshaven cool dude as I rounded the corner.

He stood up straight and removed his hands from his pockets. "I wasn't sure you'd know which apartment was mine."

"I didn't. I was going to knock on doors until I found you."

He pushed the door open and stepped back, and I walked in.

"The banker in his lair," I joked.

The apartment smelled new, even though he'd lived there a couple of years. The walls were white and the carpet dark khaki with a geometric pattern woven in. The leather couch was long and sleek with a tufted back, and the matching recliner looked like it had been lifted right out of a private jet or some expensive sports car. They shared a big corner table and a large lamp that cast a soft glow.

"Wow," I said, softly. "Nice."

It was a serene, elegant apartment that gave away nothing about its occupant except that he had good taste. There was an oversized TV on a low black cabinet and a black desk against the wall, nothing on it but a thin aluminum laptop and a mushroom-shaped lamp that gave super-white light. Nothing personal anywhere except a few books and a copy of *The Economist*.

"No blanket or pillow for napping," I pointed out. "And I thought you didn't use computers." He'd known very little about them a few months ago, when I first went to him for help in interpreting Harbor Health Care's financial statements.

"You convinced me I needed one. Now, if you're ready for dinner—" He waved toward the dining table, already set with thick white dishes. The place mats were dark wooden slats. "I knew you liked Andree's, so I got them to make sandwiches." He dimmed the lights. "Cabernet?"

"Lovely."

It was my second chicken salad sandwich of the day, but I didn't tell Riley. We had potato salad and pickle spears to go with the sandwiches and lemon bars for dessert.

Most people choose a pleasant topic for dinner conversation. We talked about murder. I told him about finding the body, dressed in bicycling attire and oddly positioned on the floor, and progressed to Montgomery's visit to the office. "She came to tell me he was strangled."

He was quiet for a moment before giving a little shrug and shake of the head. "Tough."

"She was actually chatty for a change. I don't suppose you have any idea who would've killed him, or why."

He didn't answer right away. "The spouse is usually the first choice, but with a strangling, I might rule out women. Maybe he had a boyfriend? Or somebody with a grudge against him? Strangulation takes real strength. Or rage. Road rage, maybe—you said he rides a bicycle? A lot of people dislike them."

"A yellow one, and it's missing."

His brows went up. "Odd. But I'd check out his clients first. See if he was cheating anyone. Remember Bernie Madoff?"

"He made up phony statements, didn't he? Showing people how much money they were making, when they'd actually lost everything."

"He'd *taken* everything. And people still loved him, until they learned they'd been swindled. How many clients did Wheat have?"

I didn't know. "Patti says Todd Barnwell was angry with him about a trust account."

"Who's Todd Barnwell?" he asked.

I skipped to Jim Bergen's hypothesis. "Maybe he was killed in his office and moved to the bathroom. But why?"

"Carried? Dragged? Was he a big guy? Athletic?"

"About my size."

He nodded thoughtfully. "I'm sorry you had to find him, but I'm glad Nita wasn't there alone."

"Nita's stronger than she looks."

Riley smiled. "That's not saying much."

We'd finished the food and were sipping the last of our wine when he glanced at his watch and changed the subject.

"I didn't tell you the whole story about my trip." He leaned forward, forearms resting on the table. His sleeves were pushed up and his arms were covered in brown hair that looked velvety.

"We had two family weddings. Joel's you know about, but Diane got married, too."

"I thought she was already married."

He shook his head. "She and Abby are longtime companions, but marriage wasn't a possibility until recently."

Abby? "I see. And you attended. That's really nice. Lots of men wouldn't do that."

He took my hand and held it, absently. "They're happy together. And I spent a few days with everyone. It meant something to my sons. And to me, too. Diane and I had a couple of long talks. I even learned a few things about myself."

"And what was that?" I smiled at him. There'd always been a playful chemistry between Riley and me, egged on by Nita's hints and suggestions, but a serious conversation in private was a new experience. I didn't know much about his career, not even which bank he'd worked for. I eased my hand away from his and leaned back, looking at him more attentively. He'd put on reading glasses while we ate and now he looked at me over their tops, chin down, a fetching pose. The ribbing of a black T-shirt showed at his throat. Self-possessed was the word that came to mind. I smiled back.

"Diane says I should dust off my assets, such as they are, and get back in the game."

"And that means—?"

He gave me a lingering look. "Cleo, I'd like for you to…I guess the expression is, to be more involved in my life."

"Riley, be careful," I kidded, even though half my brain was already screeching an alarm. "A girl might think you're proposing or something."

He smiled and fiddled with his empty glass, then suddenly looked at me. "Is that what you want? A proposal? And here I've been taking you for a modern woman. A feminist, even."

I grinned in spite of growing discomfort. Was he serious? No. He was smiling, relaxed, and teasing, the old banker testing his negotiating skills.

"You had a happy marriage." He had a sweet expression. "You know it can be done."

What did that mean? I fanned myself with my napkin. "You're giving me a heart attack, Riley." My hands were shaking. And just as I decided it wasn't a joke, or not entirely, he laughed, stood up, and began gathering our dishes. I blinked in surprise.

"Let's talk about it later. Right now, we're running late. Ready to learn about investment-grade automobiles?"

I'd asked for it, but I felt disappointment at the abrupt change of topic. We cleared the table in silence, except for a moment in the kitchen when he hummed to himself. Both of us wanted out of there, I was sure.

"Let's leave the dishes in the sink. I'll take care of them later."

I grabbed my shoulder bag from the floor, but he didn't open the door when I got there. Instead, he paused for a moment, then put his arms around me and gave me the kind of kiss I'd forgotten existed.

It started tentatively and, with just a little encouragement on my part, escalated. My knees went weak, and a tingle crawled up my spine. I closed my eyes and smelled his soap, felt his warmth, his arms, his body against mine. Even when it ended, I could think of nothing else.

He rested his forehead against mine for a couple of seconds, allowing me to get some oxygen in, and when he spoke, his voice was soft and resonant. "I adjusted to your ex-husband showing up all the time, but that single taxer buzzing around when I got back? That was a kick in the rear."

He kissed my temple. "I'm not going to push you, but I'll be here when you decide."

The self-possessed look came back, softened with a slight smile. He flipped the apartment lights off and opened the door.

Surprise! The rest of the world was still there.

I rushed out to meet it.

The moon was almost full behind thin, broken clouds as we walked to the big house. I still felt a little shaky and my pulse was too rapid, as though my personal power system had reversed polarity a few times in recent minutes.

"What's a type forty investment?" I asked finally, halfway to the big house and hoping to sound natural, to drown out the *oh-my-god* chorus that cranked up in my head whenever I was stressed.

"A four-oh-one-K? You know what that is."

"I'm trying to understand something Patti said. Just wondered if I was overlooking something."

"Don't overlook this night." He caught my hand and held it. "The moon's almost full."

And we were almost late. A few people were still moving through the lobby, on their way to the ballroom. The sound coming from that direction was a loud and steady hum, like a fruit tree full of bees.

Stewart came through the lobby with a couple of chairs from the dining room and gave us a knowing glance. Were we giving off some signal? Pheromones, perhaps?

"Full house again," Stewart said. "I told you. You should've sold tickets."

We followed him into the garden and entered the ballroom through the side door.

A cluster of people stood at the front, chatting with the speaker, and another group crowded around the beverage table at the back, but half the audience was already seated. Carla was placing stacks of plaid paper napkins on a second refreshment table, this one filled with pastries and fruit trays. I went to speak to her and to look over the wares. She wasn't letting anybody sneak a taste yet. The platters were still under wraps.

I asked, "Are you glad this night work is about over?"

She shook her head. "It's been so much fun." She moved one of the plates to the front and gave it a quarter turn. "That's why we like having you here, Cleo. We never know what'll happen next." She laughed and moved back against the wall, standing guard over the desserts.

Fun! Not the word I'd choose for this week.

I scanned the room and saw Patti come in from the lobby. She had skipped the first two lectures, but here she was tonight, carrying a little tray with a bottle of water and a glass of ice. She went straight to Handleman and placed the tray in front of him and they chatted animatedly, as if colluding on something. She even took off her glasses and held them out at a distance. Describing her many eyewear options, I supposed. The next time I looked, he had a goofy smile on his face and she was sitting on the first row, turned around to chat with Jim and Nita Bergen.

At that point, I shared Carla's outlook. What would happen next?

Handleman donned the microphone headset and counted off a test, and I spotted Riley. He waved. With mixed feelings, part apprehension, part anticipation, I wormed my way around the straggling members of the audience to sit beside him.

Chapter 7

Reg Handleman began his third and final performance by projecting the image of a silver elephant standing on its rear legs, its trunk lifted high in the air. "If everybody will take a seat now, we'll get started. Do we have enough chairs?"

As I took the seat beside Riley, he gave me a sly look and a smile.

How long did it take people to notice you had a new person in your life? And what did I even know about this man beside me, beyond the fact he smelled good? *Oh-my-god*, the chorus whispered. I looked away, forced my hands to give up the death grip they'd locked into, and checked out the audience.

Dolly Webb's bedtime, I knew, was only an hour away. I figured she'd leave at the break, but the lights dimmed and right away, someone got up, tiptoed in a low crouch to the lobby, and slipped out soundlessly. But it wasn't Dolly, still sitting on the second row beside Nita.

It was Patti. I couldn't tell if she headed for the parking lot or for the kitchen. Was it possible she'd come to the lecture just to cozy up to the speaker? What if the simple act of facing up to bad behavior could stamp out bigotry? I engaged in a little escapist imagining while Handleman adjusted his audio-visual equipment.

"Anybody recognize this elephant?" He gestured toward the screen.

It looked a little crude to me, like something a child might make with modeling clay or that green stuff that had stuck to my shoes when Stephanie was little. The dog ate some of it once and turned his poop green, something I'd never forget.

"This is the hood ornament of the most valuable car in the world."

Handleman was feeding it to us bit by bit but there were still no replies from the audience. I glanced at Riley and he shook his head in an I-don't-know gesture.

There was small print in a red oval below the elephant. I was sitting in the back of the room, but when I squinted I could just make out the letters...Bugatti?

It sounded Italian. I pronounced it to myself in various accents but none of them sounded particularly expensive, as Lamborghini or Ferrari did. The VW beetle had been called a bug but it wasn't a Bugatti. And Bug was never meant to be a flattering designation. Maybe I'd seen the name on one of the car show posters?

"We'll save the rest of the automobile for later and begin instead with some of the common rarities. That's a term I invented. Common rarities. An oxymoron, a smart guy like Charlie Levine might say. Raise your hand, Charlie. Where are you? Ah, Eloise is here tonight, too. Great! I'll get back to you, sweetheart. Listen, folks. Charlie's the fellow responsible for these lectures. If you've enjoyed them, or if you haven't, tell him. Now, I need three chairs up here. If some of you men will do the honors—" He rapped his knuckles on the front table. "We're going to have a little competition."

Handleman leaned over a chair where his briefcase sat open.

I heard a bell ring and he glanced over his shoulder at the audience, grinning, and turned his back again, concealing whatever he was doing.

When volunteers had arranged the requested three chairs at the front tables, Handleman turned around carrying three little call bells, the kind used to signal for service. Each one had a little button on top that, depressed, produced a loud, clear tone. He winked at us as he spaced the bells out, one in front of each chair. Then he walked down the table and rang each bell.

Ding. Dong. A long pause and another grin. *Dang.*

Three distinct sounds.

"Now, I need three volunteers, and I know just the people for the job."

He scanned the front row and finally lifted his eyebrows inquiringly and pointed to the empty chair where Patti had been.

Jim announced in a loud voice, "She went to the bathroom."

Nita gave him an elbow in the ribs and the audience laughed.

"In the kitchen," Stewart said. "Want me to get her?"

"No, no. We wouldn't want to interfere with refreshments."

Handleman moved on, looking around the room. Finally, he pointed to me. "Ms. Mack, will you come to the front?"

There was polite cheering and clapping from the Harbor Village residents, and I curtsied when I got to the front of the room. Handleman pulled out a chair for me, then went back to select another victim.

It took a minute for him to decide on a slim blond man who moved toward the front of the room in a sluggish saunter that looked familiar. When he got closer, I recognized Todd Barnwell.

"Hi there." I gave him a little wave.

He was clearly embarrassed to be singled out and didn't make eye contact. He slumped into the third chair, as far away from me as possible, and left an empty seat between us.

Handleman was pacing the aisles, looking for someone else. Someone he couldn't seem to find. Finally, with a sweeping gesture, he swooped down on his final victim. "How about you, Mr. McKenzie?"

Travis.

Naturally, Travis hammed it up, clasping his hands together above his head like a prizefighter and swaggering to the front as if he'd won already.

The crowd whistled and clapped and I rolled my eyes at him.

"No fair," I said. "I live here."

"People love an underdog."

I supposed he meant me. He was grinning like a fox. Todd Barnwell, farther down the table, looked like thunder. I turned my chair so I didn't have to see him.

"Ready?" Handleman asked. "Now, here's the deal. You're going to see ten cars on the screen, one at a time. If you can identify the car, ring your bell and I'll call on you. The first correct answer wins a point. If I rule you wrong, you're out for that item and someone else can ring in. Now, audience, don't help them. It's sink or swim for these three. Everyone ready?"

We nodded. Or Travis and I did.

I was fast with the bell and won the first item—a VW beetle—and the second one. "BMW!" I slammed my bell. I recognized the insignia even though the orange car had a dainty appearance that contrasted my mental image of BMWs. But I was right and the crowd cheered.

"Two to nothing," Handleman mugged. "Come on, guys. Wake up!" He rapped the table in front of Todd and I looked at him again, in spite of my resolve. He was clearly miserable.

Travis beat me on the third slide, a spotted Cadillac convertible with fins on the back and cow horns on the hood. The audience judged it hilarious.

Todd Barnwell actually got the fourth one, a Hummer, but forgot to ring his bell. Handleman threatened to deny credit but relented, and after that, Todd didn't try again. I had classified him as pouty the first time I encountered him. Now I felt compelled to pump up my own enthusiasm and act a fool to compensate for his bratty behavior.

Travis knew the next two automobiles instantly, a Rolls Royce followed by a Porsche, which he pronounced as a single syllable. Handleman repeated it with the two-syllable pronunciation I used, like the name Portia. My husband, Robert, had always said anyone who could afford a Porsche could call it whatever he liked.

The seventh car was a curvaceous white convertible with chrome mesh over the headlights. "Corvette!" I slammed the bell a split second ahead of Travis. Score one for Wozniak. I hoped he was there to see it. It might've been the same car we'd talked about on the poster in the Henry George Colony office.

Travis got the gull-wing Mercedes with doors that lifted up, like a bird in flight. Handleman pointed out that gull-wing doors would come in handy on some of Fairhope's narrow streets.

I got the Citroen 2CV only because Robert and I had rented one on our honeymoon and I'd liked the French pronunciation. *Deux chevaux.* Two horsepower. Seeing it unexpectedly was like a stab in the heart, but it wasn't exactly the right model, and anyway, the show must go on.

At this point, Travis and I were tied, with one car to go.

I hovered over my bell as the tenth slide popped onto the screen. It was a silver Jaguar roadster, with a long hood and red leather interior for two. I pounced on my bell and knocked it off the table.

Dong, Travis's bell chimed.

The crowd went nuts and I put my head down, sobbing and giggling until I got the hiccups. Travis clowned around while I got my emotions under control. Handleman picked up my bell, brushed it off and, with a flourish, put it back in place. I found a tissue in my pocket and dried my nose and eyes.

Todd Barnwell helped, too, by slinking out to the parking lot.

"Past his bedtime," someone said, and the audience howled with laughter again.

"All right, folks. That was fun," Handleman said. "But what's our topic tonight? Investing. So the real question is this: Of all the valuable cars we just saw—and they *were* all valuable, for one reason or another—which one has appreciated the most since it was new?"

"The Rolls Royce," Travis answered promptly. Half the audience agreed and applauded, and he turned to me with a smirk.

Handleman waited. I could feel everyone watching, wondering what I'd do now with the right answer already taken.

"And the little lady says…?"

I hated that term. Anybody younger than eighty knew it was taboo, or should be. Just hearing it made me want desperately to get the answer right. But Travis probably had it already. I cut my gaze around and saw his smug smile. I refused to agree with him. Handleman began singing the *Jeopardy* theme. I knew it wouldn't be the little French car, and I could remember only one other.

"The BMW." My voice sounded confident, but it was pure bluff.

Handleman turned on his heel. "How many of you know the BMW five-oh-seven?"

Nobody responded, and I had no clue if I'd been right or ridiculously wrong.

"Well then, how many of you know Eloise Levine?" He walked down the aisle to the row where Eloise sat beside her husband.

If they hadn't been together, no one would've guessed Charlie and Eloise were a couple. Charlie Levine was short, grumpy, and had asthma or something like it, which caused him to breathe with a wheeze and to perspire with the slightest exertion. Eloise, closing in on seventy or maybe seventy-five, was still glamorous, a big woman with shoulder-length blond hair, exotic clothes, and jewels that definitely looked real. The effort she put into her appearance probably explained why we didn't see her around Harbor Village very often. Even when they chose to patronize the dining room, Charlie generally walked over and picked up meals to take to their apartment.

"Stand up, Eloise, and come out here." Handleman held out a hand.

Eloise moved into the aisle beside him, and he put his arm around her. Now *there* was a well-matched couple—two oversized, flashy individuals. I thought about Riley and wondered how we'd look together. Drab, maybe, but not really mismatched.

"Back when I was a poor, broke college student," Handleman said, "Eloise went out with me occasionally. That was before she developed good taste and discovered Charlie. And Eloise convinced me to buy this very car." He clicked the BMW photo back on the screen and looked at Eloise. "You remember that, I hope?"

I looked at the screen and turned back to see Eloise nodding. From the smile on her face and the twinkle in her eyes, she might've been remembering more than a car.

"It took me three years to pay it off, thirty-four hundred dollars plus interest." Handleman wiped his brow in a gesture of pretended desperation. "Then later—ten years ago, I guess—I put twenty-five thousand into it for a professional renovation."

The audience groaned.

"And then I sold it, four years ago, for eight...hundred...thousand dollars."

I gulped and Travis, still sitting beside me at the front table, threw back his head and laughed.

"Thank you, Eloise!" Handleman said.

He gave her a hug and a big smooch on the cheek, and then she wiggled her way back to the seat beside Charlie. I applauded along with everyone else, and Eloise sat down and planted a big kiss on her husband, who took her hand and raised it in the air, signaling victory and managing to look slightly happier as he did it.

Handleman walked back toward the front. "That was the best car investment I ever made. Now when people ask me if there's money to be made in automobiles, I have to say yes. It helps to have money when you start out, but sometimes time can substitute for it."

Someone shouted out a question. "What do you drive now, Reggie?"

He stopped abruptly and pointed to the speaker. "I was hoping somebody would ask that. Remember when we saw Duke Ellington playing the Steinway?" He pantomimed fingers on the keyboard. "And we talked about Steinway making engines for horseless carriages? Well, that's not the only link between Steinway and the automotive industry."

He perched on the end of the table where Todd had sat. "In 2011, BMW brought out their seven-series Steinway model. Only a hundred and fifty were produced that first year, in any color you wanted so long as it was black or white. Like a keyboard, get it? For the gearheads in the audience, and I know you're here, there were two engine options. Mine is the V-twelve with five hundred forty-four horsepower and twin turbochargers. It's parked right up the street and you're welcome to look, but don't drool."

I looked at Travis.

"Nice car," he nodded. "I already looked."

I whispered, "When did you get so interested in cars?"

"When I learned you could sell them for ten times what you paid." He smirked and raised one eyebrow. "Get the right one and people beg to use it in parades. Good PR."

Handleman touched on the substantial appreciation of the other cars in our little competition before he dismissed Travis and me. "See that they get a couple of grapes during the break."

I walked down the aisle and Riley slid over, giving me the seat at the end of the row. I sat and the lights dimmed again.

And that was when Terry Wozniak slipped in from the garden and took a seat a few rows in front of me. I hadn't seen him earlier and realized he'd missed the first half of the night's presentation. Good thing he hadn't skipped Wednesday night's lecture. If he had, Mary Montgomery might be having an unpleasant little conversation with him. I wondered if he'd known Devon Wheat.

The next part of the night's program involved the photographs people had brought to the afternoon session. Handleman told us about the most interesting ones, naming automobiles I'd never heard of, like the Elmore and the Gardner, and some I had, if barely, like Cord, Auburn, and the Stutz Bearcat, the best name of all. Is there such a thing as a bearcat? He talked about what he called the chess set, naming the King and Queen, the Knight, plus two attempts to manufacture a Bishop, one in Birmingham. "No Rook, but there was a Crow and a Black Crow."

People at the afternoon session had brought photos of a few of those.

"I persuaded people to leave their photos here for you to see." He gestured to a pair of tables positioned near the wall behind him. "I'd like the people who have photos on display to come up and stand behind them, in case anyone has a question. We'll take a little longer than usual for our break so you can get something to drink and take a quick look at all the photos."

Suddenly he did a double take. "Well, there's Mr. Wozniak! I must've overlooked you earlier. I hope you're feeling better this evening?"

Wozniak nodded. Had he been unwell when I saw him in the afternoon? I couldn't remember any suggestion of that but hoped he hadn't exposed us to some bug.

"Well, as I was saying..." Handleman paced across the front. "Let's take about twenty minutes for refreshments and photos. And after that, we'll look at the most valuable cars in the world."

People stood and moved toward the front, but Riley bent toward me. "Who was that kid in the contest?" He gestured toward the parking lot door.

"His name's Todd Barnwell. I mentioned him to you earlier, remember? He'd been arguing with Devon Wheat over the management of a trust fund. And that reminds me. I need to run outside and make a quick phone call."

I left him heading for refreshments and went out to the garden. There were other people there already, chatting and stretching their legs and drinking coffee or punch or wine.

"Good work, Cleo," someone called out.

I thanked them and took out my phone. The fountain in the koi pond made a lot of noise so I went to the covered walkway outside the arts and crafts room before I keyed in the nonemergency number of the FPD.

"I'd like to leave a message for Lieutenant Montgomery," I told the night duty officer.

Montgomery had a curt outgoing message. When it ended, I gave my name and reminded her about Patti saying Todd Barnwell had harassed Devon Wheat about a trust fund. "I just remembered that Todd Barnwell was on de la Mare Street this morning, after you released Nita Bergen and me. He was there where he had a good view of the courtyard, and you said I should call if I thought of anything."

That would teach Todd Barnwell to be snotty. I clicked off and checked for calls.

Ann Slump had phoned but hadn't left a message. Why wasn't she in the ballroom helping Carla and Lizzie? I hoped nothing was wrong.

When I closed the phone case and started back inside, Terry Wozniak was standing alone near the koi pond. He was facing the ballroom, and the fountain noise kept him from hearing me, but I held back anyway, waiting to follow him inside.

He walked toward the entrance but turned right at the last minute and disappeared around the end of the building.

Suddenly I felt a little guilty. While Patti had been making friends with her nemesis, I'd been giving Wozniak the brush-off, even though he'd been so helpful about explaining the property tax business. And just now, I'd blown the whistle on Todd Barnwell, who'd done nothing except be a bratty kid. So, who was actually the bad guy? I went back into the bright lights of the ballroom feeling like a louse.

The second half of Handleman's presentation began with a photo parade of cars we were likely to see in the Grand Concours the next day.

My favorite was the Cadillac V-16, a big, luxurious car from the 1930s, with running boards and six white sidewall tires, including spares inset in the front fenders. Some of the several photos he showed had official-looking flags fluttering on its fenders.

"There's a tale about Al Capone's armored car being appropriated by FDR when he delivered the 'Day of Infamy' speech. It had three thousand pounds of armor plating and gangsters were the only ones who could afford such luxury back then. Unfortunately, the story's apocryphal."

The V-16 engines, made only by Cadillac and Marmon, were common on the show circuit, Handleman told us. "I guarantee we'll have at least one at the show tomorrow."

There were photos of spacious leather interiors, little jump seats, mohair grab ropes, and lap robes. Handleman gave price estimates for various cars that ranged up to and even exceeded a million dollars.

"Prices at the top end may be negotiated over several years and are highly confidential, but I'm giving you educated guesses."

He talked about eras and told us how to estimate the date a car was manufactured by examining its wheels. "Wooden spokes came in with wagons and were all but gone by nineteen thirty."

For the first time, I learned there would be two separate categories of cars being judged at the Fairhope-Point Clear show. "The concours will feature certified classics, almost exclusively prewar automobiles with only a few specific models from later years. But there'll be a sports car group, too. Some of the nicest cars anywhere will be here."

"Do you have an entry?" someone asked.

He shook his head. "I'm minding two entries for the museum, but they aren't mine. They don't belong to the museum, either. They're cars we display on long-term loan."

Finally, with only a few minutes remaining in his final presentation, he clicked back to the elephant slide.

"And now we come to the best, most elegant cars in history. We may see one of these tomorrow, probably not the *crème de la crème*. But who knows about next year, when word gets out about this new show."

In the United States, the best was Duesenberg. In Europe, it was Bugatti.

"Both companies were in the aircraft engine business during World War I, and both made the shift into high-performance automobiles."

He covered the Duesenberg first, showing handsome photographs and giving production numbers. "The models J and SJ are the standouts but before that, there was the Duesenberg Model A, arguably the first straight-eight automobile in the US. And I'm delighted to tell you there'll be one in the show this weekend. I'm eager for you to see it."

He then shifted to various models of Bugatti and finally to the Type 41. "These cars were manufactured for royalty. Prospective buyers were interviewed and approved by Ettore Bugatti himself."

He flipped quickly through slides of people, estates, and a few animal topiaries, and then the silver elephant hood ornament, "...crafted by a member of the Bugatti family shortly before his suicide." There was international intrigue, too—a secret, underground vault where a few prized cars were concealed throughout the war, to prevent Nazis taking them.

Handleman sat on the edge of the table and spoke, firmly and plainly, his gaze gliding person to person, mesmerizing us. As a series of six Bugatti Type 41s flashed briefly on the screen, one of them in a couple of guises, he gave us their frame numbers and the current owners or locations of each.

"Six examples of the Type Forty-One were manufactured and we've accounted for every one. Remember that. There's an investment scam that goes around every few years announcing the discovery of a seventh, previously unknown, Type Forty-One. I've heard that it's in Germany and subject to repatriation. Or it's in Alsace, still buried, or the Bugatti family sold it to a collector in Switzerland."

He took a sip from his water bottle and replaced the cap, then smiled and looked around the room, snake charmer and snake rolled into one.

"The latest story is that it's being shipped to America as soon as investors find a couple more people willing to chip in a hundred thousand to join their little consortium and share in the fortune the Royale will bring at auction. Like most scams, there's enough truth there to overpower skepticism. An unknown Type Forty-One *would* sell for millions of dollars. Tens of millions, even. But there's not one."

Another smile.

"The first Type Forty-One, the one wrecked by Ettore Bugatti, causes all the trouble. Five other examples were made, each slightly different, all of them utter perfection. The wrecked one was repaired and rebodied and then rebodied again. And some people, who had counted it number one when it was manufactured, counted it again with the new body, making it number seven. Got it? Well, don't fall for it. And why am I emphasizing this? Because the rumor has resurfaced. Be careful out there, especially if you've got a lot of money to lose. I can suggest much better things to do with it. And with that, I want to thank you for your time and interest."

He stood up. "I hope you'll have a wonderful weekend at the inaugural Fairhope/Point Clear Grand Concours. It takes place Friday and Saturday, with a gala Saturday night. Cars will be judged Friday morning. If you want to see the winners, wait and go in the afternoon or on Saturday. Does anyone know the ticket prices? I'm sorry, I don't."

"A hundred and forty bucks," someone shouted. "Give or take."

Handleman pointed toward the speaker. "There you have it."

The final round of applause was loud and long. When it ended, no one seemed anxious to leave. Even Dolly Webb was still there, which must have been a record for her. The remaining refreshments didn't last long.

Chapter 8

Riley leaned toward me. "Are you aware of the power of that man's presence?"

I told him about Patti's initial reaction to Handleman. "She spent days avoiding him, but I saw her chatting with him before the program started. I think he really wanted her for the contest." I got up.

"You were the perfect choice." Riley stood and stretched.

Nita joined us in time to hear his comment. She agreed. "Perfect. I was so impressed."

"Too bad I didn't beat Travis."

"Oh, no." She shook her head disapprovingly. "You did it exactly right, my dear. You *handed* him the victory, and he knows it."

I laughed at her assertiveness about passivity. At the front, Handleman shook hands, hugged, and posed for one photograph after another.

Patti was in the middle of everything, getting photographs for our use. Handleman was a shaggy fellow, I noticed, compared to Travis or even Jim, who had always reminded me of a silver buffalo. Could that shagginess explain Patti's ape-man reference, or whatever it was she'd called Handleman? Regardless of his parentage, I'd find it difficult to call him a person of color. Travis's complexion was definitely darker.

"He does have the most unusual eyes," I said to Riley and Nita, watching beside me. "Navy blue and penetrating. Do you suppose he's honest?"

Riley was looking at him. "Do you think he's not?"

I laughed and shrugged off suspicion. "Powerful people frighten me, even when they're museum ambassadors."

Riley had his own suspicions. "What if, instead of warning us about the scam, he's the scammer?" He smiled at me. "We'd be lined up to give him our money."

Riley had unusual eyes, too, but not alarming. Self-possessed. I smiled back and saw Nita do the same. Did she already know about his—what should I call it? Not a *proposal*, certainly, and not exactly a *proposition...* his *interest* in me? Their friendship went back a long way.

We joined the line for the refreshment table.

Patti was zipping through the crowd, getting candid shots of people with refreshments or in conversation. She arranged groups of residents beside the speaker and coaxed everyone to smile. The bulletin board would be made over tomorrow, I knew. And residents would come by throughout the day to talk about the event or get her to email photos to their family members. The effects of these lectures would reverberate for days or weeks, which was why they were so important.

A team from the Mobile FOX channel had set up in the garden and people circled around to watch. I recognized the anchorwoman who clipped a microphone to Handleman's lapel while her helper lit up the fountain and an elephant ear plant for a backdrop. Then she lobbed him a few questions. He smiled and chatted his way through the interview, plugging the car show and Harbor Village just like he was doing a commercial, and praising Fairhope.

"So wonderful for a town this size to have an international event like this. And the chief judge will be Harry Lipton, a thirty-year judge. You don't get any better than Harry and his team."

"Who's Harry Lipton?" Riley whispered to me. "The name rings a bell."

"Don't mention bells." I shivered. "Lipton sounds like tea. Let's see if there's any left."

At the refreshment table, conversation hopped from person to person.

"I haven't heard of any of those cars. Can you still buy them?"

"They're too big to fit into garages."

"Or parking spaces. Imagine driving down de la Mare in one of those land yachts."

"It's been fifty years at least since you could go to a dealership and buy something like that. Isn't that right, Riley?"

Riley laughed. "You can still buy them. There might be some for sale tomorrow. Just bring your checkbook."

"Hey, wasn't there a car named Riley?" someone asked.

"Yes," Handleman said, right behind me. "A reliable British vehicle. Respectable bordering on sporty, I'd say."

I grinned at Riley.

"Ms. Mack?" The TV newswoman touched my arm. "Can you give us a little background on the lecture program? The camera's right out here." She steered me back to the garden, pasted on her professional smile, and tugged her V-neck a little lower just as the camera's red light came on.

I remembered to mention Harbor Village and to give Charlie Levine and his community affairs committee credit for an always-stimulating lectures series. And I praised Reg Handleman's expertise and thanked him for educating us.

"Is there anything you'd like to say to Travis McKenzie, who won the automobile trivia contest tonight?" The interviewer turned syrupy sweet and reached out a hand to Travis, who'd been standing an arm's length away, listening.

He stepped into camera range, grinning and handsome. The interviewer obviously liked bad boys. She was smiling and flashing some serious cleavage, but if he took a peek, I didn't see him.

"You certainly know a lot about automobiles, Mr. McKenzie. Doesn't he, Ms. Mack?"

"Yes, he certainly does." I smiled right back.

She asked Travis another question or two, letting him show off, before she gave a signal and the camera lights went off, along with the high-wattage smile. I backed away and tried to disappear into the crowd.

"What do you think a Duesenberg would cost today?" I heard someone ask.

"Do you suppose that's where the word *doozy* comes from? Reg, do you know?"

Travis pulled me aside a minute later, no longer smiling. "Listen, Cleo, about that banquet. Get somebody else to go with you. Maybe take some of the staff if it's too late for residents to be out."

Did this mean what I thought? "Are you backing out? I thought you wanted to go. I thought you'd invited a friend."

He had the decency to look guilty. "I'm thinking I may just hit the road tomorrow. Work's piling up. I need to get back and spend the weekend in the office."

I scowled but he kept talking.

"You can put in an appearance and fly the flag for Harbor Village. Invite Reg Handleman. Here's Jim. Hey, Jim! You and Nita want to go to the banquet Saturday night? Cleo's got a bunch of tickets and needs somebody to keep her company."

Nita was diplomatic, telling Travis they wouldn't think of taking his ticket.

Jim was angling for a better deal. "Are you driving, Cleo? Should we go early to get good seats? Maybe we should sit at the back, so we can slip out when it gets boring. What's on the menu?"

Anybody who really wanted to go would have tickets already, I was thinking.

"Are you at least going to the car show tomorrow?" I asked Travis peevishly when the discussion quieted down. "It'd be a shame to come all this way and not even see it."

He shrugged and tugged at his shirt collar, not meeting my gaze. "I've been out there all afternoon. The show cars were coming in early, some of them driving around in the paddock. Might've been the best day to go. To tell you the truth, I'm pretty bummed out with cars."

I could sympathize but didn't want to say it in public. He kept talking.

"But the banquet, that's business. Publicity. You want to go high profile. Get Handleman to escort you. He's got visibility. Not your type but you can manage for a couple of hours. It's something you get used to. Want me to set it up? Where's your buddy who drives?"

Was he talking about Riley? *My buddy who drives?*

"We haven't even had a real talk, Travis." My voice had an obvious edge. "I thought you were going to look over my budget proposal."

"Well, we didn't count on having a murder, did we? And you don't want a meeting tonight. We're both tired. What about nine in the morning? We can meet at that breakfast place in town and I'll leave from there."

I agreed before he could escape and then did some mental calculations. He was usually late, which would make it closer to ten. Perfect for a coffee break, not breakfast. I could have my usual toast and jelly at seven and meet with the rental agent at eight thirty for our regular Friday review of Harbor Village rentals. And I could, and would, take some time away from the office next week to make up for this week.

Charlie and Eloise Levine were crossing the lobby when I got there. I called out to them and they stopped and looked around.

"This is last-minute planning and I apologize for that, but I'm trying to set up a table of Harbor Village people at the gala Saturday night. May I give you two tickets?"

Eloise was a head taller than me. "Cleo!" She took the tickets I held out. "Look, Charlie. What do you say?"

He shrugged. "Will we know anybody?"

"Nita and Jim Bergen will be there. Is there someone else I should include?"

"How about Reg?" Eloise asked. "You'd like to visit with Reg, wouldn't you, Charlie? For old times sake? I know I would."

Charlie Levine looked more positive than I would've expected. "Why not? He's leaving the next day, right?"

"I suppose." I didn't really know what his plans were.

"Will there be dancing?" Eloise asked.

"I'm sure. And a silent auction."

"Oh, Charlie. Let's go. How much are the tickets?"

"Free," I said. "Harbor Village has a sponsor's table. It'd be a favor to me if you'd help represent us."

She gave Charlie a pleading look.

He threw up a hand in submission. "Whatever you want, Eloise."

She looked at me and squeezed her shoulders and head together, eyes closed and lips pursed, sort of a Marilyn Monroe pose. "We'll go! What are you wearing?"

"A long blue dress with sparkles around the neckline. It's my only fancy dress."

"I'm sure you'll be beautiful. And I won't wear blue."

She probably had a closet full of fancy clothes.

I left Stewart and Patti in charge of locking up and went by my office for the budget worksheets, thinking I might go over them once more before I went to bed. Then I walked home with a little group that included Riley, everyone talking about Handleman's lectures and the excitement of the car show.

"I can't believe it's finally here," Georgina said. "And, Cleo, you're a car expert! Did y'all rehearse that quiz? I loved the way you knocked that bell across the room!" She threw a pretend punch and the group laughed.

At my porch I called out good nights.

Riley circled back and let the others walk on. "Want to take the shuttle to the show tomorrow?" He leaned against the doorjamb. "About noon?"

"That would be nice. I've got tickets for the banquet Saturday night. Will you go? Nita and Jim are going, and the Levines. I don't know who else yet."

"They don't see too well at night. If you'll hang on to Jim, I'll drive and look after Nita."

My friend who drives. I gave him a tired thumbs-up and went in.

The porch light was on at Ann's. She never stayed out late. I wondered again why she'd called me without leaving a message and hoped she wasn't sick. But she had family she could call if she'd had a problem.

Tinkerbelle was waiting in the living room. I dropped my bag on the coffee table and took out my phone. Stephanie had called a few minutes earlier and left a message telling me to call back if I got home before ten. I moved over to the desk, opened the laptop, and fired it up. While I waited, I clicked on Stephanie's number.

"You've been out late every night this week." She didn't even say hello.

"Tell me about it. But tonight's the end. Well, not really. There's a gala Saturday night and then it's done. The car expert gave his last lecture tonight. And your father managed to humiliate me in public."

"How?"

I told her about Handleman's competition and Travis's triumph, which tickled her. "It was fun, I suppose. For the audience, anyway." Tinkerbelle climbed into my lap and made a nest.

"I know you're glad it's over."

"I learned way more than I need to know about cars, but I saw a master showman at work." I told her a bit about Handleman's techniques. "Wish I'd seen him when I was still teaching. I could've used some of his techniques."

"What I want to know about is the dead man."

I had to think for a moment. "Was that just this morning? It seems like a week ago. Haven't we already talked about it?"

"You were driving and didn't tell me anything. What happened?"

My laptop was ready and waiting. I clicked on the mail icon and watched messages tumble in as I told Stephanie all about Nita and the knit shop and the body on the floor.

"And was it an aneurysm, like you thought?"

"No. He was strangled."

There was a pause. I scanned the list of messages.

"Strangled? Mom, do you mean murdered?"

"'Fraid so."

Long pause. "You wouldn't come to Birmingham because of crime and now you're in the middle of a murder investigation, for the second time in six months. This isn't normal."

I didn't disagree. "You're right. It's not. But it's not like I'm caught in a shootout or a drug bust or something. We have very civilized crime here. Murders for revenge, or jealousy, or…" Actually, I couldn't imagine why somebody would want to kill a financial advisor. "Maybe he lost somebody's savings in a shady investment. Or maybe a romance went wrong, although I can't imagine a young woman strangling her lover."

"You do know I'm married to a financial analyst." Stephanie got all huffy. "He doesn't deal with clients directly, but he makes decisions that advisors repeat, that affect people's wealth. I'd hate to think some maniac might start shooting at him."

"Devon Wheat was strangled, not shot."

"Oh, well. That's totally different." She was being sarcastic. "In his office, right?"

"Hmm, probably. But the body was left in a bathroom."

"Oh, well then, that's fine. I'll just tell Boyd to avoid offices and bathrooms."

"Maybe it was an angry wife."

She snorted. "Or a sarcastic mother. I hear they're especially deadly."

I saw a message from a former colleague and scanned it. "Kate Bradshaw sent me a note. One of the new grad students had a meltdown and had to be hospitalized. She's got to rearrange a bunch of placements to preserve confidentiality."

"See what you're missing, Mom? The campus can be dangerous, too. Maybe you can get a double dose, madness and murder. Exactly where is this knit shop where people get strangled? Is it in Fairhope? The one your neighbor's involved with?"

"Ann started it, but she's turned it over to a niece to run. It's in Royale Court, a cute little area in the middle of town. Have you seen it?"

"Hmm. I think it's for sale. Remember when I talked to Patti a few days ago and she thought I was moving to Fairhope?"

"You never did tell me what that was about. But the knit shop wouldn't be for sale." I was confident. "Ann and her family own the whole complex."

"Well, don't be too sure. One of my quilters heard me talking about Fairhope. Her husband's in commercial real estate and has a listing for a quilting shop. Guess where? Fairhope. That's what I was asking Patti about."

"A quilt shop's not the same as a knit shop."

"I know that, Mom. The listing says it's the perfect location for a knit shop or a quilt shop or an art gallery, anything like that."

"And it's in Fairhope? Ann will hate that. There couldn't be enough business for two knit shops here. She's already complaining."

"Well, check it out. Not that I'm really interested. Just curious."

I told her about the Saturday night gala and threw in a little bitching about Travis. "After I arranged for a table, your father is backing out and going home early."

"I wish I were there. I'd go to the gala and you could stay home with Barry."

"And how is Barry?"

"Teething. And he wants a dog."

"That's funny. I was thinking about T-Bone Pickens earlier tonight. Do you remember him?" T-Bone was our little beagle mix when Stephanie was young.

"Of course I do. Who could forget a dog with green poop? I don't think Barry's old enough for a dog so don't tell him about T-Bone. I'm not admitting I ever had one. He was cute, though, wasn't he? Remember those velvety ears? How's Nita? And my buddy Riley. Is he back yet?"

If she only knew. "I saw them tonight. They're all going to the banquet Saturday. We got a table for Harbor Village."

"What're you going to wear?"

"I don't have many options. Old faithful, I suppose."

"Definitely," she said. "But now that you're a big shot executive, you should have another fancy outfit. Several, in fact. Let's shop next time you're here. Okay, I take that back."

"Why?"

"Because you always weasel out of shopping trips. I'll have to spring the idea on you."

She was right about that. And now with the black pants available from Amazon, I might never see the inside of a department store again.

When we hung up, I clicked the TV on and watched the lead story on local news. Three different reporters had segments on Devon Wheat's murder, and there was footage of Royale Court that made it look rather exotic. The camera stayed on Prissy a long time. She was a pretty young woman. I wondered how well she knew Devon Wheat.

There was no report from Harbor Village about tonight's lecture. That would probably come tomorrow.

On a whim, I swiveled back to the computer and did a Google search, keying in a jumble of terms like commercial, for sale, knit shop, Alabama. I scrolled through a long list of items that went back years and had no relation to the topic but finally found one that looked promising. "Trendy Gulf Coast location." That sounded like Fairhope, but to be honest, it could be anywhere from Tampa to Brownsville.

Since I was looking up things, I keyed in Devon Wheat's name and found a dozen sites listing his office location, age, and phone number. There was only one review of his performance as a financial advisor, and it was from three years ago. It gave him three stars out of five because he kept someone waiting twenty minutes. He had a Facebook page, too, but it was all about bicycles. There was a bunch of photos from bike races and a personal section that said he was single and interested in women. Judging by the comments posted on his page, he knew a lot of trivial, semi-literate people, but the last post was months ago. I didn't see anything predicting murder.

I shut down the computer and closed up the apartment for the night.

In the bedroom, I pulled out clothes to put on in the morning, brushed Tinkerbelle, took my shower, and completed a Sudoku puzzle before I was finally ready to drop off to sleep. But as soon as I closed my eyes, I thought about Handleman's little contest and popped wide awake.

There was no chance Todd Barnwell would've known those cars. Not a kid like him, not even if he'd been a car buff. His memory might go as far back as PT Cruisers, but that was about it.

And was I really likely to do much better—a middle-aged female social worker? I'd played over my head due to coincidence, like owning a Beetle and parking between two BMWs every workday for the last four or five years. And anyway, I was pretty sure Handleman had wanted Patti for the contest, and she would've known even less than Todd.

No, our expert had selected his stooges very carefully. But why had he wanted Travis to win? What was the point of that? I couldn't think of any.

Chapter 9

I got up Friday morning and fed the cat, started the coffee, and went back to the bedroom to dress. When I came out a second time, looking presentable for the office, I usually went around the apartment opening blinds and curtains and turning on CNN to get the morning news as I made breakfast. On Friday I got to the glass door that opened to the screened porch, opened the blinds, and saw a note taped to the outside. I retrieved it.

"Help!" it said, in big letters. "Can you come for breakfast and give me some advice? Any time after six." The note was from my neighbor, Ann Slump. Since the clock said it was almost seven, I cut the coffee maker off, took the carafe along in case Ann didn't have decaf, and went next door. This had never happened before and I was hoping nothing was wrong.

There were six apartment buildings at Harbor Village, three on either side of the main boulevard. My building and the similar one across the street were now officially designated Three South and Three North, but they were called the donut buildings because they had central courtyards and looked a little like a square donut in aerial photos.

To get from my apartment to Ann's, I had a choice of the interior route, through the courtyard, or the outdoor route, which involved going through my screened porch, out onto the sidewalk, then in at Ann's screened porch. That was the route I chose.

Ann opened her door as soon as I stepped on the porch. She was wearing brown corduroy trousers and a patterned shirt, with one of Evie's fleece jackets in a bright teal color that complemented her red hair.

"I saw you called last night," I told her. "I hope nothing's wrong."

She took the carafe out of my hand.

"It's decaf."

She nodded. "I figured. I've about finished the regular."

"Then you've been up awhile. And you were out late last night."

"That's why I need to talk to you. You're the only person I know who's experienced with the police."

"Well, thanks, Ann. You make me sound like a criminal."

"You know what I mean. Come sit at the table. Breakfast is in the kitchen, staying hot. I'll get it."

Ann went to the kitchen and I looked around. Ann's apartment was a lot like her knit shop, full of interesting things, warm colors, and intriguing textures, with cozy spots for sitting. This morning the apartment had some enticing aromas, too.

The big, round table could seat eight or ten, or maybe twelve if they got along well. The couch looked like it had been expensive a long time ago. The apartment was clean but there were projects everywhere—books and magazines, baskets with yarn and knitting needles, a gallon jug half full of coins, a stack of quilted coasters, and an oval quilting frame with a lap quilt stretched tight. There was one of those rocker/glider chairs with a matching footstool, angled in front of the window. I could see that was where Ann sat most of the time. Not that she ever sat very much. A gooseneck floor lamp was close by, adjustable to illuminate knitting projects or quilting or books.

There was a stack of unopened mail on the coffee table, catalogs in one stack, letters and bills in a shorter one with a brass letter opener lying on top. There was a stack of videos, too, most of them with stickers showing they came from the Fairhope library. The one on top was *Fried Green Tomatoes*. I knew the book, written by Fannie Flagg, a sometimes resident of Fairhope.

Ann bustled in and out of the kitchen, bringing dishes to the table and muttering to herself.

"Do you know Fannie Flagg?" I asked.

"She looked at one of the houses back there but didn't want to leave the bay." She indicated the private houses on Andrews Street, across the fence from us.

"Can I help with something?"

"No. Just sit down."

She poured coffee for each of us, then itemized the components of breakfast, pointing things out as she named them. "There's scrambled eggs and bacon, sausage, and grits. I made biscuits an hour ago, but they're keeping hot. Two kinds of jelly, homemade. Fresh berries. I think they came from Florida but they're tasty. Butter. Salt. Pepper. What else do you need?"

"A few days in the gym after I eat. Now, tell me what's bothering you."

She got the biscuits from the oven and took the chair closest to the kitchen. I sat across the round table.

Soft cloth napkins. Had she made them, too?

"My brother's the problem."

"Usher," I said.

Ann looked at me. "You know him? I didn't realize that."

"No, I haven't met him. But Nita told me about the vowel names."

"Momma would die again if she knew how he's acting."

The food was hot and good. I ground some black pepper on top of my eggs because I liked the way it looked, black spots on bright yellow. Then I added pepper to the grits because I didn't usually like grits unless they had shrimp on top. But then I tried Ann's. "What did you do to the grits?"

"What's wrong with them?"

"Nothing. They're tasty."

"Of course they're tasty. And good for you, too. Something about the lye they use to make hominy. I forget the details. Did you put a little butter on them?"

There was a rogue's gallery of family photographs on the wall beside the table, maybe thirty in all. "Show me your siblings."

She smeared jelly on a biscuit, then took a bite and studied the photographs while she chewed. "Here's a picture of the five of us together, but that was a long time ago. You can pick me out. We're lined up by age. And Evie's here a couple of times, right here and down there by you, on the bottom row. Irene's dead, but here's the last photo I have of her. Olivia, let's see—here she is. Beautiful Olivia. She lives in England, you know."

I didn't know. "She is beautiful. Do you see her often?"

Olivia had large eyes and a solemn expression and was twice Ann's size. She looked like Grace Kelly, if I remembered correctly.

"Not often enough. She comes every February and stays six weeks. She's married to a snob who won't come here and thinks she shouldn't."

"But she comes anyway?" I took a bite of crisp bacon. It wasn't something I ate often but I'd never lost my appreciation.

"Of course she does. This is her home. We have our business meeting while she's here and she goes back with lots of money, so the snob's happy again."

"What kind of business meeting?"

"Royale Court, mostly. Evie and I developed it, you know. But we used family funds to get started, so it just seemed fair that the others should profit, too, and once it was set up that way, we were stuck. And they certainly have benefited. I thought it'd get everybody involved, you know, that we'd all stay here and work together. Well, we did for a while. Everybody did a stint at Royale Court, at least summers. Even Usher ran a shop for a while, but now we just say he's the manager and let him do what he wants."

"How many shops are there?"

"We've added on a couple of times and we have twelve now. I don't want thirteen. Might be bad luck." She laughed. "*More* bad luck, I mean."

"How can you look after twelve shops?"

"Honey, we've cut way back. But not as much as we need to."

She got another biscuit, split it open, and slid in a pat of butter. I thought she seemed distracted and nervous, and I still didn't know why she'd invited me.

"The family attorney thought we should have a corporation and created one for the five of us. Or four, with Irene gone. It doesn't matter to Prissy. She gets her money. She's married to an IT guy with a big income. He wants her to travel with him instead of running a shop. And the family corporation does give Olivia an excuse to come for a long visit."

"You don't have children, do you?"

"No. Evie and I never married. Not that it's a requirement for having children, but it used to be, back in our day. Irene had Prissy. Olivia has two, a boy and a girl, but I wouldn't know them if they walked in here. And Usher's got three, all with two different mamas."

"And where's Usher's photograph?"

She looked at the photo display. "Don't tell me he's not up here. Well, he's in the group photo. You can see what he looked like when he was six." She laughed.

He looked like a pale boy with a big head. I looked at my watch. "What's your problem with the police?"

She got up and brought the coffee carafe from the kitchen before she answered. Stalling. "They questioned Usher about Devon Wheat."

I gave her a chance to say more but she didn't. "They questioned me, too. Asked me some questions, anyway. Didn't they talk with you?"

She nodded. "Yes. But they picked Usher up and took him to the station. Didn't let him go until almost midnight."

"Unless there's something you haven't told me, it still doesn't sound very serious. Did Usher work closely with Devon Wheat? Were they friends? Or just landlord and tenant?"

She shook her head. "Like I said, we *call* Usher the manager. He's got problems, you know. He knew Devon Wheat, yes, but they weren't friends.

There's an age difference, for one thing, but Usher's emotionally unstable. I don't think either one of them had friends."

"Is that a clinical diagnosis?"

She nodded. "Emotionally unstable, impulsive, I forget what else. He saw a counselor once, I think, and never went back."

"Where was he Wednesday night? If he's the manager, he must know everybody in the courtyard. What has he told you about the murder?"

"Nothing. And that's the problem, the reason I'm worried. He's not talking, just says he was at home. I wonder if he's drinking, but he's admitting nothing. He's just not himself. I was hoping you'd heard something, like maybe they already have a suspect." She looked at me hopefully.

I shook my head, sorry to disappoint her. "Does Usher have an attorney? You could find someone to advise him."

"Won't the cops think that's a sign of something? I don't want to hire somebody if it's going to make him look guilty."

"Ann, do you think he might be guilty?"

She froze, watching me, and pressed her lips thin. My heart sank before she answered. "I don't know."

It looked like she knew something she didn't want to tell me. It was as though saying the words would make it true. How was I to advise her if she couldn't tell me her suspicions?

"What does Evie say?"

Ann winced and closed her eyes, as though I'd touched a nerve. "She says he took down the security cameras."

"Hmm." That did sound suspicious. "Maybe he was taking them down to give to the cops."

"I wish." She looked terribly worried now that the fact was out. Worried and old.

"When did he remove them?"

"We don't know. Evie found them late yesterday in a box under her counter. I was over at the big house all afternoon and she didn't leave a message at first, just kept calling back, trying to catch me. I came home at six to change clothes for the lecture and Usher called, wanting me to come to the police station. I missed the lecture and sat down there all evening. Did they have enough food?"

"Yes. It was very successful. The whole series was. We'll be on TV today, I guess. When did you last see the security cameras in place? And where were they?"

She shrugged. "It had to be in the last day or two. Evie says the box wasn't there Wednesday afternoon when she cleaned. You didn't see him removing cameras yesterday, did you? One of the them was right outside the knit shop."

I shook my head.

She sighed. "It had to be Wednesday night or yesterday, before you got there."

"But no one knew Devon Wheat was dead then."

She looked like she might cry. "The killer knew."

My heart sank. But she was right about that.

She sighed again and rubbed her temples. "The cops kept saying he'd be able to go soon, but it got later and later. And finally, they released him but told him not to leave town. You know what that means. He's a suspect."

"Well, maybe. But they'll have a lot of suspects. Travis was a suspect a few months ago, remember?"

"Yes, and you hated it, didn't you?"

I admitted it. "He's my daughter's father. I hated it for her."

"Evie left a message here—several, in fact. When I got home, it was almost midnight but I called anyway, so she'd be able to sleep. And she told me about the cameras. Then we both stayed awake all night. The cameras were in a box where she keeps needlepoint rugs for her little houses. When she picked it up, it was heavy and she knew something was wrong."

Nita and I had intended to visit Evie's shop and see the rugs before Devon Wheat's death changed everything.

"And now Evie has the cameras?"

She nodded. "Do we have to turn them in?"

What a spot! I nodded. "Yes, you do. Otherwise, you'll be involving yourself. Maybe..." I was thinking as fast as I could.

"Maybe what? We've got to decide now."

"Maybe you could get Usher to turn them in. He can tell the cops he took the cameras down to deliver to them. And you don't know that's not true."

She was shaking her head. "He wouldn't."

"Well, finesse it. Involve Usher, have him there with you. He doesn't have to know the cops are coming. When they get there, hand them the cameras and say he disconnected them. Do it for him if he won't do it."

Ann looked doubtful but I persisted.

"He can't very well refuse to hand them over if the cameras are there and the cops are reaching for them."

She still looked unhappy, but what choice did she have? "Well, it's better than nothing. I knew you'd come up with something."

I thanked her for breakfast and asked her to keep me informed and was already going out when she said, "Cleo! Wait a minute."

She picked up a square white envelope, about six by six inches, from her coffee table. She opened the lined flap and slid out a matching card, with a little square of onionskin paper protecting it. "The Grand gave me this by mistake. Do you know who it belongs to?"

She handed me the card and envelope.

The first thing I noticed was the quality. Heavy paper, slick gold lining in the envelope, lots of white space on the card, and little gold curlicues in raised print.

"Exclusive Offering," the heading said, in fancy letters with swirly designs on each side. There was a small oval photograph that looked something like Handleman's royalty cars. "Royale Consortium," the print said. There were words like "confidential," "exclusive," and "prototype," but Ann didn't give me time to read it all.

"They gave it to you when you were setting up the knitting workshop?"

"Don't you think it belongs to Mr. Handleman? I want to get it back to him."

I looked at the envelope, but it was blank. "Ann, isn't this what he was talking about last night? The Type Forty-One scam?"

Ann gave me a puzzled look. "I wasn't there last night. Did I miss something interesting?"

The bottom line of text said, "For a complete prospectus, contact—" There was a long blank line where something was supposed to be written in by hand.

"Where did you get this? From the hotel, you said?"

Now it was Ann's turn to look puzzled. "Well, I suppose so. She didn't say anything about it, but it was mixed in with the other stuff. I think she gave it to me because it says Royale and she was thinking Royale Court. Marjorie Zadnichek, I mean. The special events person. She's awfully busy with the holidays coming up. Overworked and distracted. She's older than I am, you know. Do you think it's a stolen car or something?"

"The one Handleman told us about doesn't actually exist. Well, some do. Six, I think he said. But people think there's a seventh that's worth ten million dollars or something outrageous. They're tricking people into investing a lot of money in hopes of getting a big payback when the car's sold."

"Tell me more. I might be interested."

"You're missing the point. They take your money and disappear. You never get it back because there's no car."

Ann tapped the envelope. "There's a photograph of it on here. How'd they get that?"

I wasn't doing too well at explaining, but her interest ran out about the time my answers did.

"Just give it to somebody, okay? Get it back wherever it belongs."

I said I'd try and thanked her for a very special breakfast. "I'm supposed to meet Travis at Julwin's in an hour. I doubt I'll even be able to drink a cup of coffee."

I went back to my apartment, picked up the paperwork I'd brought home, and checked on Tinkerbelle. The food and water dishes were half full, and the cat box was in good shape.

The cat was at her usual station, on the corner of my bed. She raised her head and looked at me, then rolled back into a fuzzy ball.

Evie's fleece jacket was on the dresser, and it looked as if Tinkerbelle had slept on it all night. I hated to return it dirty. I read the label and stuck it in the washer with a few similar items and left them washing, thinking I'd come back later and switch everything to the dryer. I locked up and walked to the office.

Chapter 10

I had a regular appointment at eight thirty on Fridays to review the current status of Harbor Village rentals with our new agent. Wilma Gomez, a sweet lady about my age who wore long skirts and bright lipstick, had a high-pitched, nervous laugh. Today she was wearing a knitted shawl, which I complimented.

"I made it." Wilma revolved slowly, arms extended to show off the full effect. "I've been dying for cool weather so I could wear it."

The shawl was triangular, lacy-looking, and changed from blues to golden browns in wide, watercolor-like stripes.

"I love it. I'm definitely going to start knitting again. Maybe if I start now I could have a shawl like that by next fall."

Wilma giggled like a jungle bird. "*Twee-hee-hee-hee.*"

We had begun the practice of meeting in her office, around the corner from Patti's desk, so we could look at the key box. It gave us a visual reference for which apartments were available and which needed attention from outside contractors or from Stewart and his maintenance crew.

The big, flat, felt-lined box was mounted on the wall. Wilma folded the doors out of the way and I turned one of her armchairs to face the box.

The black background was divided into sections representing the seven rental buildings at Harbor Village. Within each section were little pegs holding keys and an attached, color-coded tag designating the current status of that apartment. Rented units had green tags and I was happy to see a vast majority of green tags in the box.

A yellow tag meant the unit was vacant and ready to rent. There were still too many yellow tags, but fewer than a month ago, when Wilma came on staff. The vacancies were concentrated on the upper floors of the two-story buildings, and I was counting on Patti's screened porch project to cut their number substantially.

"I was wondering, do we have any flexibility about cutting rent on those second-floor units?" Wilma stood, hands on hips, looking at the key box. "Maybe give new tenants a free month, or knock off two hundred a month for a year's lease? A thousand a month is less than twelve hundred, but it's still a lot more than zero, which is what they're bringing in right now, sitting there vacant."

"But that's not fair to the residents who already live here, so it's a last resort. Let's see if Patti's porch project brings in some new people. Then we might offer free lunches for the first month. That would save the residents four hundred dollars a month, but the cost to us would be less than two, or whatever our profit amounts to. I can't believe I'm saying that."

Wilma seemed surprised. "Why? It sounds so impressive."

"I've always had this block about numbers." I waved away the compliment. "I'm getting over it finally. You know, we could make it more equitable by giving everybody a free meal ticket for the first month of a new or renewed lease. Let me think about that." I made a note for myself and looked back at the key box.

"People say we've been evicting some tenants."

I nodded. "We've relocated a few who didn't fit our tenant profile, but everyone went peacefully. We made it easy for them. And for the future, as long as one member of a couple is fifty-five or close to it, we'll be happy to have them join the community."

"What about this young man living in the houses?"

I frowned. "Todd Barnwell. What are you hearing about him?"

Wilma shrugged and her shawl fell off one shoulder. "Nothing, really. But I see him now and then, out walking or skateboarding. Does he live there alone?" She twirled the shawl and covered both shoulders, then tucked one end in at the neckline.

"So far as I know. Maybe I'd better have a little talk with him." I made another note. "It's been several months since his grandfather died and he should be making other arrangements."

Wilma counted under her breath. "Looks like we're down to eighteen red tags."

A red tag meant the apartment needed attention—paint or carpet or repairs, usually. Stewart and his crew had worked hard to whittle the number of red tags down to the current level. Wilma ran through the affected units quickly, giving me the apartment number and the problem. We were waiting for carpet in two cases, waiting for Stewart to cut out fiberglass showers and replace them with tile in two cases, and waiting for painting or new appliances or carpentry work in the others. Somebody's dog had chewed up a windowsill, but Stewart said it wouldn't be hard to fix when he got to it. In addition to the renovations, he had to keep up with appliance repairs, sticking windows, pictures to be hung, and all the other maintenance tasks.

"Not bad," I told Wilma, glancing over the red tags and nodding approval.

"Here's the official tabulation." She gave me a printed page showing buildings and numbers.

I scribbled the date in pencil at the top corner. "Have you seen the screened porches on the second floor of One South?"

"I love them. I'm showing there this afternoon. One prospective resident and one current resident who thinks she'd like to move upstairs. She says it'll be quieter, but those porches are the real draw. You know, it effectively enlarges their living space, since they can have meals out there, or parties. Mrs. Moore already moved her finch cage to the porch."

"That's just the sort of thing Patti envisioned. And it adds to the social life."

"That, too." *Twee-hee-hee-hee.*

When Wilma and I finished the review, I went to my office and added Wilma's rental report to the stack of papers I was taking with me to see Travis. I stopped at Patti's desk and asked her, "What time are you going to the car show?"

She was wearing lavender glasses today, with a purple tunic top. "Are you kidding? Did you hear Reg say what tickets cost?"

So now they were on a first-name basis? Really. "Want to go to the gala tomorrow night?"

She looked uncertain. "What does it cost?"

"Harbor Village has a table."

"You mean for free? Can I invite somebody?"

"Yes and yes. I'll be out for an hour or so. I'm meeting Travis."

"Stewart!" she crowed.

I looked over my shoulder. The maintenance man was walking in from the ballroom, carrying a stack of picture frames.

Patti waved to him. "Come here a minute!"

She had purple and orange nails today. I saw them when she pushed the driftwood and turtles aside so Stewart could balance his load on the corner of the desk.

"You want to go to the car show gala tomorrow night? For free?"

"It's at the hotel," I explained. "We'll all sit at one table and represent Harbor Village."

"Sure." Stewart wasn't nearly as enthusiastic as Patti. But neither was I. Patti clapped her hands and beamed at him.

"Somebody forgot their pictures last night." Stewart picked up a sheet of paper and read from it. "Terry Wozniak. You know him?"

I nodded and looked at the top photograph in the stack. Handleman's efforts had been wasted on me. I had no idea what kind of car it was.

"I saw him leave early last night. I guess he didn't come back." Even the enthusiasts were tired of cars. "I'm about to go into town. I can deliver them to his office, I guess."

With Travis expecting me, I'd have an excuse for a quick getaway if Wozniak should turn talkative again.

"I'll put them in your car when you're ready to go," Stewart said.

"I'm about to leave now."

We walked out together. I opened the garage and Stewart braced the frames against the back of the front seat. "You don't want them sliding around every time you touch the brakes. That should do it."

I left the garage open while I hurried to the apartment and switched the load of laundry to the dryer.

It looked like a beautiful day for the car show. Fairhope hadn't had much of a fall yet, but as I drove into town, a cluster of cypress trees looked ready to shed orange needles. A few popcorn trees glowed red and one bright yellow ginkgo had a circle of yellow leaves on the grass beneath it. Maybe Wozniak would be out at the polo field already, enjoying the day.

There wasn't much activity in town. I circled a block, lining up to park right in front of the Henry George Colony office, but I was out of luck. Hertha's was having a sale. I turned right at the corner and took the first nonhandicapped space beside the drugstore. Stewart had done a good job of wedging the frames in. I finally got the big one loose and decided they were too heavy for a single trip.

The Colony office was half a block away and the woman who'd been so helpful in arranging for a last-minute table at the gala was at the counter. "Morning, Ms. Mack. You're out early."

Through the glass partitions, I glimpsed Terry Wozniak going through a back doorway.

"I'm returning Mr. Wozniak's photographs. I've got a couple more in the car." I looked toward the back again, expecting him to come out and walk to the car with me, to save me another trip. He didn't. "I'll be right back."

I went back to the corner, rounded it, and saw Wozniak come out of the alley and turn in at the drugstore. If he recognized me, he gave no indication.

The smaller pictures weren't nearly so heavy, but I was still puffing a little by the time I got back to the Colony office.

"Tell Mr. Wozniak we appreciate his bringing the photographs."

"You just missed him." The woman glanced back toward his office, which was still empty.

"Yes. I saw him going in the drugstore."

"Burned his arm, you know. Probably getting some numbing salve."

"Sorry to hear that. How did it happen?" I started to leave.

"I don't think he said. I'll see you tomorrow night, won't I? At the gala?"

"Yes. And give Mr. Wozniak our thanks for the photos." I hurried back to the car without meeting Wozniak, did a loop of the adjacent block, and parked just down from the breakfast spot.

Julwin's was the oldest restaurant in town, according to the sign on the window. Travis liked it, and in the last four months, we'd had most of our serious discussions there, usually in the front booth of the main dining room. That space was taken today and I had to sit in the side room.

"Decaf," I ordered. "I'm waiting for someone."

While I waited, I spread out the budget sheets and stuck notes on a couple of things I wanted to remember to discuss.

Travis came in fifteen minutes later, a handsome, smiling man who looked as though he'd just come back from a two-week beach vacation and hadn't heard that suntans were bad for us. His eyes were chocolate brown, his hair and brows black and precisely groomed, with just the slightest bit of graying at the temples. As usual, he wore a suit and tie and looked like he might be about to address the legislature on some new bill affecting senior citizens.

I stacked my worksheets to one side and a server brought a cup of coffee for Travis and greeted him like an old friend.

He didn't need to see a menu. "A ham steak, well done, scrambled eggs with cheese, and a sliced tomato." He gave her a smile.

She smiled back. "Wheat toast, light butter?"

He nodded. He must eat here often.

She glanced at me like I was intruding. "And what are you having?"

I ordered tomato juice with a glass of ice.

"That's all?" Travis settled into the other side of the booth, his back to the entrance.

"My neighbor Ann had a problem and bribed me with food this morning. She's a great cook. The one who's been helping Carla."

"And what's Ann's problem this morning?"

He didn't sound very interested, but when I told him about Ann's brother being questioned in Devon Wheat's murder, he perked right up.

"These cops. They like to rope innocent people into their investigations. They'll look at surveillance video, identify everybody who walked through that courtyard in the last month, and then hassle them all to hell and back. Let the cops work out the details of the crime and then go after the one who did it. Be efficient about it."

He was speaking as someone who had been hassled. Maybe I'd feel the same way if I had personal experience?

"Well, whatever." I poured tomato juice over the ice cubes and took a drink. Tomato juice always shocked me with how good the first sip was.

"I want your opinion about the monthly fees for condos and houses. We need to cover property taxes, yard care, security, basic cable, water and sewer, insurance, and housekeeping once a month..." I counted them off on my fingers until my voice trailed off. "What am I forgetting?"

He glanced down my written list, added transportation services, and put the paperwork aside when his breakfast arrived.

Since I wasn't eating, I talked. I showed him Wilma's rental report.

"What's the occupancy rate?" he asked.

I jotted figures in the margin. "Forty vacancies out of two hundred and twenty-four units. What's that? Ten percent would be twenty-two, so twenty percent would be forty-four. I guess we're at about eighteen percent." I'd been training myself in shortcuts. Sixth grade math for grandmas.

Travis looked surprised. "Very good. The corporate average was nineteen last time I looked. You're doing a good job, Cleo." He took a sip of coffee. "I guess I forget that you ran a university department, and picture you doing casework your entire career."

"There's nothing wrong with casework."

He looked at me and gestured with his fork. "No. But I've got an idea for you to think about. How would you like a regional position? You'd be gone some but our other facilities are nice, too. You could keep your apartment here."

I was shaking my head long before he finished. "I like what I'm doing."

The server came back, poured more coffee, and left the check.

"You said no to this job at first, too. Think about it. There'd be more money."

I didn't want to think about it. "Travis, I'm making a big salary already, plus my pension. And I like Fairhope and the people here. This is where I want to be."

"Well, don't say no yet." He wiped his mouth with the napkin, picked up the check, and looked at it. "There's no such thing as too much money. Do you know what tomato juice costs?"

"I disagree. I read about lots of people who have too much money. Unless they're going to start a charity or something. What do you do with a million dollars a year? It's absurd." I noticed his expression and corrected myself. "I didn't mean *you* personally. I meant *one*. What would *one* do with a million or two a year?"

"Well, I'll tell you." He put his coffee mug down, eyebrows pulled together in indignation. "*One* would pay a boatload of money to ex-wives, and set up insurance policies to be sure the money keeps coming if *one* dies."

I tensed up at the mention of ex-wives, but he didn't seem to notice.

"And *one* would pay an expensive attorney to keep *one* from spending half his life in court, quibbling over pensions and bonuses and cosmetic surgery and condo fees."

"No," I said quietly, outraged.

"Cleo." He reached across the table and took my hand. "I'm sorry."

I jerked away.

"I didn't even think—I've never thought of you as an ex-wife. You've always been a colleague, a partner."

"No." I put my hands in my lap and rubbed them together, hard. "Oh my god," I heard and realized it wasn't the mental chorus this time. I'd actually said it out loud.

"Look." He closed his eyes and rubbed his face and I heard the scrape of whiskers. "I got off on the wrong foot here. I've never told you this, but I see how Steffi turned out and I'm embarrassed I had so little to do with it. I didn't treat you the way I should've, the way I wish I had. I thought I could make up for it with a job, but you've turned out to be good at that, too, so I feel like I still haven't done anything. Do you understand what I'm trying to say? I want you to move up in the corporation, to a vice presidency if you want it. Come to Houston. But it's your choice. Okay? You'll think about it?"

I didn't believe half of what he said and my face felt like it was on fire.

"I'm staying here. I may be getting into a new relationship." I certainly hadn't intended to tell him that. What was wrong with me?

He snapped to attention and started to say something but I interrupted.

"I've met a nice guy."

"Well, congratulations, if that's what you want. But do yourself a favor. Get a pre-nup."

"Who said anything about *nups*? Travis, why are you talking like this?" I looked around for the server or other eavesdroppers. "You're wealthy! Part of the one percent. Stephanie raves about your house. Says it's a palace."

I'd been to Houston twice, once for orientation and again for a meeting of executive directors, but both times were right after his wife had died and we weren't invited to his home.

He snorted and shook his head. "The fact is, I don't have a house. My stepdaughter has a house that I pay the mortgage on. My former sister-in-law has an expensive defense attorney. My former sister-in-law's girlfriend—wife—whatever she is—is avoiding jail by lounging around in an expensive, country-club rehab program at my expense. My—what is he? Great-uncle-in-law? Uncle Nelson pays his own way, fortunately, but I'm responsible for him. I saw him yesterday and he has no idea who I am. What I'm trying to say, Cleo, is that I make an obscene amount of money and still can't afford to retire. Not for years. But I'm not complaining. I just wish people wouldn't make assumptions. And I wish I'd thought ahead. Like you did."

"Oh, Travis. You know you've done very well."

"I admit it. I've done well. I am doing well. But not half as well as everyone assumes. And not as well as I could've, if I hadn't screwed things up."

It was no fun being hard on someone who was so hard on himself.

"I can only speak for myself, but I'll stop the assumptions and focus on being a partner. That was a nice compliment, by the way." It really was, I realized. How many ex-wives ever heard such a thing?

Travis hung his head but smiled.

* * * *

I drove back to Harbor Village and went to the apartment first. When I opened the laundry door, Ann's square white envelope was lying on the dryer. "Oh, pooh!" I'd forgotten all about it. The cat, enjoying the warm air eddying around my knees and ankles, looked at me.

There were some cotton sweaters and socks, still warm, lying in the bottom of the dryer, along with Evie's fleece jacket. I set the dial for warm-up and leaned against the rumbling machine, enjoying the heat. While I waited, I opened the square envelope and slid the card out for another look. Too bad the sender hadn't filled in the contact line. Had it actually been sent? Maybe this was a printer's proof.

After a couple of minutes, I removed the sweaters and folded them and laid the socks on top of the washer for more drying.

Ann would be in the dining room now, so no point in taking the jacket over. I put it on a hanger, hung it on the laundry rack, and picked up the white envelope. I didn't really think the invitation belonged to Handleman, but I'd like to know what he thought about it. Tinkerbelle meowed when I nudged her out of the way and closed the dryer.

It was sixty-five degrees and sunny outside, and the walk up to One South was a short one. I took the elevator to the second floor, where Patti's carpets and love seats made a great impression, even on a second viewing. At the end of the porch, I was about to knock on the guest suite, but the door swung open at the lightest touch.

The place gave off the vibe that said nobody was home, but I knocked anyway and called out. "Mr. Handleman? Reg? Anybody here?"

No answer. I stepped inside. The kitchen looked just as it had days ago. He probably hadn't used it all week. I looked toward the bedroom and called again, then walked in that direction, my steps silent on the carpet. The comforter, when I could see it, was pulled up but crooked. Used towels lay in a heap on the bathroom floor. Handleman was gone. Any luggage he'd brought had been removed from the apartment and no trace of him remained except used linens.

The Sudoku book was on the dresser with the cover folded back. I walked closer and saw that someone had used the top page for a notepad. "*Devon Wheat*," the first line said, in blue ink and a heavy scrawl. There was a phone number and, below that, what I took for directions.

"*L on Section, R on de la Mare.*"

The note hadn't been there Monday. Handleman had moved in Tuesday. And Devon Wheat died Wednesday night. I read the note again and told myself there was some perfectly innocuous explanation, but I had no idea what it was. Why would an automotive history expert visit a small-town financial advisor a thousand miles from home?

Still holding the envelope Ann had given me, I went back to the porch and sat on one of the rattan love seats, where I could look down the boulevard toward the big house. I thought for a minute, then once again dialed the FPD. Mary Montgomery was at a conference in Mobile, I learned. And so was Chief Boozer. Would I like to leave a message?

I asked for a callback from either of them, clicked off, and sat for another minute. It was cool there in the shade. One of the housekeepers, rolling a noisy cart, turned in at Riley's building. Would they show up here as soon as I left? Would they rip out the used page, as I had done a few days ago? Or maybe toss the entire book into the trash bag hooked to their cart?

I went back into the guest suite. It took a minute, rummaging through the kitchen drawers, but finally I found a box of plastic bags and pulled one out. I fiddled the bag inside out and stuck my hand in as if it were an oversized, stiff glove. Holding the corner of the Sudoku book through the bag, I popped the bag over it, dropped the square envelope in, and zipped the bag closed. Then I closed the apartment and took the elevator down.

So Handleman knew Devon Wheat and had perhaps gotten together with him at Royale Court this week. I hoped Patti's intuitions didn't turn out to be right, in spite of all my denials. I hoped he wasn't a bad guy.

I went back to my apartment, dropped the plastic bag with its contents on the coffee table, and put on a black cardigan. Maybe I'd order a couple of those fleece jackets. I'd ask Ann where Evie got them.

Chapter 11

The shuttle bus was late and half full when it finally arrived at the big house, where another twenty people were waiting. We climbed aboard and set off for the polo field.

Banners hung on rail fences all around the entrance to the event. The shuttle bus pulled in at a circular drive, and thirty-six of us were processed into the arena through side-by-side lines. Tickets to the Grand Concours were expensive, but there was a discount if you bought two days at once.

"One day," I told the man at the gate and handed over my credit card. Ridiculous. How did young families afford to go anywhere?

"My treat," Riley volunteered, as he usually did.

I refused flatly, as usual, but he paid twenty-five bucks for a slick, illustrated program and offered it to me. "Let's share one."

Every outdoor exhibit should be held at a polo club, I decided right away. There were open pastures on both sides of the road, enclosed with rail fences. One side had low hills with a few trees, a series of paddocks, and handsome ponies grazing or whinnying at the crowd from a distance. The other side, where the car show was set up, was almost flat and divided into three big paddocks.

There was a parking lot with valet service for VIPs.

I pointed to a white BMW as Riley and I walked side by side across lush, bright-green grass. "Is that Handleman's car?"

He looked where I was pointing and gave a nod. "I don't think there'd be two with Indiana tags."

The biggest field, in the middle, looked like the scene of a large wedding and accommodated both the concours exhibit and, near the entrance, a comparatively bland display of American sports cars.

A weathered wooden pavilion, draped with garlands of silk flowers and gauzy fabric that billowed in the breeze, stood on a little rise between the two exhibits and functioned as a tearoom. I didn't know about Amelia Island and Pebble Beach, but there were no port-a-potties at the Fairhope/Point Clear Grand Concours. Instead, a row of restroom trailers, with attendants, was provided for the ordinary visitors. For dignitaries, there was a clubhouse atop a little rise and a fleet of golf carts to get people there and back.

The third and smallest field was a sale paddock with an odd mixture of antique cars, about fifty in all, and three times that number of wheeler-dealers.

A few people stopped to look at the sports cars but most of the group I arrived with headed straight to the back, where the antiques and classics were on display.

It would be hard to pick a favorite among the seventy-five or eighty cars arranged in circles or squares or rows, but I tried.

The Baker Electric was cute and looked like Daisy Duck should be driving it. It was tall and glossy black, with a lot of glass, over a hundred years old, and powered by a whole flock of lead-acid batteries, according to an observer.

Nearby was a cream-colored Cord with disappearing headlights. A pair of chrome exhaust pipes curved out each side of the hood. I liked it until Riley, frowning, said, "With the headlights closed, it looks sinister."

I agreed, and we moved on.

I also liked the monstrously large red-and-silver Packard with a white top and a V-12 engine, according to a sign. I could barely see over the hood, so you can imagine how tall it was. Its running boards merged into the front fenders with a well to hold a white-sidewall spare tire, and each spare had a little rearview mirror belted to its top.

The podiatrist who came to Harbor Village once a month was looking at the Packard. I spoke to him and he introduced his wife, who told me that the Packard had once belonged to Bear Bryant.

"No, honey. Bear Bryant was the football coach. The Packard belonged to that actor, what's his name?"

I waved and moved on.

In the midst of all the old, exotic cars was a bulbous, new, red-and-black Bugatti that looked like a bomb.

"Is this a Type Forty-One?" I asked the car minder, showing off my newly acquired knowledge.

He had a pencil-thin moustache and looked down his skinny nose at me, literally. "La Finale," he said with a heavy accent. He pointed to where the word was written in script below the headlight.

There was an old Bugatti, too, a race car, more spartan than luxurious, parked facing me. From a distance, it looked like a fish with an open mouth.

My heavy breakfast was ancient history by the time we completed a slow lap around the concours exhibit and a relatively quick walk through the sports cars. I checked the time.

"Are you hungry?" Riley pointed to the tea tent. "They don't look busy now."

Reg Handleman was there, too, looking around as if he were waiting for someone.

I caught Riley's eye and jiggled my head toward Handleman. "Shall we invite him?"

Riley gave him a wave and I turned around, pretending to be surprised to see Handleman. "Reg!" I called. "We're about to have a late lunch. Won't you join us?"

"Ms. Mack," he said, "and Mister…?"

"Meddors." Riley offered his hand. "Riley Meddors. I enjoyed your lectures."

"Oh, yes! Riley. The sporty British model. You're not actually a Brit, are you?"

Progress to the pavilion was slow, delayed by the ebb and flow of the crowd. A number of people recognized Handleman and stopped to chat. Some were Harbor Village residents but not all. If Friday was—as Nita had said—the quiet before the storm of visitors, I wondered what Saturday's crowd would be like.

The Hospital Auxiliary provided lunch, which included Italian confetti pasta salad, spicy chicken skewers, a cupcake, and a choice of iced tea or lemonade. There had been chopped broccoli salad, but a line was drawn through that part of the menu. "Gone an hour ago," the women behind the counter told us. We had a big choice of tables.

The dining area was arranged to offer a choice of view: sports cars or concours. In respect for Handleman, I chose the concours, with the intention of giving him the seat looking out over the cars. The pavilion's walkways were littered with chairs. Riley put down his tray and cleared us a path.

"Are you enjoying the show?" I asked Handleman when we were seated.

"Delightful. Everything I imagined."

"I went looking for you this morning. You must've gotten here early."

He nodded. "Oh, yes. I had to prepare two cars. I hope you saw them—a Duesenberg Model A and the little Baker Electric. Now, don't confuse the Duesenberg Model A with the Ford Model A. Lots of people do that."

Riley asked, "Have winners been announced?"

Handleman grinned. "Best in show went to the Duesenberg. A Phaeton, dove gray and black."

"I've heard that term," I said, "but what's a Phaeton?" I was hungry, and the pasta was tangy and really hit the spot.

"An expensive touring car. Large enough for a family and all their luggage. This one's a particularly nice restoration with an original polished nickel radiator shell."

I pictured the winning car, with its sparkly, wire-spoke wheels and a matching, arch-topped trunk centered at the back. "A bit decadent, wouldn't you say? Gatsby-esque?"

Handleman laughed. "My dear, all luxury cars are decadent. That's the whole idea."

"I'm glad your car won," I told him. "Congratulations."

"Would that it were," he said, smiling.

My view from the pavilion was of a pair of small ponds. Between them, on a slowly revolving turntable in the middle of the pasture, was a black roadster, polished to perfection.

"There's the car I'd like." I pointed. "What is it?"

Handleman turned to see what I was looking at. "The Ferrari." He turned back. "Excellent choice. A local car. Belongs to a podiatrist, I believe. Did you pick a favorite, Riley?"

They talked about a short maroon Stutz that had looked out of proportion to my eye but both of them liked it. I looked around at the crowd and saw a BRATS bus—which stood for Baldwin Rural Area Transportation System—leaving the entry area, heading back to town. People were still arriving at the show but traffic was heavier in the homeward direction now. The temperature was dropping and the western sky had darkened slightly.

The food was good, but I was interested in a little sleuthing. How could I steer the conversation around to Devon Wheat? I wanted to find out if Handleman knew the financial advisor, and why he'd left Wheat's name and phone number in the Sudoku book. None of my business, of course, since I wasn't getting involved, but that didn't mean I wasn't curious.

The conversation at my table was still about the Baker Electric. "It was marketed as a woman's car because it didn't have to be cranked," Handleman said and glanced at me.

"Was cranking all that difficult? Not that I ever tried it, but I've seen it in movies."

Handleman made a cranking motion. "Difficult and dangerous. If you forgot to retard the spark, the engine might backfire and break your arm. What did you think of the Steamer?"

I shook my head. "That was the one with a rounded nose? Not my favorite. Maybe because it made me think about cleaning carpets."

"What would you say the fuel was?"

Riley chuckled and I looked at him. He didn't say a word, but I was tipped off to consider my answer.

"Well, steam, I suppose." I laughed. "But it needed something to heat the water, didn't it? Gasoline?"

Handleman chuckled, too. "Kerosene, more often. You'd be surprised how many people assume steam is a fuel."

"You were hoping to laugh at me again? I think you did enough of that last night." I pouted but made it clear there were no hard feelings. Handleman still looked a little embarrassed.

"I hope you didn't mind too much. You actually did very well with the identifications. You'd have won if that bell had rubber feet."

I thought about telling him my history with Travis but decided against it. He already looked embarrassed.

The breeze picked up noticeably and one of the fabric panels fluttered toward us. I pulled my cardigan up around my neck.

Handleman looked toward the concours area. "Maybe I should get back to the cars. I left someone doing double duty while I came for sustenance."

"You're staying through the weekend, aren't you? And going to the gala tomorrow night? We have a ticket for you at the Harbor Village table if you don't have other duties."

He seemed surprised. "Why, I'd be most appreciative, Cleo. I understood my suite was for the duration of the lectures, and since they're over, I thought I should look for another place tonight."

"I don't think the suite is booked again until Thanksgiving." I got out my phone to call Patti, right in front of him. "I'll ask her to be sure housekeeping gets to the guest suite before they leave for the weekend." But I couldn't get a good phone connection there in the pavilion. "I'll try again later." And if I didn't reach her in time, Handleman might just have to use towels that had been on the floor all day.

I followed him as we departed. He led the way down the steps and offered me his hand once he was on solid ground. Riley was right behind me.

"Did you say why you were looking for me this morning? Or have I forgotten already?"

"I wanted to tell you about my neighbor receiving an invitation to join a consortium that's purchasing a Bugatti Royale. I wondered if it's legitimate."

I watched closely to see Handleman's reaction. His eyes grew wide and he took a half step backward.

"Is this true? A Royale? Interesting, yes, indeed. Is your neighbor a wealthy person? Who made the offer?"

Authentic surprise? I thought so, but he was a showman.

"There's no name on the invitation but she thinks she got it from the Grand Hotel. She owns the Royale Knit Shop and thinks the people at the hotel confused the name of her shop with the name of the car."

He frowned, eyes narrowed in thought. "And they gave her the invitation by mistake? The Royale Knit Shop, you said? Located in Royale Court?"

"Exactly." I nodded, squinting.

The wind was picking up even more. Little bits of grass and grit swirled around us. We stepped to one side of the path, out of the light foot traffic, to continue our conversation. The pavilion was almost empty and only a few people went up and down the steps now, stragglers like my group. Personally, I was ready to join the line for the shuttle. I kept glancing that way in case we needed to hurry to catch a ride home.

"I was there, was it two days ago? Yes, Wednesday," Handleman volunteered. "I didn't notice a knit shop, but I might've overlooked it. I went to meet with a local financial advisor."

"Devon Wheat?" Riley asked.

Handleman turned toward him with a smile. "You know him?"

Riley and I looked at each other. If Handleman was fibbing, he had a talent for it.

"I hope he wasn't a friend of yours." Riley made it a question.

"Why? Is something wrong with him?"

"I'm afraid he's dead." I wrapped my arms around my middle for warmth.

"Murdered," Riley added.

Handleman's hand went to his heart, but he just looked surprised, not like he had a pain.

I could see the entrance gate and recognized Mary Montgomery walking our way. I gave her a little wave. She was looking right at us but didn't wave back. Maybe she was too far away to see me, but I got a bad feeling.

"Anybody call a cop?" I asked.

Handleman followed my gaze but he wouldn't know her. Riley swiveled around to look over his shoulder.

"Murdered, you said?" Handleman refocused on our conversation.

"Maybe we'd better sit down again." I turned, pulling my sweater tighter and buttoning it all the way up. We went back up the steps, sat at the first table, and filled Handleman in on the details of Devon Wheat's death.

"Cleo and Nita Bergen found the body," Riley said, after I'd given the big picture.

He nodded. "I know Mrs. Bergen. They invited me for tea after the photo session. Nice apartment."

I veered away from murder like a flash. "It was professionally decorated, with their age and lifestyle in mind. I saw it on my first visit to Fairhope and decided immediately I wanted to live at Harbor Village."

He was nodding in agreement. "They allowed me to take a photograph to send to my wife. But tell me about this poor fellow. Devon Wheat."

"If you met him, you know more than I do. He was strangled Wednesday night. Nita and I found his body yesterday morning."

He frowned and shook his head, showing the proper gravitas. "It must've been a shock."

I agreed. "But I didn't know him. That would've made it worse."

"Mr. Handleman?" Mary Montgomery and a uniformed officer stood right beside me.

Handleman looked at her inquiringly and got to his feet.

Montgomery introduced herself.

"We were just talking about Devon Wheat," I said.

She favored Handleman with her usual stare. "I understand you were looking for Mr. Wheat Wednesday. I'd like to hear about that."

Handleman waved her to a seat and stood to hold the chair, but she hesitated.

"We're about to leave." Riley nudged me.

I got up slowly and retrieved my bag and the concours program, stalling to hear Handleman's reply. "I visit brokerage houses wherever I go, informing them about automotive investment fraud. It's easy to miss the independents, but Mr. McKenzie referred me to Devon Wheat. Unfortunately, I missed him."

Travis? That sounded wrong. Why would Travis know Devon Wheat? I wanted to hear more but Riley was pacing between our table and the steps.

"There's a shuttle heading this way." I hesitated and he added, "We've got an appointment tonight."

"I got a message to call you." Montgomery looked at me abruptly. "What did you want?"

I couldn't talk about the Sudoku book in front of Handleman. I didn't want him to know I'd confiscated it.

"Ready?" Riley was already at the top of the steps.

"Umm, nothing important, I guess. I've forgotten."

She was staring at me, eyes narrowed. "Okay."

I looked at Handleman. "I'll see you at the gala."

He gave a half bow and I fled.

On the walk to the bus, Riley asked thoughtfully, "Where were Wheat's pants?"

"What?"

"You said he was wearing biking shorts, but he wouldn't have worn them to the office. If he changed for a bike ride, maybe he left his wallet in his pants and then surprised someone going after it."

I nodded. It was a reasonable possibility, I supposed—not a deliberate murder, just a robbery gone wrong. But like Jim, I knew zebras when I heard them.

Chapter 12

On Friday afternoons the office staff usually began slipping away about four, but there appeared to be a full house when I got back from the car show.

The shuttle bus was another cute BRATS bus. It looked like an old-fashioned trolley car, maroon with brass trim and big windows, and it dropped off two dozen passengers in the Harbor Village parking lot.

Riley walked to the lobby with me. Not that he had much choice. I took his hand as I came down the bus steps and continued to hang on to his arm once I was on flat ground.

"I want to know what you think of Handleman," I told him. "I didn't think we should talk about it on the bus."

"Nice guy." Riley shrugged.

The automatic door swept open and warm air rushed out to meet us.

"That feels so good." I gave an involuntary shiver.

Something else was rushing toward us, too.

"Why are the cops calling you?" Patti demanded, eyes wide and worried as she skidded to a stop. "Two calls from Lieutenant Montgomery and Chief Boozer. And you didn't answer your phone. I called at least half a dozen times. I've been so worried about you! Has something happened?"

"No." I took my phone out and examined it. "Everything looks okay." I had some voice mails, I saw, but didn't attend to them.

Riley watched over my shoulder as I probed the phone, and he explained to Patti at the same time. "Service was spotty down there." He gave her a one-armed hug. "Horses never complain when their phones don't work, have you noticed? They're like that. Do you think the coffee's still drinkable this late? We need warming up."

I agreed. "But let me call Mary Montgomery first."

"I need to talk with you." Patti tapped me with a finger. "I'll get coffee but do *not* disappear." She headed for the dining room.

Riley and I went to my office.

"Mary put me on the spot, asking what I'd called her about. I couldn't talk in front of Handleman." I punched in the number, listened to her voice mail message, and then told her when she'd be able to reach me during the evening. I put the phone down and told Riley about the two items I had in a Ziploc bag.

He grinned but there was a wary expression in his eyes. "You knew Handleman had contacted Devon Wheat even before he told us? Nice to know how devious you are."

I'd never thought of myself as devious. It didn't sound quite nice. "Naturally I was going to listen to him, to get his side of the story. I still don't know if he actually met Devon Wheat."

"But you let him tell his version so you could compare it to what you already knew."

"That doesn't seem so bad. Does it?"

He grinned and zipped his lips.

Patti brought a tray with coffee and sweetener and little cups of half-and-half plus napkins and chocolate chip cookies. "This is to make up for what I have to tell you."

"Uh-oh," I said, wondering what had gone off the tracks since noon.

"Do I need to leave?" Riley poured cream into his cup.

"No. I don't care who hears it." She stirred sweetener into her coffee and took her usual chair in front of my desk. "It's about Todd Barnwell. Has Emily talked to you?"

"I've barely seen her all week. What's up?"

"I'm just going to come right out and say it." Patti took a sip of coffee and made a face like she didn't like the taste. "Todd Barnwell's broke. I've been lending him money for months, but I can't keep doing it, and it wasn't enough anyway. Emily says I'm crazy. She says the association fees haven't been paid since Mr. Barnwell died and it's four thousand dollars already and automatically goes to collection if he doesn't do something soon. *And* she thinks he won't pay me back. I told her that's not an option."

She spoke all in a gush, ran out of breath, and then glanced out the window behind me. She jumped up, sloshing coffee onto her hand, and grabbed for a napkin. "Good grief. Here he comes already. I told him four thirty."

I looked at my watch. "It's four thirty, almost. Who's coming?" I looked out and didn't see anybody. It was getting dark.

She brushed cookie crumbs off the table into her hand and dumped them into the trash can. "I told Todd he has to talk to you, to see if you have any ideas. He's been here twice already, which shows he's getting worried. You want me to tell him to come back next week?"

I looked at Riley. "You're the banker. Why don't you advise him?"

"I don't know who you're talking about."

"He's a *kid*." Patti sounded irritated. "Just talk to him, okay? I'll get him."

Riley watched her go. "Is this a typical job for a social worker? First you're collecting evidence in a homicide case, interviewing a suspect who doesn't know he's a suspect, and now calming your staff and counseling a kid about finances?"

I waved my cookie at him. "Social work is not for sissies. But I try to eat a few pastries between problems." I glanced through the unopened mail. "At least there were no bodies today. Todd's the kid who played Handleman's game last night."

Riley frowned, checked his watch, and paced back to the corner with his coffee.

Todd Barnwell came in doing his slouchy strut, leather jacket squeaking and upper lip lifted on one side in a little sneer. Riley rolled his eyes.

"Come in, Mr. Barnwell," I greeted him formally.

Riley stepped forward and stuck out his hand. "Todd, I'm Riley Meddors."

Todd had expected a private meeting, I guessed. The sneer went away immediately, replaced by a look of wariness.

"Come in and join us, Patti," I said. "Todd, Mr. Meddors is a banker and a friend of mine. He's agreed to listen to your situation and advise me. I understand you're in a financial bind." I sounded like a family court judge. All I needed was a black robe and gavel. I stacked half a dozen letters together, put them on the desk, and gave him my full attention.

"I've got four million dollars," Todd Barnwell boasted, setting me straight. He slumped in the chair and stuck his feet out, consuming all the real estate he could. "It's just tied up in a trust right now."

"And what do you propose doing about it?" Riley swung a chair around and sat, forcing Todd to turn his head as he looked from me to Riley.

The kid shrugged, slumped a little more, and gave Riley a cautious look. "Get a lawyer, I guess. Bust the trust."

I laced my fingers together and rested my chin, and Riley took charge.

"And how much does a lawyer cost?" Riley asked.

Todd grunted and shrugged. "I dunno. A lot, probably."

"Would you say your grandfather was a stupid man?"

His head jerked up. "No. He was a smart man. He made a lotta money."

"Maybe somebody left it to him. Inheritance, I mean."

"No. He worked. He worked his whole life. He was a PE. A Professional Engineer, if you don't know. He built garment plants in Mississippi and Mexico and saved all his money. Invested it with a VP at Merrill Lynch in Atlanta. Their headquarters."

"Yeah, they're all VPs over there. Why do you suppose your grandfather didn't just give you the money outright when he died? Or even before."

Todd shrugged and aimed a smug little grin at the office carpet. "I guess he figured I'd waste it. But how much smarter am I going to be in four years?"

"You're twenty-one now?"

"Almost. Twenty and a half."

"How much does it cost you to live a year?"

Todd stared, his gaze flicking to me and then back to Riley, like he'd just sensed a trap. After a minute, he asked, "A year?"

Riley nodded. "That's what I said."

Another shrug. "I don't know. Nothing, I guess. I've been living free."

"No, you certainly have not," Patti blurted out.

I'd forgotten she was there, leaning against the worktable behind Todd, her arms folded.

"You've cost me plenty. And you're paying it all back, Todd. I don't have a trust account waiting for me. And you owe Stewart, too."

Riley jumped in before Todd could answer. "If I were going to write you a check to cover living expenses for a year, which is hypothetical and highly unlikely, you understand, how much would I need to write it for?"

After a confused pause, Todd shook his head.

"Do you expect me to figure it out for you?" There was a note of incredulity in Riley's voice and in the way he shook his head. "When you know the answers, how much you need and what you should pay for the privilege of using someone else's money, we'll talk."

"I'm paying Patti interest," he said.

She snorted.

Riley looked at his watch again. "We're going to have to wrap this up. We've got people waiting for us. We'll get together tomorrow if you're interested in assistance. Bring me a list. What are your assets? You say you've got four million dollars. Where is it? Who's managing it now? How is it invested? I ask because I want to know if there's likely to be anything left in four-and-a-half years, if there's any chance you might be able to repay me. Some managers actually lose trust funds, you know. Sometimes all of it."

Todd was instantly agitated. "So, who does have it now? The guy that did is dead. Where's my money?"

Riley shrugged.

Jeez, I thought. He was being hard on the boy.

"We'll find out, but you can't come in empty-handed. You have trust papers? An attorney? A guardian? Bring all that information to show me. Make a list of how much money you need for a year, and what you'll do with it. What does an apartment cost? What's the deposit for utilities? What does it cost you to eat? Do you have a car? How much are your payments, maintenance, and operating expense? Tuition? Health insurance? When you know where you stand, you can start figuring out what to do about the problem."

Todd made a feeble attempt at protest. "You eat. You know what it costs."

Riley grinned at him. "You don't get the senior discount."

He tried again. "I've got a house, I don't need an apartment."

"A house you can't afford," Patti snapped at him. "You're about to have a claim filed against you for overdue fees."

Todd gradually sank into a limp and defeated posture. He sighed and looked at Patti. "You going to help me?"

Riley stood up and pulled out his wallet. He peeled off five twenties and tossed them onto the worktable beside Patti. "Write me an IOU, sign, and date it. Patti can be a witness. Then take her out to dinner and beg her for help, because you're going to need it. What time will you be ready tomorrow?"

Todd looked from Riley to Patti.

She stood up straight, fists on her hips, and cocked her head at Todd. After a pause, she threw him a lifeline, employing more authority than I knew she possessed. "Two? I've got plans for the evening."

"Two," Todd repeated.

"Two," Riley agreed. "I'm having lunch in the dining room tomorrow and I'll be in the lobby at two." He looked at me. "You ready to go?"

The two of us laughed all the way to my apartment.

"You were wonderful," I told him between giggles. "That sneer disappeared in about two seconds. And he's already trying to impress you. That never would've happened with me."

Riley smiled, enjoying the afterglow. "I had two boys, remember."

"Patti was good, too. Did you see how she stood up to him? Priceless! I'll call and tell her."

Riley shook his head. "Wait until they've had dinner. You don't want him to know you're enjoying this."

I fed the cat and changed clothes, and we crossed the street to Nita and Jim's apartment, where four of us—Nita, Dolly, Riley, and I—played Mexican Trains for three hours every Friday night. After the first hour, we always took a break for food and Jim joined us then. Sometimes a fifth person played with us, but never Jim; he met us as we arrived, said hello, and retreated to his study until Subway delivered the sandwiches at six thirty.

Same routine, every Friday night. Unless something else was going on.

"Come in, come in," Jim called out as he threw the door wide for Riley and me. He closed and locked it behind us and shook Riley's hand in that two-handed thing they always did. "People, we've got a murder on our hands!" He almost crowed. Jim Bergen meant to enjoy whatever life brought, up to and including murder.

Nita didn't really disagree with him, but she wanted more decorum in her world. She rolled her eyes at him and gave me a hug. "Are you getting enough rest, Cleo? Late nights all week, plus a murder and now this car show."

"I'm feeling it." That was an understatement. "I'm going to take it easy this weekend."

"But you've got the gala."

I hadn't forgotten. "Maybe we'll slip out early."

"Hello, Riley dear. How are you?" She gave him a kiss and whispered something that left him smiling.

I spoke to Dolly, who waved back as she headed around the corner, aimed for the dining table. I admired her hair, white as Nita's but cut short and turned under all around. She'd spent her entire career in Washington, she'd told me, working in a windowless basement. I liked to imagine her as a spy or code breaker or something romantic, but like Jim with his naval career, the past was past for Dolly, never to be thought of again. Maybe that was the secret to a happy retirement.

As usual, I drank in details of the Bergen apartment. "It's so pretty in here, Nita. The lighting is perfect." There was a brass lamp on the mahogany secretary, two pharmacy lamps and a tall, translucent stone lamp in the seating area, plus a crystal chandelier and sconces in the dining area, where an illuminated painting hung in the little nook with the buffet. And as always, I admired the angled, plush carpet, woven in muted shades of red and acid green. The clock chimed the half hour.

"You must see Dolly's apartment." Nita waved us toward the dining table. "She's having it painted."

"You'll have to come see, Cleo." Dolly picked up the box of dominoes. "But wait until Wednesday when everything gets put back together.

The color's called burnished shrimp, and there'll be an accent wall in dark cinnamon."

I always admired Nita's weeping fig tree, covered with white twinkle lights. It stretched upward almost to the skylight and one branch draped gracefully across the pass-through to the kitchen. "It looks like Christmas in here."

The tree had looked just about the same since July, lights and all, but with Christmas only a few weeks away, the tree assumed more prominence now, giving the apartment a festive, happy look. The dining table, oval and mahogany, had some special transparent coating that kept it looking new and glossy, in spite of all the sliding and scraping of dominoes.

Jim followed us. "We've all had a busy week. I'll bet we didn't get to bed before ten a single night."

"No," Nita shook a finger at him, "but we had a nap every afternoon while Cleo worked." She glanced at Riley and me. "Did you two get to the car show before it turned cold?"

I shook my head, Riley nodded yes, and we laughed at the lack of agreement.

"We got there, but the temperature was dropping." I gave a little shiver that wasn't entirely pretend.

Nita asked, "Is it warm enough in here?"

I said it was. Nita had known Riley's wife, too, I remembered as I sat down at the table. I wondered if she knew about Diane's new marriage. And had she learned yet about Riley's proposal, or proposition, or whatever I'd received? Probably not. I looked at her. She wouldn't keep something like that to herself.

"The sandwiches will be here in an hour." She offered us coffee or wine or water in the meantime. Nobody wanted anything.

Dolly had dumped out the domino tiles and now she began turning them facedown. "I'll tell you what I want. I want to know who murdered that stockbroker and why nobody's talking about it. I almost put my money with that man. Has anybody lost anything?"

"Whoa there." Jim held out both hands like a traffic cop, one toward Dolly, one toward Nita. "We don't want to start this discussion until the food gets here. Talk about the car show, if you need a topic. Or the weather. It's getting cool out there, did you notice?"

"The moon's almost full," I said.

Jim nodded approval of the topic. "A waxing gibbous moon. Good night for a murder, if we hadn't already had it. But don't talk about it yet."

The four Mexican Train players settled in at the dining table. Riley held Nita's chair for her, then set up to keep score, as usual. Dolly and I got all the tiles turned facedown and then made a lot of noise stirring them before everyone began to draw out their fifteen starters.

We always played off the double twelve first and worked our way downward during the course of the evening. We'd completed four rounds when the food arrived, a few minutes late.

Nobody had said a word about the elephant in the room, the late Devon Wheat, but I had heard the landline, Jim and Nita's only phone, ring while we were playing the first round. Jim had answered in his office and talked for a few minutes, but he hadn't come out until the doorbell sounded.

"Forty dollars." He set several plastic bags on the table. "I adjusted the tip to make it come out even. Eight dollars each."

"Why do we never pay for drinks?" Dolly asked. "You're shortchanging yourself, Jim."

Nita and I went to the kitchen to prepare the food, while Riley and Dolly cleared the table, moving the game pieces to the center and freeing up the perimeter for dining. Jim got out wineglasses and brought them to the kitchen, where he filled them from a bottle on the counter. I put ice cubes into two tall glasses and topped them up with Coke.

"I called Subway a few days ago and they told me they don't deliver." Dolly spoke loudly so we could hear her through the pass-through. "Now how do you explain that? They've been coming here every week for a year or two. Is it just on Fridays?"

Nita smiled at me and told Dolly, "Ask Jim."

Dolly did. "Jim?"

He laughed, too, as he delivered wineglasses to the table and was brought the fifth chair from beside the buffet. "I'm a good customer, Dolly. Piggly Wiggly delivers, too. Did you know that?"

"No. Are you sure? Nita, is that true?"

Nita winked at me as she unwrapped the last sandwich, lined them up on the cutting board, and began slicing them into quarters. She arranged the pieces on two platters of the desert rose pattern.

My aunt Jo had the same china pattern when I was a child and she was a newlywed. I always loved it. Aunt Jo was hard on dishes, and other things. She gave me her last surviving desert rose soup bowl as a dog food dish when Stephanie got T-Bone Pickens. That was the second time I'd thought of T-Bone this week, but I thought of my aunt every time I saw Nita's dishes.

"Jim stays on good terms with all the managers around here." Nita handed me a platter and we went to the dining room.

Someone had moved my chair to Riley's side of the table so Jim could have his usual place at the end.

"It pays off," Jim was saying, about his cultivation of good relations of the local shop managers.

I laid out small plates, forks, and pink napkins. Jim put another stack of napkins on top of the mound of dominoes.

"The barbecue is going to be messy," Nita warned us.

We sat down and began passing food. Something smelled delicious.

"Before I forget…" Jim was looking at me. "Lieutenant Montgomery will be here at eight thirty. She said you aren't answering your phone tonight."

"Is that phone quitting on me?" I got up again. "It didn't work at the car show today but we thought it was a lack of service down there."

I wanted to get my bag and check the phone, but it wasn't on the floor beside the secretary, where I usually dropped it. And it wasn't in the desk chair, or beside the couch. Nowhere in the dining room.

I looked at Riley. "I didn't bring my purse. I'm locked out." It was such a helpless feeling.

"I'm so sorry, honey," Nita said. "It's overwork."

"Sorry," Riley echoed, with a sweet smile and a pat on my shoulder. "Does someone have a spare?"

"Mary says you know something," Jim said.

I sighed and looked at Nita. "You have my spare key, don't you?" I'd left one with her when I moved in. "I knew this would happen sooner or later."

"Certainly," she said. "I'll get it when we finish. Now eat and don't worry."

Riley held the platter and I took one segment of a barbecue sub. "Don't you want more than that?" He still held the platter beside my plate.

I took a second segment, this one with hot, sautéed Mediterranean veggies spilling out.

"What does Mary Montgomery want?" Dolly reached across the table and took the platter from Riley. She took two sections of barbecue sandwich and ignored Jim's scowl of disapproval. "I hope you're helping her solve this murder. Seems like nobody's the least bit concerned about it."

"No, I'm not helping her. I have no connection to this investigation, except for being there when the body was discovered, just like Nita. I never even heard of the man when he was alive."

Dolly picked up her fork. "I knew about him but never met him face-to-face. But you've got the right equipment, Cleo. Not many people understand the criminal mind like you do."

Riley made a funny noise, like he'd inhaled some of his wine. I looked to see if he needed me to pound on his back, but he was grinning and avoiding my look.

Jim grinned, too. "I'm not sure I'd take that as a compliment, Cleo."

I looked at Dolly, thinking she might be kidding.

She was holding her fork sideways, cutting off a bit of sandwich. "This is messy."

I shrugged. "Ann said something similar, about me being experienced with the cops. Made me sound like a criminal. Did you hear she got an invitation to join a consortium to purchase some expensive car?"

"Hold on." It was unusual for Jim to ignore food, but he did. "Mary said you've got something for her but she didn't know what. This is it?"

I described the invitation Ann had given to me. "It's a square envelope and matching card. Expensive-looking card stock, with a gold lining inside the envelope, but there's no address on it. No return address, nothing written on the line that's supposed to tell you who to contact."

"How do you know where it came from? Or who it's meant for?" Jim asked.

"I don't."

"And how'd you get it?" Dolly asked.

"Ann got it somehow. She thinks the people at the Grand Hotel gave it to her by mistake. She met with Marjorie Zadnichek about a retreat Royale Knit Shop is sponsoring in February, and the invitation has the word *Royale* in the headline. Ann thinks the two things ran together for Marjorie. And the invitation mentions the Type Forty-One Handleman talked about."

"Is that so? Did you call Marjorie and confirm?" Jim asked.

I shook my head. "No, I'm not involved. Remember?"

Nita nodded approval. "Don't let them rope you into something."

"I didn't see Ann at the lecture last night," Dolly said.

"She wasn't there. That's why she didn't know Handleman talked about this very thing," I said. "But she thought he'd know about the invitation. And since she's busy with her brother, she gave it to me to take care of."

"What's wrong with Usher?" Nita asked.

Jim ignored her. "I don't know if Handleman had any hard evidence of how they operate. What did he say when he saw this invitation?"

I chewed and swallowed before answering. "That's an awkward point. I was going to give it to him and took it to the guest suite this morning. But he'd moved out. The only thing left was a note with Devon Wheat's name and directions to Royale Court."

Four forks went down onto plates. Four people stared at me, blinking, heads tilting quizzically. They looked at one another.

I laughed. "I thought I'd give both items to Mary, just in case—the invitation and the note. But she asked me about it right in front of Handleman. Put me on the spot, and I couldn't think what to say. I hope Handleman didn't notice anything."

Jim whistled softly and squirmed in his chair. "Well, that's interesting. You're sure it's Handleman's handwriting? If it is, you're doing the right thing." He began eating again but looked at me and gave a thumbs-up.

"We know Handleman tried to see Wheat." Riley glanced at me, perhaps recalling my duplicity. "He told us about it this afternoon. Said he went to Wheat's office and no one was there, but I don't know if anyone can confirm that."

Jim chewed and swallowed. "We'll leave the investigation to the authorities, of course. But Handleman isn't stupid. If he strangled somebody, he's not going to go around saying he paid the man a visit."

"Isn't Wednesday the day he came here?" Nita asked.

Jim nodded. "Yes, Wednesday afternoon. Had tea and cookies and left about four thirty."

"I was here," Dolly said.

"He told us he left here and went to Royale Court," I said, "and someone steered him around back to Wheat's office. I think Patti made me suspicious by reacting to him so negatively."

Jim chuckled. "Looked like they were buddies last night. But the police should be informed. Mary'll be here soon. We'll find out if there's anything new."

I remembered something else. "Here's something you can think about. Handleman told Montgomery he learned about Wheat from Travis. Do you believe that?" I was looking at Jim. "Why would Travis know anything about a Fairhope financial advisor?"

Jim shook his head. "No telling. But they'll find out." He scooped up the final bit of steak and cheese.

"His sister-in-law lived here," Nita thought out loud. "Wasn't she about Devon's age? Jim, did she ever say anything about that restaurant, the Bistro?"

His answer was muffled. "Don't know."

Nita looked at me. "What's wrong with Usher, Cleo? You said Ann's busy with him."

I had finished eating. I dabbed at my lips and put the crumpled napkin on my empty plate. "The cops interviewed him for hours last night, with Ann there, waiting."

"Interesting," Jim nodded.

Nita frowned at him.

"They've got to talk to everybody, honey. Don't draw any conclusions. Not yet."

She glanced over his shoulder, to the big wall clock, just as it clicked to seven. "I'm drawing a conclusion about our game. We should get back to it."

The clock began to chime and we moved the dirty dishes to the kitchen. Jim set my chair against the wall and when I returned from the kitchen, I took his spot at the end of the table. We spread the tiles out again, mixed them up, and drew out fifteen each.

"Where's the double-eight?" Dolly asked.

Nita handed it over.

At eight thirty-five we finished the threes. It'd been one of our faster games. Riley totaled up the scores while Nita and Dolly watched over his shoulders.

Dolly swatted him when it was apparent that he'd won, as usual. "How do you always do that?"

Nita went out of the room while Dolly and Riley packed up the dominoes and stored them away. I went to the kitchen to rinse dishes and then arranged them in the dishwasher, following her routine. After a minute, Nita came back from the bedroom and held up my apartment key.

"Thank you! I'll bring it back tomorrow. I'd hate to have to call security to let me in. It seems so unprofessional."

Jim carried a little black flashlight when he came out of his office. He went to the front closet, took out our jackets and his windbreaker, and called to Nita. "I'm going to walk home with Cleo and take a look at this invitation." He reached up to the shelf and took down a Navy Veteran cap.

"Jim." Nita followed me out of the kitchen, still drying her hands. "Let Mary take care of it."

He seemed determined. "I'm going to have a look. Riley, if you're not interested, you can go on home."

"Jim!" Nita's voice had developed a real edge.

Riley grinned at her. "Did he ever send you home with another man, Nita? I can imagine what my mama would think of that."

Jim grinned sheepishly. "Have you seen these new tactical lights? Fits in a pocket. Rechargeable."

"Listen to your mama," Nita told Riley and gave each of us a kiss on the cheek. "Good night, Cleo. Sleep late tomorrow, okay?"

The doorbell rang.

Jim, already standing with his hand on the knob, jerked the door open, surprising Lieutenant Mary Montgomery.

"Whoa!" she said, starting in. "You trying to get shot?"

"Let me outta here!" Dolly charged forward with only one arm in her jacket. "G'night, everybody, I enjoyed it. Jim, here's eight dollars." She stuck some bills in his hand as she went by. "Don't shoot, Mary. I'm just going home."

Chapter 13

The four of us walked to my apartment—Lieutenant Montgomery, Jim Bergen, Riley, and me. Jim flashed his new light here and there as we walked between buildings to my screened porch, but the main discussion was about the moon.

"Don't really need a flashlight tonight," Mary said.

"Do you find in police work, Mary, that the full moon brings out lunacy?" Jim asked.

"Maybe so," she answered. "Now explain what causes it the rest of the month."

There was a note taped to the glass again. I took it down and glanced at it as I inserted the key. "Ann wants to feed me breakfast again. Wonder what's up. I'm going to get fat if this keeps up."

"Don't you always try the knob before you unlock it?" Jim asked. "You saw how Nita does it. Might be a good idea, isolated back here like this."

I could see the back doors of several houses across the short fence, plus windows of a number of apartments on my side of the fence. It always felt perfectly safe to me, but Jim meant well.

"Maybe I'll start doing that when I'm alone." Actually, the inside entry to the apartment was of more concern to me than this one, out in the open as it was, with plenty of eyes around to monitor it. Sometimes I felt too exposed.

Tinkerbelle was waiting inside but was overwhelmed when so many people came in at once. She retreated to the kitchen to guard her food dish and watch me turn on lamps.

"Have a seat, everybody. Can I get something to drink? Make coffee?"

"A cup of coffee? That'd be good," Jim said.

I went to the kitchen, put in a filter, added the aromatic grounds with hazelnut flavor, and poured in water.

Riley joined me. "Can I help? Where are the cups?"

I showed him and poured some milk into a cream pitcher. Jim was prowling around the apartment and Mary sat on the couch with her head thrown back.

"I could go to sleep right here."

"There's sweetener and sugar up there, too," I told Riley, and got out a package of almond thins. By the time we were ready, the coffee was, too. I poured, and we moved to the living room and passed the goodies around.

The plastic bag was on the coffee table.

"Everything's been handled," I said, "so the plastic bag's probably pointless. Any fingerprints would be ruined."

I unzipped the bag and allowed the invitation to slide out onto the tabletop. Montgomery took the Sudoku book, still in the bag, and read the note.

"I tore out all the used pages Monday, so this note was added after that. Handleman moved in Tuesday."

"Hmm," she said.

I continued. "When Riley and I told him Wheat was dead, he seemed genuinely surprised. He said he'd looked for him but didn't find him."

She asked where the guest suite was located and what Handleman's car looked like, then pointed to the invitation. "And what's this? Somebody getting married?"

"You've heard about the Type Forty-One scam?" I asked.

She hadn't, so we filled her in while she examined the invitation without touching it. Then she summarized the details.

"Somebody went to a lot of trouble, printing up formal offers to participate in a fraud. Ann Slump found this one, she's not sure where. It's not addressed to her and she doesn't know where it came from, but she wants you to find out and return the evidence to the perpetrator."

She looked at me. "Is that about it?"

Jim chuckled. "When you put it like that…"

It was an unflattering view but not exactly wrong.

Riley had been standing at the door, looking out through the screened porch. He joined us at that point, seeming displeased. "Cleo realized the invitation might indicate someone was attempting to defraud a Harbor Village resident. She thought the police department ought to look into it."

Montgomery widened her eyes. "Oh, I got it. I got it." She poked at the envelope. "That gold stuff looks like it might hold a print. You got any rubber gloves?"

I didn't, but I went to the kitchen and returned with another plastic bag.

Montgomery was sitting on the edge of the couch when I got back, holding the envelope by pressing her fingers against each side. She flexed it, shook a couple of times, and the card slid out and landed flat on the coffee table.

Montgomery and Jim bent over to read but Jim backed away immediately. "Cleo, read it out loud. The print's too small."

I bent over the invitation and read aloud. And then I went back and read part of it silently, attempting to commit it to memory while the others speculated about print shops and mail fraud.

Exclusive Offering
The Royale Consortium
Type 41

A confidential invitation to
Select Investors
interested in protecting
the prototype of the world's
rarest and most valuable
classic automobile.

If you belong to this exclusive group
and are interested in making
a significant investment in
anticipation of commensurate return,
please request a complete prospectus from

_____

"Engraved," Jim said. "What does something like that cost? And how many went out?"

"Bag it up," Mary Montgomery said.

We watched her lift the card and then the envelope, pressing just the tips of her fingers against the paper edges. Jim held the bag and, when both pieces were inside, zipped it shut.

"Good day's work," he told her, handing the bag over.

"A night's work." She drank the last of her coffee. "The good part remains to be seen." She got up. "Ann Slump's one of Wheat's clients. Maybe he gave it to her. We'll ask if any other client got one. Or maybe Wheat himself is the *select investor*. You got any ideas, Mr. Federal Reserve?"

I winced at what seemed like a snide remark, but Riley didn't seem to mind.

He sounded thoughtful. "It's an attempt to appear exclusive, so I'd expect the investment to be steep. If multiple brokers are involved, that explains the blank line—everyone uses the same card and writes in their own name. That allows the scam to be widespread, as Handleman thought. Not just in Fairhope. Maybe Wheat was involved in a dispute with some other broker."

Jim had another idea. "I'd talk to people at the hotel since that's where Ann got it. See if they're giving them out to their guests. And talk with Handleman. He's the car expert. He said last night he's heard something since he got here."

Montgomery nodded and got up to go. "Ready, Jim? I'll walk back with you since my car's over there."

Jim looked at Riley. "You coming?"

"I won't go back with you. Good night, Jim. Good night, Lieutenant." He put our dirty cups on the tray and took it to the kitchen while I walked out with them.

"Sorry it took all day to make connections, Mary. I went to the car show and my phone didn't work down there. Then I left it at home tonight."

"Well, stuff happens." She called back, "'Night, Riley. Let's go, Jim."

I had another thought. "I don't suppose you'd like a ticket to the banquet tomorrow night. Jim and Nita and a few of us are going. I've got two tickets left."

She shook her head. "I'm working. But if they're going to waste, Chief Boozer might want them. His wife wants to go."

"Can you deliver the tickets? Let me get them." I ran to the bedroom for my bag and came back with two tickets. Jim was telling her our table would be near the kitchen.

"We'll look forward to meeting Chief Boozer's wife," I said.

"She's fun," Montgomery said. "He's a wet blanket at a party, but she's good."

Jim had his new flashlight out. "This might interest you, Mary," I heard him telling Montgomery as they walked away. "This little flashlight is actually a defensive tool."

"I'm going, too." Riley was right behind me. "I wanted to say good night in private."

We shared a hug and a kiss but then he left. I've never been quick about hopping into bed with a new guy, and I didn't intend to start at this point in life, but the thought did occur to me. To him, too, if I was any judge.

Once again, I found myself wondering why such a nice guy was available. Was I missing something?

I smiled as I locked up and closed the blinds. But I wouldn't be sleeping late on Saturday. Ann's note had said breakfast would be ready at seven. I thought cooking was probably a therapeutic task for her right now, but my to-do list for Saturday was twice as long as usual, after this busy week. At least breakfast shouldn't take much time.

Stephanie called while I was in the shower. I called her back once I got into bed.

She answered, giggling. "Guess where I am."

Her voice sounded odd, like she was in a metal barrel. I was never going to get used to cell phones. "Birmingham?"

"Halfway to Houston. That sounds like a country song, don't you think? Boyd and Barry and Dad and I are taking a mini vacation."

Travis hadn't said anything about going through Birmingham. What about his plans to spend the weekend in the office, catching up on work? What about Stephanie's shop?

"Well, that's wonderful. But what about work? I thought you were super busy right now."

Stephanie talked fast. "I told Amy if she can't hold the fort tomorrow, she can just put up a closed sign. I'm taking a mental health day. We'll fly home Sunday afternoon. How was the car show? And Mexican Trains? Did I tell you about my friend's husband having a business for sale down there?"

"Umm, I think so."

"Well, let me tell you this. This same guy's mother lives in the Harbor Village in Tampa and she told him it's a *hotbed of geriatric romance*. Her words. Don't you love it? *A hotbed of geriatric romance*? I told Dad he needs to use that in all the marketing brochures."

"Have a safe trip, honey. Give Barry a kiss for me."

* * * *

I got up at the usual time Saturday morning, put on old jeans and a faded cotton sweater, fed the cat, made a pot of decaf in case Ann didn't have any, and went next door exactly at seven.

A man opened Ann's door and reached for the coffee. "I'm Usher Slump." He ended with a little smack of the tongue. "Let me take that."

I didn't know what I'd expected Ann's brother to be like. He was younger than Ann, late fifties, maybe, with the skin of a nocturnal creature, someone who never saw the sun. His voice was theatrical and he had an oversized, Charlie Brown head. I tried to recall what the young Truman Capote had looked like and decided the link wasn't appearance or sexual orientation, but a certain exaggerated Southern-ness.

"You're Cleo, I take it. And you're the head of Harbor Village?" He sniffed. "Just be glad you don't work for my sister. Ann would shoot me if I showed up for work in blue jeans." Smack.

I looked down. My jeans looked fine. Faded, but no rips, no stains, and breakfast with a neighbor wasn't exactly work. What did Usher Slump wear for Saturday breakfast with his sister? I took inventory: dark corduroy trousers, tassel loafers, an untucked polo shirt in maroon and gray stripes. He had thin, pale hair, black-framed glasses, and none of Ann's spritely energy.

"Come right this way while I put this carafe in the kitchen to stay warm. Ann, your neighbor's here."

Ann came out of the kitchen wearing quilted oven mitts that came almost to her elbows and carrying a sausage and egg casserole. She leaned across the circular table and put the ceramic dish on a cork trivet. The tablescape looked like a magazine photograph. There was a white tablecloth with stitchery-filled cutouts around its edge, bright yellow place mats with ruffles, blue and white dishes, and a bright blue vase of yellow asters.

"Good morning, Cleo. Did Usher introduce himself? Evie's here, too. Evie, come out."

Evie followed Ann from the kitchen. She was smiling and balancing two cups of coffee on saucers, looking like a walking accident. "Hello, Cleo. I'm glad to see you in a happy situation this time."

I grabbed one of the cups and looked for a place to put it down.

"Sit down, everybody." Ann seemed tense, or peeved. She assigned seats. "Usher, you sit against the wall. Push the table out if you need to. Before Evie puts the coffee down, please. I don't want it sloshing. Cleo, you can sit beside him. I'll take the seat by the kitchen. The jump seat, I call it, so I can jump and run. Evie, you sit here. Move the flowers so Cleo can see them."

The menu was totally different from Friday's breakfast but equally extravagant. There were pancakes with a choice of two warm compotes, blueberry or citrus with walnut, and whipped cream. Conecuh sausages and, in keeping with the color palette, a sausage and egg casserole covered with melted yellow cheese. Ann and Evie made more trips to and from the kitchen while Usher raved, addressing me with frequent eye rolls and smacks.

"And you moved here from Atlanta, Cleo? Why would any *sane* person do that? Are you married? I'm single. *Ah*-gain. Maybe I'd have better luck in Atlanta. But I can't leave my dear old sisters alone, can I? I thought when Ann moved to a retirement home we'd be able to relax some, but no, it's worse than ever. Busy, busy, busy. And now, tragedy."

"Pass the pancakes, Usher," Ann told him.

"Are these our kumquats?" I spooned the citrus-walnut sauce over a perfectly browned pancake.

Ann nodded. "They're the sweet variety. There's a sour kumquat, too, sort of oblong. Usher, pass the whipped cream. Cleo, won't you have more than one pancake? That's not enough to sustain anybody."

"I get the sugar shakes if I eat only pancakes. I'm going to try the casserole, too."

"The whipped cream, ma'am," Usher mimicked, holding the big pottery bowl, still cold from the refrigerator. "Let me hold this while you serve."

A wooden spoon stuck out of the mound of whipped cream. I put two scoops on my pancake.

"Now, give me three times that amount." He moved the bowl closer to his plate.

The food was the happy part of breakfast. The people part left something to be desired. Ann seemed angry with her brother and was doing a poor job of concealing it.

"I wanted you to meet Usher, Cleo, so you'll know what we're up against."

"Ooh, that sounds bad. Doesn't it, Cleo? Please, Sister, don't tell people you're up against me. It makes me think I'm about to be flattened."

Ann ignored him. "Usher owns a share of Royale Court, same as the rest of us. And he thinks we should sell." She gave him a frown.

Evie's attention stayed on her plate. Did she agree with Ann? I couldn't tell.

"Well, that's not *exactly* what I said. And I don't think Cleo wants us washing family linen at breakfast."

"Cleo's a busy woman. And a businesswoman. I'm asking her advice, so I want her to know what I'm talking about. You want to tell her yourself?"

Usher looked at me, leaned back, and put his guard up. "Exactly what do you want to know?"

"Whatever you'd like to tell me. I understand you're the manager of Royale Court."

He sighed. "Have you ever tried managing people who outrank you? A diplomatic *nightmare*. Any *sane* man would get out of that deal immediately. So, you know what that makes me, after twenty years." He laughed and began to eat, relaxing as he shifted back to banter. Over the next few minutes, while we ate, he confirmed that he managed the courtyard and described duties that involved hanging around the premises and interacting with tenants and shoppers. "The T-shirt shop is laundering money, but it's none of my business. I need caffeine."

He got up and went to the kitchen. Ann and I looked at each other and smiled. The refrigerator closed and Usher returned, opening a can of Mountain Dew.

"Get a glass," Ann said.

"This is fine." He took a swig and put the sweat-beaded can on the quilted place mat. "My sisters have always taken advantage of my youth and inexperience." He laughed and resumed his monologue, interspersing long swigs from the can.

I wondered what his sisters were thinking, and finally Evie spoke up. "The police talked with Usher about Devon's murder, but he doesn't know anything about it. Those security cameras haven't worked in years."

"That's too bad," I said. "They might've recorded crucial information."

"Yes, isn't it," Ann said coldly. She looked at Usher.

"Devon Wheat." Usher leaned back, covered his face with his hands, and laughed. "I wish to God I'd never heard that man's name." He shook his head side to side. "I've spent hours at the police station. Hours! How am I supposed to know who his friends were? Not me, that's for sure. For *damn* sure!"

"Usher," Ann warned.

"Oh, Sister. Cleo's heard the word *damn* before." He looked at me. "She might even have uttered a damn or two herself, am I right, Cleo? A woman who wears blue jeans to breakfast? My sisters never wore blue jeans in their lives, did you?"

Okay, I decided, he must be drunk. Or high on something.

He picked up the empty drink can and crushed it, creating a loud pop. "Look at that. Remember who taught us to do that?"

They didn't respond.

"He met with a real estate man to talk about selling Royale Court." Ann scowled at him. "Didn't even invite us."

No wonder she was angry. I looked at Usher and he swiveled to face me.

"Cleo, you're a perceptive woman, I'm sure. You have no doubt noticed we're old. I'm old. My sisters are even older. There is absolutely no way on God's green earth I could run Royale Court without their participation. That's the nice word for what they do. Participate. Day and night." He closed his eyes and shook his head, then continued.

"It's simple prudence to have a succession plan. That's the real estate term. A succession plan. I agree we need it. Prissy agrees. And we, Prissy and I, we are the success-*ees*, if I may invent a term. The day Ann and Evie hang up their hats, Royale Court goes on the market! And Usher is off to see the world! We've got a family fortune in Europe. Did Ann tell you? Just waiting for us." He laughed.

He seemed to be taunting Ann, who put her elbows on the table and rested her head in her hands.

"Remember, I am your faithful servant, Ann, and you know it. Evie, too. But it's time for a change." He took his crumpled drink can to the kitchen, and I heard it land in an empty bin.

Breakfast was finished.

I thanked Ann, told Evie good-bye, and offered my hand to Usher. "It was nice to meet you, Usher." What else was I going to say?

Ann said, "There's something I'd like you to look at, Cleo."

She pushed her chair back, as I did, but didn't get up right away. Instead, she swiveled toward the green china cabinet in the corner and pulled out a green folder. "Take this with you, if you will. Just look at it when you have a chance."

Usher reached for the folder—to pass it to me, I assumed—but Ann jerked it out of his reach and put it into my hands directly.

"Don't look now. Save it for a rainy day, when you can't go out to play. It's just some personal papers, but I'd like your opinion."

I was curious about the contents of Ann's folder, but the morning was passing quickly. I went back to my apartment and, without even looking to see what was inside, dropped the folder on my coffee table. I got the shopping list from the kitchen and drove to the pier. Not the fastest way to get the chores done, but good exercise. If my daughter could take mental health days, surely I deserved a walk on the pier. I put on the canvas windbreaker I keep in the car and made two trips down the pier and back, getting in a mile of walking. Pitiful for a week's effort, but this hadn't been a normal week. Then I drove two miles north to Publix.

I stopped for gas on the way home, then washed veggies, put away the paper products and canned goods, stripped the bed, put on fresh linens while the dirty stuff washed, and worked through the routine Saturday chores, including the litter box. Eventually I got tired and sat at the desk beside the living room window, but that was work, too. I went online to pay the credit card bill and, while I was there, did a search for *Type 41*. Patti had said Todd Barnwell wanted an investment named something like that, and the term had appeared in the invitation I'd passed along to

Lieutenant Montgomery the previous night. I threw in the word *automobile* for extra precision, since that was what the invitation was about. Right away, Google popped up with the answer.

The Bugatti Type 41, the most elegant car ever built, was better known as the Royale, Wikipedia said. Bugatti had been able to sell only three of seven Royales manufactured. Six still existed and the seventh was wrecked by Ettore Bugatti. The picture on the website might've been the same one used on the invitation, but the colors looked brighter on screen.

I leaned back and looked out the window. So, who was right, Reg Handleman or Wikipedia? Six Royales or seven? And why did Todd Barnwell, an automotive dunce, want his trust money invested in a Type 41? *Scam, scam, scam.* I didn't understand it.

I gathered up garbage and recycling, took the garbage to bins at the garage, and walked on to the recycling shed with scrap paper and a few aluminum cans and glass bottles. When I got back to the apartment, I washed up and changed clothes, ran a comb through my hair, then went to test out the first ever Saturday lunch at the Harbor Village dining room.

I was late. At a quarter past noon, the dining room was just as full as it usually was on a weekday. Many people had finished lunch already and stayed to talk. Most of the diners were residents, some with visitors or family members in tow, which altered the usual atmosphere.

Carla was buzzing around in a happy daze. "Do you think we'd get this many people every Saturday?" she asked.

I didn't know.

Ann Slump hurried across the room when she saw me. "I'm so sorry, Cleo. I spent a lot of time with him yesterday and last night, and this broker business is just now coming to light. I'm in shock, I think. Thank you for coming this morning. I hope you'll advise me. I value your opinions, you know."

"I know it must be stressful for you."

She nodded and stacked dirty dishes, clearing a small table. "Like pulling teeth to get information out of him. He's so much worse lately and I can't decide what to do. I went to your apartment to apologize after he left but you weren't there."

I told her I'd gone to the grocery store. "I haven't looked at your folder yet."

She stood still and gazed off into space. "It says Usher has a health-care proxy and power of attorney and handles the wills when we go. For me and Evie both. But I don't trust him now." She had a somber expression. "I don't think he can handle it."

"No," I agreed. "Does he drink?"

She jumped and did a double take. "Did you smell something on his breath?"

"No. But I didn't get that close."

I was toying with the idea of telling her what Stephanie had told me, about the knit shop for sale somewhere along the coast. Ann had said Usher talked with a real estate broker and she thought he was just gathering information, but had he actually signed a listing agreement? Without Ann's knowledge? That didn't seem possible.

Nita saved me from making a decision. "Honey, the soup's running low. Can I get you a bowl while there's some left?"

I walked with her to the steam table. Soup, salad, and sandwiches. Turkey and cheese or ham and cheese. Going once, going twice…almost gone.

There was a crowd at the big table and smaller groups at some of the little ones.

"Let's go sit by the window," Nita said. "So we can talk."

Nita had already eaten but she pointed out the little table Ann had just cleaned, which had a view of sorts, and led the way. Nita was wearing a purple velour pants suit with long sleeves and a high neck, and it looked gorgeous with her silver hair and big smile.

The moment we sat down, she leaned across the table. "Did Riley spend the night? You don't have to tell me if you don't want to, but Jim said—"

I was shaking my head. "No, no. Riley left right after Jim and Mary did. He was home before Jim was."

"Oh, Cleo." She sounded terribly disappointed.

Probably all of Harbor Village monitored who spent time together, who went out to dinner, and where residents spent their nights. Of course they did. But Nita was eighty and disappointed that her friends weren't having an affair?

"He did talk with me a few days ago."

She was immediately all ears. "Oh? Can you tell me?"

I did, speaking softly, our heads bent together. "He was wonderfully sweet and invited me into his life. And I was an idiot, Nita. I did everything wrong. I didn't expect it. I thought he was joking, I joked back. But then he gave me the sweetest kiss." Not sweet exactly, but close enough. Did she quiz Riley this way, too?

Nita was beaming. "I'm so happy. My two favorite people! Of course, I know you wouldn't do this just for me, but you two are so perfect for each other, I wouldn't care if you did. I don't suppose you've…" She looked at me, raised her eyebrows, and wiggled her fingers.

I shook my head. "No!" Whatever she was thinking, the answer was no. My cheeks were on fire.

"Well, remember, dear. Happy couples make sex a priority." She looked down and smiled. "I'm no expert, but I do know a thing or two."

Oh-my-god, the chorus chirped.

Crawling under the table would attract too much attention, but I wasn't prepared for this. I recalled what Stephanie had said last night and asked Nita, "Are overnight visits common occurrences here?"

She looked startled. "Here? Of course not." She hesitated. "Not that there'd be anything wrong with it."

We looked at each other and she grinned. A tryst between her friends? It was like a sporting event where she could cheer for both sides.

Chapter 14

Saturday was an off day for the office staff, but Patti was with Todd when he arrived for the two o'clock meeting. She wore olive green leggings with a colorful top and carried a jacket, and when they got closer, I heard Todd's leather jacket squeaking. He carried a stack of manila folders bound with rubber bands.

Riley greeted them politely, put on skinny reading glasses, and began arranging Todd's folders, taking out documents, reading aloud from their cover pages: Grandfather Barnwell's last will and testament, an assortment of trust documents. "Prepared by the law firm of Ehlers and Leff," he read at one point, and then looked at me and raised his brows.

"A local firm," I said. "I've seen the name."

"Yeah," Todd said. "They think they're in charge now."

Riley grinned at him, nodded, and went back to laying out the documents, arranging them in the center of the table. "Bill of sale. A lease for the property." He looked over his glasses at the youngsters as he put those two documents in a separate stack. "Just so you know, there's no deed when a house sits on Colony property. Just a bill of sale and a ninety-nine year lease."

"Ninety-nine years?" Todd groaned, slapping a hand over his eyes and slumping onto one elbow. "I won't live that long. Is it already paid? I hope."

"What happens after ninety-nine years?" Patti asked. "Does everything go back to the Colony?"

Riley leaned back. "I think the average life for a lease is actually seven years, before it's canceled or modified." Todd perked up and Riley continued: "Rent is paid annually in lieu of property tax, and there's a premium, a demonstration fee they call it, used to benefit the community. When you sell, a bill of sale transfers the improvements—that's everything except the land—and the Colony issues the next owner a new ninety-nine year lease for the land."

Todd, energized, latched on to the selling part. "So I *can* sell the house? And Grandpa's lease gets canceled? Or…what?"

"Hold on until we find out if it's yours to sell." He continued emptying the folders. There were court documents and communications from attorneys. Eventually he came across a few financial statements and gave Todd an inquiring look.

"Those are from Devon Wheat." Todd tapped the thin collection of reports. "They come to me. Or did."

"Still in the mailbox," smarty Patti said. "It was stuffed full and they'd started using a package box, which was filling up, too."

All the private homes on Andrews Street received mail at a little kiosk on the corner. The actual mailboxes were small, but if a resident received a package, the carrier put it in one of several large boxes and left the key in the individual box. All Harbor Village apartment buildings and condos had similar arrangements. But collecting mail had apparently not been part of Todd's basic coping skills.

One thing about the situation was a surprise to me. I had assumed that if any resident's mail accumulated for more than a couple of days, the carrier would let us know so we could investigate. I took out my phone and sent myself a message to check on procedures when mail wasn't picked up. Come to think of it, when did I last check my own mail? Everything had been off schedule this week.

The last folder in Todd's materials, the one with financial statements, contained a handwritten document on lined paper. "That's my budget." He looked proud but nervous and paid close attention as Riley scanned the document.

Riley nodded and looked over his glasses again. "A good start. Feels good, doesn't it? Having a plan and knowing where you stand?" He flipped the page to the back, which was blank. "I don't see any goals here."

"You didn't say anything about goals," Todd said.

"No rush. You've got plenty of time. Now, folks, I'm going to sit here and read awhile. Why don't the three of you do something productive? Check back in thirty minutes."

I encountered a crowd of people in front of the big house, waiting for the shuttle to the car show.

"Come with us," someone proposed.

"I went yesterday." I greeted a few Harbor Village residents I recognized. "Loved it! You'll need that jacket, I'll bet."

"Enjoy it while you can," someone said. "It'll be hot again next week."

I walked on across the street, past the garages, and entered the lobby of my building. My mailbox was almost full. I pulled everything out and sat beside the fireplace to sort it. The gas logs were off and the sitting room felt a little chilly.

I'd received hearing aid offers, ACLU renewals, cell phone deals if I'd add another line, a pizza special, and a notice about a new dentist in town. I remembered I needed to return my spare key to Nita. When I finished with the mail, I went inside to get it. There was a note on the door to my apartment, inviting me to Ann's for breakfast this morning. I stuck it in with the junk mail. Guess she hadn't known which door I'd use last night and left notes in both places to be sure I'd find one.

I put all the junk into the recycling basket I'd just emptied and placed the few pieces of real mail on the desk beside the computer. Then I got the spare key, locked up again, and walked across the street to Nita's apartment.

Jim let me in. "She's taking a nap." His hair stood straight up in several spots. He'd probably been napping, too. "Any news about the murder?"

I told him about Usher Slump removing the security cameras at Royale Court. "Apparently they didn't work but it doesn't look good and Ann's worried about him."

Jim looked sheepish but shook his head. "Not the right type. I don't picture Usher strangling anybody."

I wasn't so sure. "I saw him crush a soft drink can with his bare hands."

Jim grinned but shook his head again. "Showing off. Look for a physical type. Macho."

I left my apartment key with him and walked through the parking lot, which was crowded with the vehicles of shuttle riders. At the pool house I spoke with a few swimmers and continued on to Assisted Living, where two residents were working a jigsaw puzzle at a card table in the sitting room. An aide stood by to kibitz, and a couple of cats slept coiled together in one chair. We chatted for a minute and I tried, without success, to help with the puzzle. When I returned to the big house. Riley, Patti, and Todd were already at work.

"I own the house," Todd crowed when I walked up.

"And he can sell it," Patti said, "as soon as it goes through probate."

"Subject to probate," Riley corrected absently, jotting a note on a legal pad. Todd looked at him. "I'm not sure what that means."

Riley looked up. "It means you can sell now if you find a buyer who agrees to let the title transfer at a later date, after the court is satisfied that all conditions of the will have been met."

"I can sell now? So what are we waiting for? Let's do it!" Todd bounced forward eagerly, grinning. "How much? I need sixteen thousand."

Riley's eyebrows shot up. "For what?"

"Next year." Todd tapped the budget folder.

"Plus..." Patti reminded, flipping the folder open and pointing to a lower section of the budget page.

"Oh, yeah. Right. I've got some loans to repay, too. Say eighteen thousand. Maybe nineteen. Let's just make it twenty. That's easy to remember."

Riley nodded, his attention moving on to another document. "That takes care of year one. What do you do for the next three and a half years, until you turn twenty-five?"

"Hmm." Todd shrugged. "Bust the trust, I guess. But here's what I don't understand. How can there even *be* a trust, with Devon Wheat gone? If I sell the house and hire some lawyers—oh, yeah. I need money for lawyers, too. Is that what you were thinking?"

Riley laid a document aside, laced his fingers together, and looked over his glasses at Todd. "Why not take your time and sell the house for what it's worth, which may be substantial. You said your grandfather was a smart man. Maybe he made some good decisions for you—what do you think? Leave the trust in place, take all that money the lawyers would charge you, and put it in your pocket."

Todd whined, "But I've gotta live."

Riley frowned and shook his head. "The house money should tide you over for a while."

"Years?" Todd didn't buy it initially but he appeared concerned that he might look foolish. "Okay. Yeah, either way. Whatever makes sense."

Riley nodded and looked at me, eyebrows raised. "You know any good Realtors, Cleo? Todd needs one."

"Well, he's in luck. I do, actually. Want me to call her? She probably won't be in on Saturday afternoon, but we can see."

It took me a minute to find her number in my contact list, and Vickie Wiltshire answered immediately. She was in her car, on her way back to the office after a showing. Since her office was in the shopping center next to Harbor Village, it'd be no trouble to zip by and talk with us in person. She could be with us in five minutes.

I relayed her offer. Todd nodded. Patti shrugged and nodded.

"Sure," Riley accepted. "Does she know where we are?"

I told her to come to the lobby.

Vickie Wiltshire was a friend of Nita's. She'd shown me a few houses and condos last summer when I was trying to decide if I wanted to move to Fairhope. She was a pretty young woman, and smart, but what my aunt Jo would've called skin and bones.

Vickie was also a hard worker and very good at her job, but she complained about it constantly. I'd felt so bad for her that, when the rental agent's position at Harbor Village came available, I'd called immediately to offer her the job.

She'd laughed at me. The pay was far too low, she loved her job, the real estate profession was ideal for someone who worked as hard as she did.

But she'd found Wilma Gomez for the Harbor Village job. I suspected they had some arrangement to direct listings to Vickie when local residents began the process of moving to Harbor Village, but that didn't seem to violate any licensure rules. It paid to have friends.

While we waited for Vickie to arrive, Patti and I went to get drinks for everyone.

"Do you have time to look at some photos for me?" Patti asked. "We've got hundreds and need to select some for publicity—for the newsletter, the website, the bulletin board. Ann usually helps but she's tied up with family stuff right now. You were there all three nights, weren't you?"

"I was. And I'd enjoy looking at your photos. They're on your phone?"

"I made SD chips. Can you use those?"

I nodded. "Am I looking for anything special?"

We started back to the lobby, Patti carrying two Cokes in red plastic cups. I had two mugs of coffee, each one with a dab of sweetener and some half-and-half. I took a sip from one to keep it from spilling.

"Remind me to give you the chips. They're in my car. And just look for anybody who was entertaining. I've got a really good one of you and Todd and Mr. McKenzie playing that game, but Todd refuses to let it go on the bulletin board." She dropped her voice as we turned toward the table where Riley and Todd sat talking. "He thinks people are laughing at him."

"Probably right." I smiled, remembering.

"What's funny?" Patti asked.

I wiped the smile away.

Riley was summarizing Todd's financial position. I heard thirty thousand and saw Todd do a couple of fist pumps.

Patti snapped her fingers. "Napkins."

Vickie arrived, wearing red lipstick and a swingy black outfit that echoed straight, swingy blond hair, cut longer in front so that it accentuated her heart-shaped face. I introduced her to Riley and Todd, verified that she knew Patti, and offered her something to drink.

"Just water, if you have it."

"Water," Patti repeated. She headed back to the dining room.

Vickie took Patti's chair. "Now, who's the client?"

She looked at Riley and raised her eyebrows expectantly. He pointed, and Todd raised his hand. Vickie swung toward him like the arrow on a compass, catching him in the middle of a sip.

He downed half his Coke in the one big gulp. Vickie seemed to make him nervous.

I got the real estate ball rolling. "Todd is inheriting his grandfather's house. The will hasn't been probated yet, but he'd like to sell it."

"Aren't you lucky?" Vickie gave him a big smile. "So, you'd like to sell now with a pending title. And where is this house?"

He swallowed and blinked but managed to mumble an address on Andrews Street.

"Good location. And how large is it?"

He was stumped. He cut his gaze to me and shook his head vaguely.

"How many bedrooms?" Vickie clarified.

"Uh, two, I guess. One for him, one for me."

"How many baths?"

He inhaled and shook his head. "It doesn't have a shower. Well, it does, but there's a tub. You know?"

"Do you have a half bath?" She was nodding at everything he said and jotting notes on a printed form.

Poor Todd. So naive.

Patti returned and set a bottle of water and a napkin in front of Vickie, then dealt out cookies and napkins for everyone. Todd got two, I noticed.

Patti leaned close to my ear. "Do you need me for this part?"

"Did you look at Todd's house?"

She nodded, looking puzzled.

"Maybe you can help with the description." I got up and gave her my chair and Riley intercepted me on the way to fetch another one, apologizing for not anticipating it. Mr. Courtesy today.

"How many bathrooms, Patti?" Todd asked.

"Hmm, three? No, that one by the pantry is a half bath. And there's another one out in...what do you call that, a laundry? The back of the house, where the garage is."

"Two baths and two half baths, then? Plus a laundry." Vickie jotted a note. She looked at Patti. "Is it furnished?"

"Yes. Full of stuff."

"Old stuff," Todd said. "Junk."

"Antiques," Patti corrected.

"Any other heirs? Maybe some of the antiques were bequeathed to family members?"

"No." Riley tapped the stack of folders in front of him. "Todd gets everything."

Vickie patted Riley's arm, either in thanks or to shut him up, and gave Todd another entrancing smile. "Have you decided which items you want to keep? What about an estate sale?"

"Sell everything. As soon as possible." He didn't seem to misunderstand intentionally. He was just totally out of his depth and eager to get this process completed. And smitten with Vickie, of course.

She smiled at him and pushed the swingy blond veil back over one ear. "I'm thinking we should go look at the house."

"Okay." He stood up abruptly. If she'd proposed jumping in a lake, he'd be wet already.

Riley sorted documents back into folders.

"You want to keep this stuff?" Todd shoveled documents toward him. "I don't need any of it."

"Yes you do!" Riley took rubber bands off his wrist and placed them around groups of folders. "This is all vitally important to you right now. But I would like to take another look through it, if you don't mind. How about I get it back to you tomorrow? And I'll keep the IOU."

He pulled out a single page with large printing and held it for me to read. *IOU* was printed in big letters followed by one hundred dollars in numerals. Todd's signature was in the same handwriting on a line beneath the amount. At the bottom, the word *Witness* was followed by another line with Patti's small, tidy signature. Riley nodded to Todd, folded the page, and stuck it in his pocket.

There was no reason for me to go along on the house tour, especially since the hour was later than I'd imagined, but I was curious about the private residences on the street behind my apartment.

"I'm going home," Patti said. "I need to get ready for tonight."

"Don't forget your tickets," I reminded.

She smiled. "Stewart has them."

"I'd like to see the house." Riley surprised me. "Just out of curiosity."

Vickie said, "I'm going to drive so I won't have to come back here. Anybody want to ride with me? There's room for one."

"I will," Todd said immediately.

Riley and I walked. He carried the stack of folders under one arm.

"I want to talk with Todd if there's an opportunity," I told him. "You saw the reference to a Type Forty-One in that invitation last night? I think he and Wheat talked about it."

A shout came from behind us. "Cleo! Cleo!"

Patti was running after us. She waved her hand and quickly caught up. "Don't forget the photos." She gave me two small plastic cases with SD chips inside. "Mark the ones you like best."

I stuck the little cases into my pocket. "I'll bring them to you Monday."

She turned back toward her car but shouted again, "What're you wearing tonight?"

"A blue dress. Long."

"Oh, Cleo! A dress?" She threw her head back and laughed delightedly. "Are you sure? You really want to wear a dress?"

"Why not? Is there something wrong with a dress?"

"You'll make me lose a bet. I told Stewart you'd wear black pants." She didn't wait for a reply but danced toward her car, still laughing.

I turned back toward Andrews Street and saw Riley hide a smile. "And what are you wearing, smarty?" I asked.

He grinned. "Black pants."

The walk to Todd's house took us past two handsome jelly palms at the corner beside the mail kiosk. The old leaf stems created a crisscross pattern up the trunk of the palms, which were ten or twelve feet tall. Their sweeping fronds reached almost to the ground, where the grounds crew had used pine straw to mulch large, interlocking circles around the trunks. It looked very attractive.

"I'm thinking about the Type Forty-One," I resumed. "That's another name for the Royale, and Patti says Todd badgered Devon Wheat about investing in something like that."

"Todd didn't seem to know much about cars Thursday night."

I agreed. "I suppose it was Wheat's idea, but that's what I want to find out. I can't imagine Todd knowing about it otherwise. He came to just the last Handleman lecture, right?"

Riley shook his head. "I wasn't there Tuesday and didn't see him Wednesday."

I checked a house number. We were almost there.

"Think it was a coincidence, his showing up the only night Handleman talked about investments? Maybe that was all he cared about."

Riley shrugged. "You've thought about it more than I have. Maybe he just went because his friends did. Patti and Stewart, I mean."

That was a possibility I hadn't considered. "Well, I'm going to quiz him a little, if the opportunity arises."

We got to Todd's house and he met us on the porch. Vickie wasn't visible but I heard odd noises coming from inside the house.

We entered directly into a large, dark living room with a brick fireplace, old rosy-beige wall-to-wall carpeting, a musty smell, and too much antique furniture. Some of it had intricate carving that made me think German, although the name Barnwell didn't sound very German. Family photographs hung on every wall.

"Who are these people?" I asked Todd as I moved slowly around the room.

He shrugged and looked at the photographs as if he'd never noticed them.

Riley had stopped in front of a mirrored sideboard. On top, a brass tray held a collection of half-empty booze bottles. An enormous cuckoo clock hung on the wall above scotch and bourbon and Irish whiskey, its weights shaped like pinecones, sprawled on the floor.

"Wonder what it sounds like," Riley said.

I looked at the sideboard instead. It was oak, unlike the rest of the furniture in the room. Everything felt dirty. I swiped a finger across the wood and left a clean streak.

"Does housekeeping come here?"

Todd shook his head. "They *wanted* to. At, like, *eight* in the morning. I didn't need that."

Vickie was in the kitchen, beeping an electronic measuring device, writing down dimensions, and snapping photos. "Nice big rooms. I assume you're selling as is?"

Todd looked at me. I nodded.

"Um, I guess," he told her.

Vickie laughed. "I didn't think you'd want to do any updating. Even if it'd gain you some money."

Was she chiding him for avoiding the work or congratulating him on not being greedy? Whatever her intent, it caused him to reconsider.

"What would I have to do?"

"Just pay, mostly." She laughed again. "And it would add a few months to the process."

"No," he decided immediately.

There was a large master bedroom with more of the oversized, dark furniture, including a king-size bed stripped to the mattress. The master bath was big enough to hold a party, and a big closet was jammed with men's clothing and boxes, many of them bearing marks from QVC. It didn't appear that anything had been disposed of, not even medication bottles lined up on the bathroom counter.

What Vickie called a Jack-and-Jill bath was shared by two bedrooms at the opposite end of the house. One of the small bedrooms was set up as an office. I breezed through it and the basic bathroom to the third bedroom.

"This is my room. Sort of messy." Todd looked around with me. I saw a single bed, an electric treadmill draped with clothing, and a large TV on a dresser. We moved on.

The kitchen was unusually large, with an extra row of cabinets in the middle of the room. Some builder probably thought it was a great idea but it looked cluttered and rather like a barrier, just something to walk around between the stove and refrigerator.

There was a pantry full of food and household supplies and, beside it, a powder room with black fixtures and striped metallic wallpaper. I debated the era. Eighties? I didn't know Harbor Village went back that far.

A separate dining room at the back of the house was light and bright with one wall of windows and another mirrored, but it was oddly proportioned, long and narrow with barely enough room to push chairs away from the oversized table. A big china cabinet on the mirrored wall displayed lots of china and fancy glassware.

I was wondering what the dishes would bring in an estate sale when I heard my name called. Riley stood in the hallway, motioning for me to follow him. We backtracked to the office and he stopped beside the big, messy desk.

"Did you see this?" He pointed.

A white envelope with a square flap and gold lining stuck out of the clutter of paperwork. The envelope was empty and blank.

I looked at Riley. "Aha!"

"I don't see a card," he said.

I looked around, pushed a few papers aside, even stuck a finger into the paper sprawl at the same geologic level as the envelope, lifted slightly and leaned over for a close look. I didn't see a card, either.

"Do you think it's the same thing?"

He shrugged. "Might be a wedding invitation."

We caught up with Vickie again in the kitchen.

Riley leaned through the doorway to look into the dining room. "Is this representative of all the houses along here?"

Vickie made an unhappy face and nodded. "The ones still occupied by original residents. New buyers are modernizing, but I worry about resale. The houses are on the big side, so renovation is costly and raises prices pretty high, once you factor in Harbor Village's monthly fees. I don't suppose the fees are likely to decrease?"

I shook my head. "They'll go up eventually."

She flapped a hand dismissively. "Everyone likes an updated house, but they don't like paying for it. But don't worry, it'll sell fast. We don't have a lot on the market right now."

There was a little passageway off the kitchen, filled with natural sunlight, laundry equipment, a forest of mops and brooms, vacuum cleaners, carpet sweepers, shelves holding outdoor shoes and other stuff I couldn't identify, and three doors in addition to the one I'd entered through. One opened to a drab powder room, another to the garage. The two spaces were taken up by a Cadillac, a few years old and, beyond it, something covered with a blue plastic tarp. The third door opened to the driveway. We walked out beside Vickie's car.

"Well, I think I've got what I need," she said.

"So? How much?" Todd sounded nervous again.

Vickie quickly fell into the business side of real estate sales. "I have to do some calculations, but in the neighborhood of three. It'll take longer to empty than to sell, so you'd better get started. Right now, you need to select an estate sale specialist. I'll bring you a list of the people I recommend. Take whatever you want out of the house and go. They'll take care of everything else. Are you staying here? Got an apartment picked out? Or do you want to buy? A condo, perhaps?"

He opened his mouth but no words came out.

"I can show you some things." She smiled prettily.

I took pity on him. "Give him a day to think about it. The estate sale people will need two or three weeks?" I based that on my recent experience. "And you'll start showing after that?"

Vickie nodded. "We'll get a cleaning crew in as soon as the stuff's out. Unless you want to do the cleaning yourself?" She looked at Todd.

He shook his head.

"He's on a tight budget." I wondered if he wasn't making a mistake but realized he wouldn't know anything about cleaning, either. Better bring in the professionals.

"No problem. I'll run a tab and he can reimburse me at closing. I'm already thinking of a client who wants investment property. I may show it to him right away." She tapped Todd on the chest. "It'll be sold before Christmas if you stay focused and we don't run into termites or mold or something. Whatever you do, keep the HVAC going. Don't try to economize there. What's the best time to catch you tomorrow?" She unlocked her car and looked back at him.

"Hmm, whenever. You pick."

"Two o'clock." She stuck out her hand. "Thanks for calling me, Cleo. I'll take good care of your friend. Nice to meet you, Todd. And Riley." She moved to shake his hand, too, then swung into her car and zoomed away.

"We need to go," Riley said.

"What's HVAC?" Todd asked him.

"Umm. We'd better walk back through the house." Riley found the thermostat on the wall near the pantry and showed Todd what temperature it was set for. "Just leave it exactly like it is. If you get hot or cold, adjust your clothing. Put on socks. Wear pajamas. How've you been paying the utilities?"

Todd didn't know.

"Automatic deductions?" I asked.

Riley shook his head. "The account owner's dead. How's that still working?"

Todd looked from one of us to the other. "Are you talking about paying bills? Well, this lawyer guy...guardian, you said? I guess he wants to tell me about that stuff. He leaves messages on the phone or taped to the door. I told him whatever, just take care of it, but he keeps coming around."

I looked at Riley. He'd raised two boys. I was willing to bet they'd known about thermostats and paying bills by age twenty. My daughter, on the other hand...I wasn't so sure about her, and thermostats were tricky. Did she know even now?

"Ready?" Riley moved toward the front door.

I motioned to Todd. "Walk with us a little way. I want to ask you something."

He swiped his hair back, jammed his hands into his pockets, and walked with his head down. "Boy! So much to think about."

"Do you want to put it off for a while?"

"No! I want it over with."

He acted a lot like Barry, my toddler grandson. And at twenty, he was closer to Barry's age than to mine, with no family left to advise him. I was still a softie where kids were concerned, even when they neared adulthood. "Tell me about your family. Did you know your grandfather well?"

Todd nodded. "We lived with Pops and Mimi when I was little, me and my mom."

"Where's your mom now?"

"Gone. A boating accident. It's just me now."

"What happened with college?"

He laughed sarcastically. "Didn't work out. So, how am I going to move out, with no money and no place to go? I don't know where to start."

I tried to come up with a reply that didn't sound like a motivational poster, but Riley answered first.

"We'll tide you over financially. You focus on a career. It doesn't have to be a profession. Maybe you'd like to drive a truck, or be a surveyor, or a chef. There's training for anything. Rent an apartment, get a job. Wait tables or cut grass while you're deciding. We'll talk when you're ready."

He sounded impatient, so I stepped in with the nurturing. "And you might get some counseling. Vocational or grief. Or motivational."

"So, how much is the house worth? She said three—what does that mean?"

"Three hundred thousand. There'll be a fee for the Realtor and for cleaning, plus some legal work you'll have to pay for. Maybe you'll get two fifty when the dust settles. I mean, two hundred and fifty thousand dollars."

"Whew!" His eyes were wide and he took a step back, blinking. "More than I thought. Isn't that, like, half a million?"

"*Half* of half a million," Riley answered sharply. "And it's what you live on until your trust comes through. It'll be adequate, if you don't do anything stupid."

He jingled keys in his pocket and looked at me. We had stopped at the corner beside the mail kiosk. Todd cut his gaze toward Riley and smiled.

"Thanks, you guys."

"Are you using the office?" Riley still sounded gruff. "Or does all that stuff belong to your grandfather?"

He shuffled his feet. "Me and Patti got some papers out of a drawer. I don't know anything about that stuff. He was in there all the time, reading or talking on the phone."

"I'll go through it tomorrow, if you like," Riley volunteered. "Organize the desk and see if there's any more paperwork you'll need to sell the house."

"Okay." He sounded indifferent.

I raised the topic I'd been thinking about. "I heard you wanted to invest in a Type Forty-One. Where did that idea come from?"

Sand had washed out of the soil and covered a corner of the sidewalk. Todd drew a line with the toe of his shoe. "Aw, it was his idea." He glanced up, then back at the sand. "Told me the money would double, I'd get eight million instead of four. I said sure, do it, but the lawyers..." He shook his head. "They said no. The investments had to be on some list and the only car was Tesla." He looked at Riley. "I didn't know Pops ever heard of Tesla. Okay by me. I wouldn't mind having one. But Tesla's not going to double. Probably."

Did he know the difference between owning stock and owning a car? I had my doubts. "When you talked about the Type Forty-One, did Devon Wheat give you any paperwork? A prospectus, or a projection of how much you could earn? An invitation to invest? Anything?"

He looked blank.

"He said your money would double. You weren't going to put all your funds into that one investment, were you?"

He shook his head. "We were just friends, you know, talking at the Bistro. All I've got is that stuff in the folders." He jerked his head toward Riley, who still held the stack of folders.

"I'll look when I organize the desk," Riley offered. "Are you ready?"

I took a step toward him.

"She's coming tomorrow at two, right?" Todd asked. "You can come, too, if you want."

"I'll come in the morning and work on the desk," Riley said. "Cleo has plans."

It was news to me.

We told him good-bye and walked past the jelly palms, which sounded lonely, whistling and rattling in the breeze. I felt lonely, too. Riley was annoyed with me, but I'd learned a few things. I took his arm.

"What was that about the Type Forty-One not being on the list? What's the list?"

Riley smiled. "His grandfather was a smart old guy. Specified exactly how the trust monies could be invested. Gave him a list of forty good companies. Good thing, too. Otherwise, Todd and his accomplice would've blown it."

"Who's his accomplice?"

"Devon Wheat."

"You think? Maybe it's a list of buggy whip manufacturers." It was a reference to controlling ancestors who tied up estates, protecting the funds from heirs until there was nothing left.

"I think." His voice was firm. "And I'll bet that invitation is on the desk. Or filed away somewhere."

"How do you explain a detail-oriented guy having a desk like a garbage dump?"

He laughed at that. "I think Todd rooted through the whole place, looking for cash. And I think you're incredibly naïve where he's concerned."

I was shocked and dropped his arm to stare at him. "Nobody's ever accused me of being naïve." No one except my daughter, who exaggerated.

We walked on, reaching the sidewalk and turning toward my apartment.

Riley kept talking. "Where was Todd the night Wheat was killed, do you know? You heard he argued with Wheat. How do you know he didn't kill him? You can see he lacks all self-discipline. Women ignore how dangerous, how volatile, young men can be."

I rolled my eyes. "How about the quiet, competent, mature version?"

He flicked a glance in my direction and smiled grudgingly. "The worst kind. What did you think of the house?"

"Depressing," I said automatically, picturing the desk and the dirty carpet.

"Really?"

He seemed genuinely surprised. But what else would anybody think about such a musty, disheveled, dirty place? If I were representative of her target market, Vickie Wiltshire had a big job on her hands. Finding a buyer might take a while.

Chapter 15

"Poor Tinkerbelle. You've been neglected all week, haven't you, pretty girl?"

The cat meowed and twisted around my ankles while I tried to brush her. I wound up sitting on the floor to corral her. "And I'm going out again tonight." She flopped on her side and stretched out. As I brushed, I told her all about banquets and she squirmed and squinted and slithered on her side.

I gave Tinkerbelle a thorough brushing for the first time in days, scooped the litter box again and walked the garbage to the containers, removed Patti's SD chips from my pocket and left them beside the computer, and finally hopped into the shower, setting the temperature on hot.

I washed and shampooed and steamed until I was lobster pink. My hair was too short for braids or jewels, but a few poofs of styling goo and careful drying coaxed maximum volume out of it. I put on a few clothes and then took my time applying moisturizer, foundation, blush, lipstick, and mascara. Finally, I slid old faithful carefully over my head.

My one fancy dress, a long, bright-teal, silk column with elbow-length sleeves, had Swarovski crystals and pendants outlining the neckline. I looked in the long mirror and sucked my tummy in, turning one way and then the other, swishing my fanny and smiling. Not bad for an old lady, assuming my eyesight could still be trusted.

My pashmina wrap was several shades lighter than the dress, its color selected to look good with a wardrobe that leaned heavily toward black. I laid it out and transferred keys and a few essentials, plus a couple of tissues, to a little silver bag with a wrist strap.

Riley drove, with Jim riding shotgun. "You clean up real nice," Jim told me and laughed when Nita called him impertinent.

Riley cocked an eyebrow and smiled like he was trapped with squabbling children. No comment, no wink, no nothing.

Nita and Dolly and I gushed and twittered and complimented one another's appearance. The three of us sat in the back. Being the youngest and theoretically the most flexible, I was stuck in the middle. I was also the only one wearing a long skirt, which might've been as much of a handicap as the age difference but didn't earn me one bit of sympathy. Nita and Dolly wore black pants with glitzy tops.

The Grand Hotel was at Point Clear, a few miles south of Fairhope. The drive along the bay was gorgeous, with a speed limit of twenty-five, so it took a few minutes to get there and involved a lot of oohing and aahing. Live oaks reached out over the winding road, dangling tendrils of Spanish moss. To the west, beyond Mobile Bay, the orange remains of sunset were visible in flashes between trees and homes set well back from the road. Addresses were communicated not with numbers but by wooden signs bearing whimsical names: Day's End, Bay Breeze, Malpractice. One sign bore the legend "The Green's" and disturbed former teachers like me. There should be a rule that anyone who failed to master the plural possessive would never be allowed to own an estate with a name.

Nita pointed out a cute little covered bridge walkway at the hotel marina.

Jim looked at the collection of yachts in the basin. "Good opportunities for the smuggling business down here. Customs agents may live on this side of the bay, but they don't work here."

Riley hadn't needed to worry about Jim and Nita's safety in a dark parking lot. He stopped at the glass guard shack for directions and then drove straight to the hotel entrance, where we stepped out on a well-lit, flat sidewalk and were immediately surrounded by solicitous attendants in dinner jackets. What he should've worried about was his car, whisked away by a kid who might've been old enough to have a license.

Things functioned perfectly at the Grand Hotel, even with multiple events and a major remodeling going on. And our event, high profile as it was, wasn't their featured attraction of the night, which explained why we didn't get the main ballroom, but a substitute dining room with a view of the bay and a small dance floor a few steps lower than the dining level.

It turned out that a last-minute table by the kitchen wasn't a bad location. We weren't near the coveted spots, cradled in the curve of the room's expansive windows, but it was dark outside and the bay wasn't really visible. I told myself it might be a little cool on that side of the room, with all that glass. We were in the skinny part of the room, off to the side and with only one table between the head table and us. And right beside us was a view over the rail to the dance floor and the little band already entertaining us.

The five of us were the first to arrive at the Harbor Village table, but servers materialized immediately to fill water glasses and pour wine. Jim calculated which seat would give him the best view of the entrance and sat with his back to the head table. The band was playing softly by this time.

"I'd better sit with our other guests." I moved toward the kitchen end of the long table.

"I'll go with you," Nita decided. "Dolly, you look after Riley and Jim."

"Do you dance?" I asked Nita.

"Oh, no, honey. Not since Jim's knee replacement. Not for ten years before that, now that I think about it. But you go."

"You and Riley dance," Dolly shouted. "We want to watch."

But I had hostess chores to attend to. I put Nita on one side of the table, and when Reg Handleman arrived, courtly but distracted by business, I asked him to sit beside her. He excused himself long enough to speak to the honchos at the head table, then returned to charm Nita and everyone passing by.

Patti and Stewart arrived, and then Eloise and Charlie Levine. I had worked out a seating chart earlier and was trying to remember who went where. It kept me on the go, verifying that all our guests knew one another, but my chart quickly gave way to individual preferences.

I had anticipated that Tasha Boozer would be the difficult one, if she and Chief Boozer actually came, because none of us had ever met her. I was wrong. Tasha Boozer was a big, beautiful, black, dramatic firecracker, and she was wearing a formfitting, gold lamé outfit.

"Put me somewhere else," she said to me, with her husband listening and grinning. "Don't make me sit with Ray. He's the biggest party pooper in Baldwin County."

She blew him a kiss and I selfishly put her across from me at the middle of the table.

"Mary Montgomery said you'd be the life of the party."

Tasha twinkled at me. "I saw Mary outside. Maybe she'll come in later. She's a good dancer."

Really? That was hard to believe, but maybe I'd ask to see a few moves the next time the glum, grouchy lieutenant showed up.

The office manager from the Henry George Utopian Tax Colony was at the silent auction table.

I went over to say hello. "I thought we'd be in a bad location, signing up at the last minute like we did, but this is perfect. Good view of the head table, good view of the dance floor."

"Some people don't like all the traffic coming and going, but I'm glad you're happy." She introduced her husband, who had a long, gray ponytail, and said another of her staff members, a woman I hadn't met, was on the dance floor.

"Is Terry Wozniak here?" I looked toward the dining tables but didn't see him. "I ought to say hello."

She shook her head. "If he were here, I wouldn't be. I got his tickets."

"Well, wasn't that nice of him."

She poked my arm and shook her head. "Don't get any ideas about Wozniak. He *sold* me his tickets." She laughed. "He didn't charge me a premium, but I wouldn't want you mistaking him for a nice person."

"Or generous," her husband seconded and moved away.

"Mr. Wozniak didn't want to come? I thought he was really excited about the car show." It reminded me of Travis.

"He *was* excited about it, for a solid year. I heard it every day—automobiles and auctions and exhibitors. The only time I've seen him in days was when you were there returning his photographs. And he never came back to get them. I guess he's been at the polo club. Maybe he's depressed about the big show coming to an end."

We talked about the crowd and about the cruise being raffled off, and I went back to the Harbor Village table.

Tasha was dancing, first with Reg Handleman and then a slow number with a man from the head table, and finally, briefly, with her husband, who moved around awkwardly while she did spins and smiled at him. She knew the band members and the hotel staff and talked with everybody. Dolly, Nita, and I stood beside the rail for a while, watching dancers and sipping our wine.

With a slow version of the old standard "Moonlight Serenade" beginning, Reg Handleman came to ask if one of the "lovely ladies from Harbor Village" would like to dance. Nita and Dolly pushed me forward.

Handleman was nimble for such a big guy, tall and broad, but he wasn't young. Could he have overpowered Devon Wheat in a life-or-death struggle? Was it possible the hand I held had strangled a man? With my thoughts veering in that direction, I didn't dare look at him, lest he sense my suspicion.

"I expected to see more lecture participants here," he said, looking around.

"You have the most unusual eyes," I heard myself say. That should've been a clue I was drinking too much wine.

He laughed. "I'll tell you a secret. People think I'm a mind reader."

I laughed, even though I was guilty. "More of a hypnotist, I'd think. You're quite a good speaker, you know."

"Well, thank you, Cleo. It's a skill set, like any other. Hard won, in my case." He looked across the room to where Chief Boozer talked with the evening's emcee. "Do you know Ken Pierce, the master of ceremonies? I just met him this week. Chief of surgery at the medical school across the bay. Lots of surgeons are car collectors, for some reason. His Stutz was runner-up to the Duesenberg. Both Indiana cars, both with beautiful, straight-eight engines—I can just imagine the nice write-ups they're going to get in the automotive press. I really expected Pierce's car to win. It would've if I'd been judging."

"Did I understand that the Duesenberg doesn't belong to you?"

"Right. I'm a gear head, not an investor. People like Pierce are much more important to the industry."

"That sounds odd, a surgeon being essential to the automotive industry."

Handleman shook his head. "I should've been more precise. Not the auto industry. We're more of a hybrid. Tourism and the trades."

The number ended and we strolled back to the main level but paused beside the steps, still talking.

Handleman explained the world of antique automobiles to me. "All sorts of specialists work on old cars, and owners spend big bucks keeping one show-ready. All they get in return is trophies and parties like this and perhaps some good press. Museums accept the completed cars on loan, maybe fifty of them at any given time at an average-sized museum. We keep the car in the public eye, and in exchange, the museum and its community benefit from the visitor stream—lodging and sales taxes, restaurants, motels, amusement parks. The total effect is quite impressive."

"And you take cars to shows?"

He nodded. "All the time. We select appropriate shows for the cars we're holding and assist with transportation or represent the owner if he can't attend. He might be stuck in court, you know, or running an ER somewhere." He laughed. "Everybody likes to support new shows like this one. It's the sign of a healthy industry."

"I hope this show succeeds. Do you have any report yet?"

Handleman nodded agreeably. "A new show isn't expected to be profitable, but there's support here. I'll let you in on a little secret. I've been thinking someone should put an auto museum in this area. That's the real reason I invited myself down this last week, to check out some possibilities. Alabama has a big automobile industry now. And that golf trail brings a lot of visitors. Snowbirds all winter, families at the beach in summer."

He hesitated, then indicated Boozer standing at the other side of the steps. "You know, I'd like to get a photo of that police chief. Will you pose with him, so I don't have to explain? Tasha, too."

"For your wife?"

"My wife, and maybe an investor or two. Do you know any wealthy people who'd like their name on an automobile museum?" He smiled conspiratorially and then glanced toward the band, which was just starting into a Boz Skaggs number. "Would you...?"

I shook my head. "When it comes to dancing, I'm a good observer."

He offered his arm and we started back toward the Harbor Village table. "Where's Mr. Wozniak tonight? I understood he was one of the organizers of this show, but I haven't seen him in days."

"That's odd." We stopped again and I told him what the Colony office manager had said about Wozniak's disappearing act. "She told me yesterday he'd burned himself, but it didn't sound serious. She assumed he'd been at the show. But you didn't see him there?"

"I wasn't there all the time, of course. Did you hear how he tried to fool me with the Royale? Claimed to know the Schlumpfs personally."

"Really? What was that name?"

He said it again. "Fritz and Hans were textile moguls from Switzerland, who acquired every Bugatti they could find back in the seventies. Wozniak insists the family has the original wrecked Royale under wraps in France. He showed me a dark, blurry photograph and said the heirs are inviting offers and he's joining some mysterious group to buy it and bring it to the US for auction." He laughed.

"That name reminds me of Ann's last name—Slump. Wozniak actually knows these people?"

He closed his eyes and shook his head. "Hell, no. He drank the Kool-Aid. Thinks this local man is a close relative and just being coy. I talked with Usher at Royale Court and I guarantee you there's nothing there. I tried to tell Wozniak, but he became quite angry. Charged off and left his photographs, then skipped the final lecture, or most of it. I wanted him in your little competition Thursday night. He would've won and maybe forgiven me, but he came in too late."

"Too bad."

"I hate to leave bad feelings. Do you know where to find him? I'd like to apologize before I go. Or maybe it's best to just leave him alone."

I didn't know where to find him, other than at the colony office. "I owe him an apology, too, I'm afraid. I've been rude to him, after he assisted me."

He smiled. "I find that difficult to believe. And where's your boss? Travis sided with Wozniak in our little *contretemps*, but I don't think he was angry. I expected him to be here tonight."

I nodded again, amused at the idea of Travis being my boss, even though it was true. "He decided to go home early, for some reason. He lives in Houston. Our daughter went with him."

Handleman's eyes widened and he stared at me. "*Our* daughter? You and Mr. McKenzie have a child together?"

I laughed. "Not a child exactly. She's twenty-five. A youthful indiscretion on our part—marriage, I mean, not the child. It lasted a couple of years."

"And you've stayed friends? How very nice."

"Better say we've become friends again. Did I understand that Travis sent you to visit Devon Wheat?"

Handleman nodded. "The lieutenant asked about that, too. Maybe I remember wrong. I could've confused him with someone. Easy to do, with the crowds at the lectures."

"You didn't really want Travis to win the competition, did you? You intended for Wozniak to defeat me." I smiled.

Handleman laughed and winced in embarrassment. "Nothing about that competition went according to plan. But I had no idea I'd created a family feud. You're a good sport, Cleo. I'm sorry the young man wasn't, but the audience enjoyed his antics, too."

We rejoined my friends.

"I'd like to be in the suite until Monday, if you're sure that's okay. I'll come by your office before I go."

"I'll be there by eight Monday. Or at my apartment tomorrow, if you need anything. I hope you'll persuade your wife to visit us sometime. Fairhope might look pretty nice when it's ten below and icy in Indiana. Just imagine the wisteria and azaleas in bloom."

Nita and Dolly chimed in, singing the praises of Fairhope.

"You paint a lovely picture," Handleman agreed.

Nita, Dolly, and I returned to the table. I sat in Handleman's seat for a while, keeping Nita company, and Eloise Levine favored us with a running commentary on the fashions surrounding us. Then the servers began to deliver food and everyone returned to the table. I went back to my self-assigned seat across from Tasha and was entertained by the group.

After dinner I posed with Chief Boozer while Handleman photographed us. They didn't seem to have much rapport and I wondered if they'd already discussed the note in the Sudoku book.

The Realtor Vickie Wiltshire stopped by our table, drop-dead gorgeous in a slinky, cream-colored dress and emerald jewelry to die for. Clearly the real estate business could be lucrative. She hugged Nita, then went to the other end of the table and surprised Jim with a hug and a kiss on the cheek. He hopped to his feet with just a little wobbling and almost bowed to her. But the diners at the Harbor Village table didn't hold her attention for long. She knew most of us were out of the real estate market.

In a mischievous moment, I called her back and introduced her to Handleman, identifying him as a prospective resident of Fairhope. He demurred, but Vickie smelled a buyer. I could only hope Mrs. Handleman wouldn't be allergic to azaleas.

The presentation of awards was handled quickly and professionally. Terry Wozniak was on the list of locals who got special recognition in the printed program. I scanned the other names while the emcee gave a brief tribute to Devon Wheat, never saying his death was due to anything other than natural causes or that he'd been only thirty-two. Wheat Wealth Management was identified as an original sponsor of the Fairhope/Point Clear Grand Concours, listed in the platinum category in the program. I wondered how many dollars that meant.

Handleman accepted the Best in Show prize—a beautiful art glass bowl—on behalf of the owner of the Duesenberg. Dessert was served while photographs were taken.

Like others at our table, I ate three bites of the bread pudding with rum sauce and asked for a takeout box. The Grand Hotel had really nice, plastic takeout boxes with see-through tops, and each box came with a separate cup containing a little extra whipped cream. "Put it in the fridge as soon as you get home," the servers told us as they transferred the desserts from plate to box and clicked the tops into grooves.

"We should get these for the dining room." Jim was taking what appeared to be a leisurely postprandial stroll around the table. "Nita, are you going to eat the rest of that bread pudding? I'll finish it up if you're not going to, and you can save your takeout box for Carla to see."

When Nita and Dolly and Eloise went to see the Nall paintings on exhibit throughout the main floor of the hotel, and Charlie Levine went in search of the facilities, I was left alone with Chief Boozer. We stood at the rail and watched the dancing.

"How's the investigation going?" I asked. "Got any good suspects?"

He shook his head. "We've ruled out a few people. All of Wheat's clients were happy with him, they say. And any printer can do cards like the one Ann Slump found, but nobody in town claims it. The envelopes come in boxes of two hundred and fifty, so that's a likely number for a minimum order." He shrugged. "So far we haven't found another one."

I told him about the envelope Riley discovered on the desk in Todd Barnwell's house. Boozer knew Riley but not Todd, so I gave him a brief account, mentioning that he was only twenty.

"Probably a wedding invitation," he said.

"Riley's doing some work over there tomorrow, getting the paperwork under control. Maybe he'll come across a matching card. We do know Todd badgered Wheat to invest in a Bugatti."

Boozer shifted his gaze to me. "Where'd you get that?"

I was happy to have told him something he didn't know. "Somebody overheard them talking at the Bistro."

Boozer nodded. "We'd better talk with him."

I asked if he'd interviewed Handleman. "He says he's leaving Monday."

He leaned forward, arms on the rail, his gaze blank. "That man has a lot to say without telling much. The gift of gab, Lieutenant Montgomery called it."

"He told me he's black."

Ray Boozer looked at me. I looked at him. We grinned. Chief Boozer might not like Handleman, but he didn't seem suspicious of him. So why should I be?

I chatted with Charlie Levine. He was ready to leave, but Eloise was still going strong. Then the photographer's assistant came looking for me, saying Handleman wanted me in a photograph with him and his prize.

The award for Best in Show was displayed on a table, a stunningly beautiful piece of handblown, blue art glass, a foot tall, with a narrow, asymmetric opening and curving rows of intricate, geometric designs in cinnamon and white. I had no idea how anybody made such things, especially after I'd taken a close look at it. I teased Handleman about wanting me there because my dress matched its color perfectly.

At least half the crowd had already gone when I got back to our table. Nita lifted her eyebrows in an unspoken question, and I nodded I was ready to go. The band was beginning to pack up, too, leaving just a trio—piano, bass, and drums—to accompany a young vocalist who'd just come in. Her first number was slow and jazzy. I followed Nita and Eloise to the rail when the singer began in a lovely, clear, torchy voice, and Riley was suddenly beside me, leaning close to my ear.

"This is slow. I think I can manage if you're interested."

I returned my wineglass to the table. How many was this? I didn't remember but was glad to have him holding my hand as we went down the steps.

Lots of people had the same idea. The dance floor was crowded when we got there, giving us just enough room to stand together, touching lightly, encapsulated in bass vibrations, pierced by the achy perfection of voice and lyrics. She was a great singer. Amid a sensuous list of colors and clouds and body parts, the word *miraculously* bubbled out in what struck me as miraculous syncopation. And just like that, the word was stuck in my head.

"Come home with me," Riley murmured, his head against mine.

His breath tickled my ear and I felt a little thrill, the kind that usually came with goose bumps. I stepped closer and leaned against him, moving with the music. It was entirely too slow for any fanny swishing, even during the swingy piano riffs that set my spirit soaring. Riley's hairy cheek brushed against my temple.

I was already feeling my reply, about to whisper it, when I glanced up. Nita and Dolly and Jim and Eloise were side by side at the rail, all of them beaming down at us.

I stiffened and completely lost the rhythm.

Riley steered me to face the band and I was sure he saw the same little audience watching us. I felt him chuckle. And when the number ended, he arranged to give them a thrill, too. He looked into my eyes, pulled me close, kissed my brow, and then pressed his cheek against the kissed spot as he gave me a quick hug. My face warmed, and I smiled and dropped my gaze like some teenager caught in the glare of the porch light by her parents.

"Damn," he said, so softly I might've imagined the word.

We were home by ten. Riley stopped in front of the Bergens' apartment and walked them and Dolly to the porch while I moved to the front seat and threw the wrap around my shoulders. He got back into the car and looked at me, and we broke into laughter.

"I can't go home with you," I said.

"Yes. We've got a little problem here." He shook his head and drove around the median to our side of the street.

We parked in his usual place and he walked me home, gave me a good-night kiss—medium hot but no fireworks—and waited for me to get inside and lock up. Then he walked up the slope toward his building as I watched through the blinds. My mental soundtrack was looping the word of the night, chopping it into syllables. *Mi-rac-u-lous-ly.*

Stephanie called a few minutes later, after I'd washed my face and changed into pajamas. "So? How was your big affair?"

"Haven't had it yet. The gala, if that's what you meant, was very gay. And *la.* I might've had too much wine."

"Get a good night's sleep. I've been meaning to ask you something. You do know about STDs, don't you?"

"Stephanie!" I gasped, sobering up instantly.

She giggled. "Just checking. It's been a while since you were out there, you know."

"I don't think anything's changed."

"But it has, Mom. It really has." She actually sounded serious for once in her life. "That's why I brought it up. Be careful and have fun. Does that sound familiar?"

I thought about her being at Travis's home in Houston and panicked. "I hope nobody's there hearing you," I hissed into the phone.

She giggled again. "You mean Dad? No, he's not here. But I'll tell him you asked about him."

I was wide-awake after that, thinking I was too young to be changing roles with my child. And too old to manage the intricacies of romance, dang it. I got a warm terry robe from the closet and padded barefoot to the computer. There was email, none of it particularly interesting. A *Washington Post* article about Russian hacking. I wasn't ready for doom and gloom yet. I quizzed YouTube for "Midnight Sun" and clicked on a vocal rendition that happened to sound much like the vocalist I'd heard earlier in the evening. Lyrics by Johnny Mercer, the site said. It seemed that I liked a lot of his music. I ought to learn more about him. Maybe go to that famous murder house he'd owned in Savannah.

Patti's photograph chips lay beside the computer. I left the music playing and plugged in one of the little black chips, downloaded the photos from the chip to my computer, and repeated the process with the second chip. Then I looked through dozens of images from Handleman's first lecture. Patti hadn't been there the first two nights, before her truce with the speaker, but Emily had done a good job filling in as official photographer. I queued up the photographs and clicked through the lineup. There were good shots of a lot of Harbor Villagers, including quite a few men I barely recognized, but at least half the people weren't our residents. I selected several of the best images, thinking Patti could decide if they deserved to be featured somewhere.

Terry Wozniak was in the mix, wearing a bright-yellow shirt with the sleeves rolled up and a hand-knit wool vest, this one in a colorful pattern. I wondered who made his vests, since he didn't seem to have a wife. But I didn't add his photo to my selections. "Midnight Sun" ended and I clicked to play it again.

Another photo included Wozniak in a little group gathered around Travis and Handleman. Travis looked annoyed, almost angry. Then there was a photo of me standing beside Wozniak, our backs to the camera. I looked as broad as a barn and Wozniak looked like he had his arm around me. It had to be some trick of perspective, but I dragged that photo to the trash anyway.

And there was Devon Wheat—my first glimpse of him alive, and he looked even younger than he had the next day as a corpse. He'd been a short, slight man with blond hair, broad features, and what's known as a deer-in-the-headlights look.

Tears came to my eyes as the YouTube vocalist sang about stars forgetting to shine. Lord, I didn't want that song ruined by association with Devon Wheat. I grabbed the mouse and clicked pause, then stared at Wheat's image. He was beside Travis in one photograph, both of them frowning at someone out of camera range. He'd had another twenty-four hours to live, more or less. So sad. Maybe I really was a little drunk.

I moved to the photographs from the second lecture and looked for Wheat. This would've been Wednesday night, the night he was murdered.

I found Travis, looking like a movie star, a plastic cup in his hand. And there was Wozniak, bending someone's ear, hand raised to emphasize a point. Jim and Nita and Dolly were lined up and smiling, three kids out after bedtime. And then Riley, staring past the camera and wearing an unusually stern expression. What had he been looking at?

I clicked the music on again and got my mood back.

No Devon Wheat in the Wednesday night photos. Out riding his bicycle, probably. Should've been at the lecture.

I waited for the song to end before I shut down the computer and then went through the apartment, checking doors and lights. When I came back through the living room, Ann's green folder was lying on the coffee table. I took it to bed with me.

There was an elegant simplicity to the ownership structure devised for Royale Court. There were five equal shares, one for each of the five Slump siblings with their vowel initials: Ann, Evie, Irene, Olivia, and Usher. Each of the five was granted a voting membership on the management board. Upon the demise or incapacity of any member, his or her board seat and the attached vote disappeared. Which meant that, with Irene already dead, control now resided in the hands of the four surviving siblings. A handwritten note from Ann explained that Prissy worked in the knit shop and received both a salary and a share of the income generated by the complex but had no vote in business decisions. I wondered what had happened to Irene. I didn't think Ann had said.

Usher received a salary to act as manager of the complex, and in that capacity, he had the authority to enter into contracts on behalf of Royale Court. He had received a small raise every April for six years and now earned a mere $32,000 per year, in addition to his share of any profits. That seemed like a low salary for a shopping center manager, especially in light of his benefits, which were itemized and minimal. Maybe that explained why he didn't take the job seriously.

Ann and Evie had apparently never married. Usher held medical proxy and power of attorney for them, and he was listed as personal representative (executor) on their wills. Ann's and Evie's heirs were their surviving siblings or the issue of such siblings, which meant Prissy would receive Irene's share of their estates. Another note listed Olivia's heirs as her husband and children. Usher was listed, too. He was single, with two former wives and two children, all living in New York. I looked for more information about him, but that was it. No explanation for his unusual behavior, no mention of substance abuse. He was sixteen years younger than Ann.

I wasn't sure why Ann wanted me to know all this. She was looking for someone to trust, I supposed, which social workers were always advising seniors to do. Or it might mean she'd lost confidence in her brother. I could certainly understand that.

I put all the papers back into the folder, put it on the bedside table, and turned the light off. When I slid down into the bed, my feet bumped against the cat.

My dreams were about a maze of hotel corridors, tender kisses, and a blue glass bowl.

Chapter 16

I woke up at the usual time Sunday, rolled onto my stomach, and pulled the covers up to my ears. Thirty minutes later, I woke for the second time, with Tinkerbelle sitting on my shoulder, purring and reaching one paw out occasionally to pat my cheek.

I got up then but took revenge on the cat by delaying my first trip to the kitchen until I had dressed. She darted toward the kitchen every time I moved in that direction, hurrying me along. When I finally got to her food dish, I found the entire bottom of the bowl exposed, a true feline emergency. I poured in half a cup of dry food and she purred while she crunched. I put on coffee and went to open the blinds.

Ann Slump was sitting on my screened porch, crying.

I opened the door and stuck my head out, and she jumped with surprise and wiped her cheeks.

"You okay?"

"Yup."

It was chilly and there was a mound of wet tissues on the table. Ann added another one to the stack.

"Be right back," I said.

I went to the bathroom for a box of tissues and to the bedroom for a cardigan and then returned to the kitchen and poured two cups of decaf and took them out to the porch with me. If I'd spent the night with Riley, I'd be waltzing in here about now, still wearing my fancy dress, and finding Ann crying on the porch. Lucky me.

"I came to tell you what Usher's done," Ann said. "But the blinds were closed and I thought I'd wait. Didn't know you slept late on Sundays."

It was barely seven, and judging by the tissues, she'd been waiting quite a while.

I put the coffee cups on the corner table, turned the heron light on, and pulled a chair closer. "Has something happened?"

"No." She sniffed and wiped her eyes. "Not really. Well, yes, I guess it has. I found out Usher has sold Royale Court out from under me."

Now she really cried. I took a sip of coffee, then held the steaming cup under my chin and inhaled while Ann sniffled and blew her nose.

"How could he do that?" I asked.

She shook her head and dabbed at her eyes.

A Carolina Wren landed on the fence, looked at us, and flew away.

After a minute, she blew her nose again. "I don't understand it."

I detected traces of anger.

"Everything he has came from Royale Court. Our whole life is in those shops."

"I looked at your folder last night. Did the owners vote to sell?"

She shook her head. "None of us knew a thing. I called Olivia in England. He's signed papers and he's got the money, he says. Part of it, anyway. But he won't admit it's sold."

This was going to take some time, and probably some skills I didn't have. "Let's call your lawyer."

She stuck her hands into the opposite sleeves of her sweater. "I tried already. He's in England, too. For Anastasia."

"Anastasia?"

She nodded. "You know. Ballet. He's addicted. Won't be back until Friday."

Oh, of course. Fairhope lawyers went to London for a week of ballet! I should've known!

I took a sip of coffee and slid down into the cocoon of my sweater. I had a sudden image of Usher, blathering away at breakfast yesterday. Where was he now? Had Ann's distress been building all night?

"I've had my cry." She slapped her thigh in what I took to be a shifting of mental gears. "I need to do something, but I've got to figure out what. That's why I'm here."

I waited, but she didn't seem to have any more to say. "What do you want to do, Ann? Swear out a warrant? Theft by taking, or something like that? I'm sure it's a felony. Fraud? Your attorney could file some action to have the sale vacated, I suppose. Or do you want to protect him? Haven't you been thinking about selling?"

She didn't answer right away, but the tears seemed to be gone. "I've considered all those. If I could wring his neck, I would. Now I'm back to worrying about him. This Devon Wheat business…we still don't know. Have you learned anything? Do they know who did it? What if Usher's involved somehow? I need you to help me." She sighed.

I sat quietly, trying to think. It'd been twenty years since I'd had even a trace of a hangover. Did Usher kill Devon Wheat?

Ann watched me. "I've got leftovers if you want to eat. I'll tell you the whole thing."

I got up. I was curious about what else there was to tell. And I was curious about what she thought I could do.

I took the coffee cups and tissue box inside and Ann cleaned up the used ones. I got the carafe from the kitchen and her green folder from the table beside my bed. Tinkerbelle was curled up in the folds of the quilt and duvet and didn't even raise her head. That cat knew how to do off days.

We went to Ann's apartment, which yesterday had been all cozy and comfortable. Today it was warm but sad, filled with anxiety and depression. The curtains and blinds were open, letting in the morning sun, but the light looked pale and sickly.

"Let's get the drama out of the way and then enjoy the food. Okay?"

Ann went to her chair at the window and I sat on the couch and pulled a yellow afghan across my legs.

"Okay," I said. "Tell me all about it."

It was a brief story. Usher had committed to sell Royale Court.

"Weeks ago. Agreed to a price, agreed to finance the deal. The buyer's already making payments."

"That doesn't seem possible." I shook my head in disbelief.

Ann threw her hands in the air. "He's the manager. He can negotiate contracts."

Paper rained down. She'd been shredding a tissue, ripping off strips and twisting them into tight little pills. They'd flown into the air with her gesture. While she talked, she gathered them up and stuffed them into her sweater pocket.

"We gave him authority, as manager, so he could sign contracts for yard work or a new roof, routine things. Not to sell us out. He tried to convince me nothing's really changed and the actual date of transfer isn't set. But there's nothing left to decide."

The payments were accumulating in an escrow account controlled by a Birmingham business brokerage.

I wondered if it was the man Stephanie knew.

"As soon as Evie and I are out of the way, dead or demented, whichever comes first, he'll get Olivia to sign off. She'd do it today if her husband gave the word. And just like that..." She snapped her fingers. "It's a done deal. When twenty percent of the sales price is in escrow, ownership transfers to the buyer. He can charge us any rent he likes and pay off the balance with our money. It's the craziest thing I ever heard."

It didn't sound unreasonable to me, but I had no experience with such things. "Is that a common way of selling commercial property?"

Ann shrugged. "I created commercial property. I didn't buy and sell it."

I remembered what Riley had told us yesterday about Henry George Colony leases and bills of sale. "Is Royale Court on Colony property?"

Ann nodded. "Yes. He took care of that, too. Signed an agreement to transfer the lease at the date of sale. The agreement's already recorded."

"Recorded where?"

"Wherever they record things. The courthouse? The Colony office? I don't know. Maybe both places. I feel so violated."

"Yes, I can understand that."

"Betrayed by both of them. All three, actually."

"Usher and...who? Olivia? Evie?"

"Olivia knew nothing about it. I can't speak for her husband. I wouldn't put anything past him. But Prissy knew and didn't say a word to me. She's decided she wants to retire and move to Highlands where her bridesmaids live. And Devon Wheat."

"Devon Wheat? He's not moving to Highlands. What does he have to do with it?"

She gave me a startled look. "Didn't I say? He's the buyer."

I was stunned, but Ann didn't seem to notice.

"And now he's dead and Usher's got us tied up in it. There's a sales agreement recorded for Royale Court, which would have to be undone before we could sell to anybody else if we wanted to. And here I sit twiddling my thumbs. No business, no money, no buyer, no lawyer. Might as well say no brother. And no sister right now. Evie's getting a cold so she's staying in bed all day. Maybe I'll go over and get exposed. Maybe it's the flu and will kill us all."

Maybe she'd already caught the drama bug from Stephanie and Patti. And I was no help. I felt like she'd dropped a ton of bricks on me. I reached over and patted her arm.

The anger was gone, replaced by confusion and sadness. We sat quietly for several minutes and then we had breakfast.

Ann had prepared a big bowl of fruit—melon, halved strawberries, pears, blueberries, and an orange yogurt sauce. She nuked the sausage and egg casserole left over from the day before and made some hot and buttery toast. Ann cranked out good food, even when her world was collapsing.

While she worked, I set the table for two and told her the highlights of the Saturday night gala.

"I saw your photograph," she said.

"My photograph?"

"You made the front page. You haven't seen it?" She sent me to the coffee table for the Sunday newspaper and we sat down and applied ourselves to the feast.

Ann refolded the newspaper and propped it against the vase of asters. There I was in living color, standing beside Reg Handleman, with the Best in Show prize bowl on a table in front of us.

"It's a beautiful bowl," I said. "I would've expected silver, but maybe that's out of style."

"We've got lots of artists here. They probably wanted a prize made locally."

"Why do you suppose they put me in the paper? Why not the judges or the winning cars? Or people who actually worked to put on the show."

It was nice to see Ann smile. "I guess Harbor Village has some clout."

I smiled, too, but shook my head. "We don't have a real PR person. Just Patti, among all her other duties."

She smiled even bigger. "I'm sure she did it."

I knew in my bones she was right, but the pieces took a minute to fall into place. I nodded finally. "She knows all the newspaper people and feeds them announcements and human interest stories. I wonder why she didn't warn me."

"There's probably some editor who had the final say. But it's a pretty picture. I almost didn't recognize you." We giggled at the implication.

We ate without much appetite and went back to the softer seats, where I pulled the yellow afghan across my lap again.

Ann noticed. "Is it warm enough in here?"

"Perfect. I just like snuggling."

"Too bad you don't have someone to snuggle with. I think my brother has turned me against men."

"It must've happened a long time ago." I smiled, getting back at her.

"I was engaged once," she said. "Did I ever tell you?"

"No. What happened?"

"My daddy thought he wasn't dependable. He was probably right."

She sat in her glider rocker, put her feet on the ottoman, and handed me the folded newspaper. "You can have this, but you'll probably want more copies. There's a box in Royale Court if you've got quarters. If not, the drugstore has them."

"I need one for Stephanie. And one for corporate, to show them Harbor Village is involved in community life." That last came out in a poor imitation of Travis's voice. I put the paper on the coffee table in front of me, on top of Ann's green folder.

"Where's Usher?" I didn't really want to know. It was just something to say.

"I sent him home. I don't want to see him for a while."

"Where does he live?"

She gave me another look, like I should've known. "Royale Court. Over the T-shirt shop."

"Do you think the cops know about the sale? Is that why they questioned him so long Thursday night?"

Ann stared, then leaped out of the chair, eyes brimming with tears. She took a step to the couch and hugged me. "Oh, Cleo, I knew you'd figure it out. Now, tell me how we're going to get out of this mess."

I stayed a few minutes longer, trying to remember something I'd wanted to ask Ann. I never did, but she wound up telling me about her niece Prissy. I learned that Prissy and her family lived in one of the old bay houses we'd passed driving to the Grand Hotel.

"It was our summer house, growing up, but it's winterized now. Still drafty and costs a fortune to heat. But there's a glassed-in porch all across the back, with the prettiest views of the sunset, and manatees under the pier in the summer. Evie and I lived there until a few years ago."

"Alligators?"

"Are there alligators there?" She rolled her eyes. "Lord, yes. Go out at night with a flashlight if you want to know how many. Eyes shining everywhere."

"And where does Evie live now?"

"We built granny pods at the front of the lot a few years ago and let Prissy and Michael take the house. Evie still lives in her pod, but I decided I wanted a little more social life, so I moved to Harbor Village. Delaying senility, I hope."

"You're still going strong."

Ann gave me a grim little smile. "To tell the truth, I think Evie and I will outlast Usher. You saw how he was yesterday. He needs help."

"You said he's seen a therapist?"

She nodded. "It's sad, in a way. The therapist told him he was emotionally unstable and that was just the excuse he needed. Never went back."

"Prissy has children?"

"Three. I don't want to cut them off, but I don't know how I'll deal with their mother now."

"How do you know she knew what Usher was doing?"

"She came over last night. Matter-of-fact, just like nothing had happened. Asked if I was all right. Pretended she'd tried to get Usher to tell me."

"And he did tell you?"

She nodded. "Said he can't run Royale Court without Evie and me."

"That's probably true."

"I know. He can't even steal without help."

Ann's apartment was right next to mine, so you'd think we would've seen or heard anyone who came to my porch. But we didn't, and when I got home, three copies of the Sunday newspaper were on the love seat. My carryout box of bread pudding was on top of them, still cold from someone's refrigerator. Riley's, I supposed, since the box was in his car the last time I saw it. I took it to my refrigerator.

I was out of my routine after the busy week and breakfasts with Ann for three days, but somehow my kitchen had gotten messy. I tidied up, Swiffered the floor, then dusted the bedroom and started a load of laundry before I sat down at the computer.

I refolded Ann's newspaper, flattened it on the scanner/printer, and scanned in my photograph with Handleman. Then I emailed it to Yolanda in the Houston office and to Stephanie. The instant I hit send, I thought how humiliated I was going to be if Handleman turned out to be a murderer. He'd seemed perfectly legitimate last night, with all his talk about an automotive museum for Alabama, but I should've waited a few days before sending the photo. Let the cops finish their investigations.

Vickie Wiltshire called a minute later and I had to search for the phone. "Did I wake you?"

"I wish."

"You going to be home today? I'll come by if you are."

I told her how to find my apartment and wondered what she was up to. Digging for info on Handleman and his wife, I decided, but I didn't know anything else to tell her.

I was changing laundry from washer to dryer when someone knocked at the door. But it wasn't Vickie.

"I'm not coming in." Ann handed me the green folder. "I wanted you to keep this, just in case. And I couldn't remember if I told you about somebody getting in the knit shop Thursday night."

"Wednesday night, you mean."

"No. Thursday. The night after Devon. We've never had any security problems before, nothing but kids drinking or making out, and now a murder and a prowler in two days. It's an unkind coincidence. I guess it was kids, larking around. They didn't even take the bait money."

Bait money sounded like something she left out for a thief to find. I wondered if she kept larger sums in the shop, too. Maybe it wasn't too big a risk, with her brother living on the premises.

"What did the cops say about the prowler?"

She shook her head. "Nothing. I didn't tell them yet. I'm going to help Carla with lunch and then go by Publix and to Evie's and make her some soup. You want anything?"

I told her I'd done my shopping the day before.

Ann hadn't been gone five minutes when there was another knock at the door. I thought it was Ann again, that she'd forgotten something.

It was Usher, looking disheveled, his eyes bloodshot. There was no doubt he'd had something to drink this time. I pulled the front door closed and stood on the porch with him, appreciative for all the windows I could see.

"I'm looking for my sister." He bent to peer around me, into the living room. "Is she hiding out over here?"

"She just left for the dining room. Want me to give her a message when I see her?"

"Well…" He cast a long look at the love seat. "I guess I could tell you. If you've got time."

We sat on the porch for the next hour. It was warmer than it had been for Ann's early visit, and Usher didn't cry, but he pretty much told his life story. All I had to do was nod occasionally. Two marriages and two babies before the love of his life decided she was lesbian and he was gay and, who knew, he probably was, or maybe bi.

I'd heard it all before, lots of times, from friends and students and clients, so it didn't shock me. Not the way Nita's comments about sex had. Did I have some unresolved feelings about Riley? Was I worried about what our children would think? Afraid we'd be unhappy?

I dragged my attention back to the moment and listened to Usher until the tale became redundant. Then I asked questions to move him along, skipping right past the warping of his psyche to ask if he'd been drinking and driving this morning—he said no—and how he'd gone about selling Royale Court. "Did you contact the business broker, or did he find you? He didn't ask you about the other owners? How long did it take him to find a buyer?"

He was making the little smacking sound again, punctuating sentences. "I found the buyer myself and took him to the broker, who didn't do a damn thing but talk." Smack. "Then Devon decided we should cut the broker out of the deal, to save himself the commission, but that guy wouldn't even give him a break. He was still handling all the business stuff and making it work, even though Devon was pretty much broke." Smack. "Just imagine... broke and buying million-dollar properties. The two of them figured out how to make it work. I just said whatever and left it to them." Smack.

"What do you know about Devon's death?" I was pretty sure he'd claim ignorance, regardless of the facts, but he didn't.

Usher stared at me. "You're thinking about Irene."

That threw me off. I wasn't thinking of her and saw no connection between Irene and Devon's death. But I did want to know what had happened to her. That was the question I'd intended to ask Ann and forgotten.

"Tell me about her."

He sighed and slid down, resting his head against the back of the love seat and gazing off into space. There was a long pause before he spoke again, but when he did, the smacking was gone. "She hanged herself. Accidentally." Tears welled in his eyes but he blinked them away. "We were building the new shop on de la Mare, putting the apartment upstairs so I could get away from that nuthouse at the bay."

There was bitterness in his voice. After a moment, he went on.

"Irene and I were sitting up on the second-floor framing one evening, after the crew left. She started climbing down but slipped, somehow, and fell. She had this necklace, a big chain thing, looped twice around her neck and it caught on something. Tightened up with her dangling in the air. No way for me to get to her." He paused with tears sparkling on his cheeks. "That's the gods' own truth."

"I am so sorry." I resisted the impulse to put my arms around him. "It must've been tough for you. How long ago?"

He seemed to be living in the past. "She was my favorite, you know. Olivia was closer in age, but she was always the ice queen. Irene was fun. But her neck snapped. I heard it. They say that wasn't likely, but I know what I heard. The fire truck got her down. I've never talked about it before, you know."

"A terrible accident. And it happened where you live now?"

Usher nodded and drew a ragged breath. It was a tragedy Shakespeare might've composed. His problems ran quite the gamut, I realized, from grief to anxiety, depression, trauma, substance abuse—how would he ever find a counselor with such a range of competencies?

"Southern Gothic. And now Devon Wheat gets strangled fifty feet away. I can't wait to be rid of that gee-dee place. I'm going to call the broker first thing tomorrow and tell him to find another buyer immediately. I wish he worked Sundays. I'd call him right now."

I'm usually pretty nondirective as a counselor, so my answer surprised me. "Most people use cell phones now. He'd probably answer today, wherever he is."

It surprised Usher, too. "I didn't think about that. I'll call him when I get home."

"Before you go…" I was thinking half a second ahead of talking. "Were you in Ann's shop Thursday night?"

"Thursday? Absolutely not. Did she say I was?"

"No. She said somebody was, but she's not concerned about it."

He shook his head. "Not me. I have zero business in a knit shop, day or night." He reflected for a moment. "You want the truth? It's a long story."

"Sure."

He drew a deep breath and launched into a new story, seeming to enjoy talking now that he'd gotten the hang of it. "I walk around town sometimes and check on things. Wednesday night it was about ten, and Devon's bike was in the alley behind the Bistro." He looked at me. "I thought it'd be fun to ride, but it was too tall and had all those gears. I thought somebody was hiding it from him and went to leave him a note, telling him where it was. But he was dead." He leaned his head back and closed his eyes for a minute.

We sat in silence. Usher didn't seem especially distressed. He slid lower in his seat, pushing the cushions out of position.

I thought about the scene he was creating. I wouldn't go into a bathroom I believed to be occupied; would he? Had the bathroom door been open when he got there? Or had he moved the body?

I asked, "The bathroom door was open?"

"I closed it so Evie wouldn't find him. But she did anyway."

I nodded. He'd wanted Ann to find the body. But it didn't seem to have bothered Evie much.

"Did you leave the building through Lilliput, too?" I thought about the missing security camera.

He shook his head. "No. I went through the knit shop. That's when I saw the camera was gone. They're trail cameras, not connected to anything, but I had to take the other ones down."

He pushed himself upright and continued talking while he wiggled around, getting comfortable again. "The camera in front of the knit shop was the only one that ever worked and it wasn't dependable. Went out all the time, I never figured out why. But Wednesday night it was gone." Smack. He was getting wound up. "Whoever strangled Devon took it to keep us from seeing him. Ergo, it's somebody we know. But with no camera, who are the cops going to suspect? *I'm* the one who lives there. *I'm* the one who knows which camera works. And it's me who just set off World War Three with my sisters. No way they'll suspect anyone else. So, I took the other ones down, too."

He paused, anxiety giving way to dejection.

He'd succeeded in convincing me. I asked him, "Nobody else knows how many cameras were in Royale Court?"

Usher slid down again, leaned his head against the love seat, and looked at the ceiling. "Are you kidding? Even Ann wouldn't know. I got a box from Lilliput and put the cameras in it, but wouldn't you know? Evie found it immediately and gave it to Ann, and she gave it to the gee-dee cops. Didn't even consider what that might do to me."

He was indignant at the turn of fate, and I felt a need to confess my role in turning the cameras over to the cops.

"I thought it was a good idea, Usher, to give the cameras up before the cops asked for them. Ann told me they didn't work."

He shrugged. "Well, one did, but that one was gone." Smack. "Do you agree the murderer took it?"

"That seems likely, if you didn't. Somebody thought he'd been detected and wanted to destroy the evidence."

He nodded. "That's precisely what I think. If we find the camera, we find the murderer. But think about this. What if he hacked it somehow and put me on there? Can they do that? I think so. What if he hid it to make it look like I'd done it?"

"Did you find it?"

Usher shook his head. "I haven't looked. I'm terrified I *will* find it. Afraid it'll incriminate me. I don't know where it is and I don't want to know. I hope nobody ever sees it again."

We sat quietly for a moment.

He looked at me and grinned. "I have an excellent imagination. I scare myself."

"That's not necessarily bad. It helps sometimes, to anticipate the future."

I dredged up an old therapy technique and had him practice a few statements to use when he talked with his sisters. "It's smart to be prepared, in case the situation is upsetting and throws you off balance."

I asked questions and he practiced. He was thinking proactively when he lined up a buyer for the shop. He was anticipating the day when Royale

Court would be a burden to all of them. He hadn't actually consummated the sale and wouldn't until everyone was ready.

"And that's the gods' own truth," he said emphatically, persuading me if not himself. But his voice became calmer, more natural, as he practiced.

"I have some photographs I'd like you to look at before you go, Usher."

The look in his eyes shifted to alarm. "Pictures of me?"

"No, no. Photographs my assistant made this week. I'm wondering if you'll recognize people, if they've been around Royale Court in recent days. If you'll wait here, I'll get them."

"Sure."

He'd be glad to look at Patti's photographs. But I had a problem.

The photographs were on the computer in my apartment, and I was reluctant to be in there alone with Usher. Whatever story he was telling, and believing, Usher Slump was still high on my list of murder suspects.

I remembered distinctly the way he had crushed a Mountain Dew can, and Usher Slump wasn't the only one with a good imagination.

Chapter 17

I put on my most innocent expression and looked around, wondering if any of the windows I could see from my porch had people looking out.

Ann was over at the big house, I knew. It was Sunday, so Harvey and Lynne from the next apartment would be at the Unitarian Fellowship a couple of blocks away, singing folk songs. Gloria was with her family most weekends—that took care of the four apartments closest to mine. Across the fence, I could see portions of six or eight houses, but was anyone at home? And were they looking out, ready to rush to my rescue if things took a bad turn?

In the other direction was Riley's building, with two apartments on the ground floor and two upstairs. I didn't even know if the upstairs units were occupied.

Maybe I should just ask Usher to come back later?

"Yoo-hoo!"

I swiveled around and looked toward the sound.

Vickie Wiltshire was striding up the wide sidewalk from the garages, wearing a beige cape and a pair of suede ankle boots with high heels. She carried a newspaper and a rust-colored briefcase, and I'd never been so glad to see anybody.

"Are you receiving?" she called.

"Come join us, Vickie." I went to open the screen door for her. "You know Usher Slump, I'm sure."

Usher asked, "Are you here for therapy, too? I'll give you the patient's chair. I'm about to go." But he didn't get up.

"Not yet." I tapped his arm. "I want you to look at those photographs. It won't take long. Come inside, Vickie, and wait while we finish up our discussion. Five minutes."

I put her in the living room, got my laptop off the desk, and went back to the porch.

Vickie opened the door immediately. "What's your Wi-Fi password?"

I told her and she disappeared inside.

"This won't take long," I promised Usher, sitting beside him and balancing the laptop. He watched as I called up photos from the Handleman lectures. "Just point out anybody you've seen in Royale Court in the last week or so."

"Day or night? It's different crowds, you know. Shoppers in the day, dog walkers and neighborhood people in the evening. And kids, but not so bad as in the summer. Skateboards mostly."

"Any time of day."

I displayed several photographs at one time and turned the screen toward him. The photos weren't quite large enough for viewing, but that didn't deter Usher.

"This little jerk," he said, right off the bat. He was looking at the bottom row and pointing to Todd Barnwell. "Who is he?"

I told him and he nodded.

"Yeah. Devon had Boudreau's girls feeding him half the time. They run a tab for Todd and Devon pays. Not out of his own pocket, I'm sure. The little jerk never appreciated anything, always complaining and arguing. He used to come in with an old man, but I think he must've died. Quit coming, anyway."

"You've got a good memory. That was probably Mr. Barnwell. He died last spring. I never met him."

"Big talker. Came by himself at first but then Todd started having lunch with him. Todd's the one who was riding Devon's bike the next day."

"What day was that?"

"Last Thursday. After Devon was dead."

That was news to me. I supposed the bike had been located by now. But did the cops know Todd had been riding it? Or was it true?

"Did Devon handle investments for the old man?"

Usher shrugged. "They talked business sometimes, but World War II was the old man's thing. Every time I saw him, he'd tell some long story. His ship got caught in a typhoon or they shot Japs down in a friendly fashion after the cease-fire. *Bor-ing.*"

We scrolled through a dozen photos before he picked another one.

"Him." It was Handleman.

He remembered Handleman's visit to Royale Court very clearly and pretty much as Handleman had described it.

"A big guy, came in late one day, by himself. Looked like an investor. You get so you can tell. He asked for Devon and I showed him where the office was and told him to come back, that Devon was out. I didn't say Devon was off on a bike ride. We all knew not to tell anybody that, in case he'd forgotten an appointment. This guy walked around back and I went along. Just talking, keeping an eye on him. He didn't stay."

I scrolled on slowly.

He signaled. "Wait a minute. Back up."

I scrolled back.

Usher pointed. "Yep, saw him two or three times last week and before that, too, weeks ago. I got the idea he was looking for Devon but he didn't say. Didn't look like a shopper. Maybe here for the car show. We had a lot of extra traffic, you know, but this guy was around before."

"That's Travis McKenzie. Our CEO." The photograph was the one where he looked like a movie star.

"Oh, yeah? I think Ann knows him."

He scanned more photos, picking out the same people multiple times. Lots of the photographs showed women or couples. We got to Devon Wheat and he grunted.

"Hmph. The late, great Devon Wheat. Guess we won't be going to Europe after all."

"You were going to Europe?" I asked.

He laughed. "He told me all that crap about a family fortune and some Nazi car he was going to sell for multimillions. Wanted me to invest. Said we'd go look at it."

"Slump. Is that their name? Is it your family?"

Usher shook his head. "Sounded like it, but not really. A German name. Sloop? Sleuth? I don't remember."

"I don't suppose he gave you any written information about the car? Maybe a printed invitation to invest?"

"How'd you know?"

My pulse rate spiked. "Can I see it?"

"Well, sure, if I've still got it. You can have it. But why do you care?"

"Just looking for information that might explain his death."

Usher smiled. "Maybe my wealthy German relatives came to Fairhope and strangled him."

He glanced at the computer screen and tapped another photo. "Wozniak's in there *all* the damn time, pardon my French. Not just last week, pretty much every day. Meeting people, planning the car show, eating at Boudreau's. He used to hang out with Devon but not so much lately. They had a spat, I think. He brought a stack of car posters and wanted me to put them up. I told him, 'Put 'em up yourself.' Jackass."

I was excited at the prospect of another investment invitation. Had Usher told the cops? Why had Wozniak quarreled with Wheat? Two promising leads—had the cops followed up?

"What was their spat about?"

He shrugged. "Money, probably. What else."

"Devon Wheat was Wozniak's financial advisor?"

Usher shook his head. "I don't think so. Wozniak was into real estate. They had a contest going—which was a better investment, real estate or the stock market? They were going to settle up at the end of the year. I guess Wozniak wins now."

He picked out a couple more photos and called them regulars at Royale Court. One was Jim Bergen. "He's a regular. Buys candy and sits in the courtyard, talking to everybody while his wife visits Ann. Done it for years."

Yep, that was Jim.

"Sometimes his wife comes by herself."

"You know she was with me when we found Devon."

He was solemn. "I'm really sorry about that. Were you upset?"

I shrugged. "Some, naturally. But we didn't know him."

We reached the end of the photos. I closed the laptop and thanked Usher for his help. "Any other strange men last week? Someone who wasn't in the photos?"

He shrugged. "Nobody special. There's always people I don't know."

"Who knits those vests for Terry Wozniak?"

He looked at me, surprised. "He buys Ann's samples. How'd you know?"

"I didn't. Just thought they looked nice."

"She used to give them to me but I only need so many. It's never cold enough to wear them." He got up. "Maybe we can talk again sometime. You're a good listener."

"Thank you."

"I'm going to call that broker now, and then I'm going to work on my sisters. Maybe I'll see Evie, get her on my side."

He grinned weakly. Confronting Ann had been an ordeal on both sides, I was sure.

I walked to the porch door with him. "I heard Evie's sick. Maybe the flu."

"Well, in that case, I'll call. Thank you, Cleo."

He shuffled down the sidewalk toward the garages, and I went inside and learned very quickly that Vickie was there to quiz me about Todd Barnwell. How old was he? Did he have a guardian? Or somebody who could sign legal documents with him? Could I do it, as a Harbor Village official?

I shook my head. "He's twenty, Vickie. That's the age of majority in Alabama."

"Yeah, but how often does a twenty-year-old sell a house? I've never handled a sale for somebody so young, with no family, only legal by a couple of months. I'm going to ask for a copy of his birth certificate."

I got us 7 Up and she used the napkin to blot her lipstick.

"I hate lipstick on glasses, don't you? How'd you like the gala last night?"

"It was nice. Nice venue, nice people, good food."

"I saw you dancing with Tasha's buddy."

"Reg Handleman? He's a good dancer."

"That's a good photo in the paper. Know what that bowl cost? Thirty-five hundred. I brought you my paper, but I see you already have some."

The papers were stacked on the bookcase. I wondered what else she'd discovered in my apartment.

"A friend brought them by earlier," I said. And that friend was going to a lot of trouble at my request, trying to help Todd. I needed to do my part. I sighed. "You saw the mess in Todd's house. Where do you think he's going to find a birth certificate?"

"That's his problem. You have any pink paper?"

"No."

She had an apartment in mind for him, too. "A little complex near the amphitheater. But I need a reference to show the owner. Can you write one?"

"I guess I can, but you've known him as long as I have."

"Really? I thought he lived in that house on Andrews."

"I think he does. But I just met him a few days ago." I didn't say he'd been snooping around Patti's desk the first time I saw him.

"Are you advising him about the sale of his house?" She had a miniature keyboard and kept her fingers straight as she keyed numbers into an iPad.

"If he asked anything I knew about. Riley's helping him, too."

"Oh, no, not Riley. I don't want Riley dealing with Todd. You do it."

I couldn't believe that. "Why can't Riley do it? He's a banker. He knows more about finance than I do."

"I can't answer any questions, Cleo. Ethics, you know. But I really don't want Riley involved. Now, how much rent can Todd afford? I could give him a little break on this apartment I have in mind if his house weren't such a pigsty." Her voice went thoughtful. "Maybe I'll raise the security deposit enough to cover a deep cleaning when he leaves. The girlfriend seemed reliable, but she's too old for him, don't you think?"

"Are you talking about Patti? She's not his girlfriend. She's trying to help him."

"Hmm," she said. "Think she's got a job?"

I'd had enough.

"She's the director of resident services here. And she's engaged to a wonderful man." Wishes she were, I meant. I wondered why Vickie hadn't seen Patti and Stewart at last night's gala. Maybe her radar just kicked in at a certain income level?

She laughed. "What do you plan to tell Todd about the fast versus high question? I can sell it this week if he'll accept a low offer from an investor, or I can sell it for ten or fifteen percent more if he's willing to wait a few months. The season really begins about March, when the snowbirds start thinking about how cold it is at home."

"I'm sure he wants both fast and high." I sighed. "Maybe he should get a second opinion."

Vickie rolled her eyes. "Anybody else will ask the exact same questions. And he likes me. I've already got the estate sale woman tied up. No pink paper? What colors do you have?"

I didn't have any colored paper, just white.

"I guess I'll have to run to the office. I thought everybody had pink paper."

I walked to her car with her. "Vickie, I'm curious." She got in and I was about to close the door. "Do you really know something about Riley Meddors?"

"Nothing bad." She smiled at me. "You two aren't a couple, are you?"

I gave my head a maybe shake and shrugged. "Too early to say."

"He's cute, with that little beard. Thanks for the contact last night. I thought Dr. Handleman might be interested in Todd's house but sounds like he's thinking bay front. We've been out looking this morning." She grinned and grabbed for the car door. "I'd better go. Lots to do and I hate to be late."

Dr. Handleman. It was the first time I'd heard that. A PhD in engineering, I supposed. Two days ago, he'd been thinking of renting a Harbor Village apartment, but after a few hours with Vickie, he was thinking bay front. Or somebody was. I smiled to myself.

Ann was backing out of her garage. I waved to Vickie and turned to see Ann's window going down. She stuck her head out.

"You're missing lunch in the dining room. I didn't eat, either. Looks like Carla might set a new record, even without us. I'm going to the grocery store and then to Evie's."

"Usher came by. We had a nice talk."

"Did you learn anything?"

"I really don't know. Vickie came before he left. I haven't had time to think yet."

I went back to the apartment, picked up glasses and dirty napkins, and took them to the kitchen. One glass had lipstick all over it. "Don't you just hate that?" I asked the cat. I cleaned it off before putting the glass into the dishwasher.

I wasn't hungry, but I made a cup of tea. Then I took a few sheets of paper—white—out of the printer tray and stretched out on the couch. It was pretty much the first free minute I'd had all week, and it felt heavenly. I could feel myself winding down, like a feather floating to earth. Tinkerbelle came in and sniffed around, then hopped up beside my feet. Now, what had I learned in the last few hours? And was I finally ready to accept Handleman as one of the good guys?

I raised my head and stretched to reach a book on the coffee table and stuck it under the papers for a make-do desk. Then I began writing down the names of men Usher had noticed in Royale Court this week, men with the strength to strangle someone: Handleman, Todd Barnwell, Terry Wozniak, Travis, and Jim. Could the murderer be someone I'd never heard of? Certainly, and I sincerely hoped that would be the case. I wrote a big X on the list to denote those unknown individuals. Then I added another name. Usher Slump had been in Royale Court, with ample opportunity to commit murder. Did he have the physical ability? I might've doubted it before I saw him crush a can with his hands yesterday. But there was someone else I'd wanted there, too. Who was it?

I closed my eyes, thinking. My pencil slipped and drew a curved line that dribbled off to nothing before it reached the edge of the paper. I heard the phone ringing at some point, but I didn't bother waking up to answer it.

An hour later Vickie called, rousing me from the first nap I'd had all week. I was freezing and needed to pee.

"Just thought I'd let you know, all Todd's paperwork is signed. I'm putting a sale sign in the yard right now, and I'll run some flyers off for Wilma in case she knows somebody looking for a house. Help me spread the word, okay?"

"Okay," I muttered, dropping my feet to the floor and struggling to a vertical position.

"I've got two prospects already. Neither one's jumping at it yet, even though Terry's been hounding me for months to get him a house or a condo at Harbor Village. I'll give him a few days to get over this stupid car show and try again. We're going to do the estate sale next weekend. Can you distribute notices to all your residents if I send you the text? It's really short notice, but I want to be ready if things move fast."

"Did you get his birth certificate?"

"Naw. I think he's safe." She laughed. "Sweet little Todd's not going to sue me. Can you believe he asked me out?"

Yes, I could believe it. I could even believe she'd encouraged it.

We hung up and I raced to the bathroom. When I got back to the living room, I noticed my list of names still on the couch. I picked it up and added a note.

Vickie had clearly said that *Terry* had hounded her for months. It wasn't a common name, and Wozniak was definitely the hounding type. I wrote under his name: *interested in Todd's house?* Usher had just told me Wozniak invested in real estate and was engaged in some kind of investment competition with Devon Wheat. Why would he stall around when Vickie called him about Todd Barnwell's house?

Handleman's name was on the list, too. I thought about striking it but remembered his claim that Travis sent him to see Wheat.

How likely was that?

Perhaps he'd masterminded the scam with Devon Wheat's assistance.

Then why warn us against it?

I went back and forth. Scams went wrong sometimes. If law enforcement was hot on the trail, guilty people might look for scapegoats, and dead men didn't defend themselves.

I wavered but left Handleman's name on the list and took my cup of tea to the kitchen.

While it nuked for a minute, I checked phone messages.

Nita had called, inviting me to dinner. "Just the four of us. Come about five thirty and we'll eat at six."

She didn't say who the fourth was, but I guessed Riley and I were now officially a couple in her view. She didn't even ask for a confirmation call, but with the lecture series squeezing out our usual visits last week, and with a murder now in our midst, we did have a lot to talk about.

The microwave beeped and I removed my cup, walked back to the living room, sat at the computer, and changed my Wi-Fi password. When I looked up, Riley was coming up the sidewalk. We reached the porch at the same time.

He stepped inside and, without saying a word, presented a plastic bag with one of the printed announcements in it. I put my cup down and he handed over another bag holding the envelope.

"On the desk," he said. "Both of them."

The blank line on the invitation had a name written in pretty script. Wheat Wealth Management.

"No phone number, no address." I looked at Riley. "Which wouldn't be necessary if the recipient was in frequent contact. Like Todd's grandfather."

He nodded.

There was a third item, too, in its own bag: a thin little pamphlet titled *Prospectus*. "The old man didn't bite on many offers, but he kept everything."

Riley put his hands on my waist and we kissed, once and then again. Nice. I could get used to that. I was smiling when I pulled away and looked back at the invitation.

"Usher Slump says he got one, too, but he might've thrown it away. And a Birmingham business broker he's dealing with got one. Devon Wheat was squeezing people for funds, and I think I know why. Want a cup of tea?"

"I was thinking about lunch. Does Usher Slump have money? Enough for a share of a Royale?"

"Good question. He doesn't have a big salary, I know. And he tried to sell Royale Court without Ann's knowledge. Unfortunately, the buyer he found was Devon Wheat."

Riley's brows went up and he whistled softly. "Do you know what a Fairhope retail shop sells for?"

"How about a dozen shops?" I looked at the time. "Nita's invited us at five thirty. Can you wait until then to eat? Or I can fix you something."

"I've got another surprise for you. Guess what's under that blue tarp in Todd's garage."

"What?"

"A yellow bicycle."

A shiver of dread slithered down my spine. "Really? Devon Wheat's bike? In Todd's garage?"

He held up a finger, cautioning me. "I don't know that it's Wheat's. I do know it's a yellow bicycle."

"Well, what do we do about it? Call the cops again?"

"Are they looking for a yellow bicycle?"

"I suppose. They were."

He grimaced and shrugged. "I guess you call them. The worst she'll do is harangue you if they've already found it."

Mary Montgomery answered this time, and it wasn't a bad call. "Riley's got something to tell you." I passed the phone to him.

Chapter 18

Riley told Montgomery about the bike in Todd's garage and then returned the phone to me.

"He found another one of those printed investment invitations on the desk," I told her. "It's here at my apartment now and Wheat's business name is written in."

"I want it. I hope you didn't handle it. I may need a search warrant for the bike." Montgomery sounded weary. "It would be a Sunday."

"Want to go to the pier?" Riley asked when I hung up. "I'd like to keep some distance from Todd until the bike's out of here."

I got a jacket and my phone, hung my bag on my shoulder, and locked the door. As we stepped from the porch to the sidewalk, I glanced toward Riley's apartment. "Can you look out your kitchen window and see me on my porch?"

He shook his head. "I can't even walk down the sidewalk without feeling like I'm stalking you."

I laughed. "So, if I were sitting here on my porch with somebody—a murderer, let's say—I'm on my own?"

He winced. "Cleo. I think you're getting obsessed with this murder."

I thought so, too. And there was only one way out.

It was breezy, and there were lots of cars still in front of L'Etoile Bistro for Sunday brunch. But in an interesting reversal, half the parking spaces around the circular drive at the pier were empty.

"We should've asked if Nita wanted to ride with us," I said.

"It's too cold for her. It may be too cold for us, too. You're sure you want to walk?"

"Let's go."

It was cool but not too cool. The wind was out of the southwest, often a sign of approaching rain and definitely an indication that my hair would be in my face on the return walk. I pulled my jacket close and walked fast, thinking we could make one trip out and back, then warm up in the car.

"Sailboats." Riley pointed to the north, toward the yacht club. Half a dozen small boats were lined up and racing for shore. He got his hand back into a jacket pocket right away. The wind was stiff and my cheeks and lips were chapping with every step.

We passed the restaurant at the middle of the pier and the little marina beyond it. Ten or fifteen boats were tied up there, bobbing with the waves, lines jingling and clanking.

We met a group of walkers as we approached the fishing platform at the end of the pier. One woman spoke to me but kept walking. I'd gone several steps before I realized who she was.

Prissy!

The same age as Devon Wheat. Worked in the shop where his body was found. Knew he was buying Royale Court. Why wasn't she on my list of suspects? There was the matter of physical capability—was Prissy physically strong enough to strangle someone? I turned to take another look at her, but her group had rearranged itself and I couldn't identify her at such a distance.

Riley watched. "What's up?"

"Ann's niece. Could someone my size have strangled Devon Wheat?"

He grimaced and shook his head. "You're full of troubling questions today. I prefer to think that's not possible."

A few people stood on the fishing platform at the end of the pier, a quarter of a mile out in the bay. All were bundled up, their lines strung out taut to the north. The resident pelican was there, too, supervising. It looked gigantic up close and hopped away when anyone came near.

The sun was almost obscured by clouds. It was still hours away, but there seemed to be little prospect for a magnificent sunset today.

"I guess they're rare this time of year," Riley said.

We didn't linger, just turned around and headed for shore, shoulders hunched against the wind. It didn't feel quite so fierce coming from our back, but I was already half frozen.

My phone rang before we reached the restaurant on the return leg. The ID was a surprise. Travis McKenzie? On a weekend? But Stephanie was in Houston, flying back to Birmingham about now. I signaled a stop to Riley, pulled my collar up in an attempt to shield the phone from the wind, and answered.

"Hi," Travis said. "How was the banquet?"

"Good. Is there a problem?"

"Does there have to be a problem for me to call?"

"Sorry. I'm on the pier and it's windy. But I'm glad you called. I wanted to ask you something."

"Shoot."

"Did you know Devon Wheat? The man who was killed."

He hesitated but sounded normal when he answered. "I talked with him a few times. He was a friend of my sister-in-law when she lived there. We'd run into him at restaurants."

There was a long pause. So long that I thought I'd lost the connection, which happened sometimes at the pier. "I bought into that scam, Cleo. A quarter of a million. I can't believe I did it. I've kicked myself to Waco and back, but yes, I knew him. Not well, obviously. Not nearly well enough."

"I'm so sorry." I paced back and forth, a few steps in each direction. It was easier to hear when I faced east. "I guess that explains why you left early."

"My attorney's working on it now. I hope he can salvage something, and I've learned my lesson. I'll stick with what I know from now on."

"You visited him in Royale Court last week? It's a good thing the security cameras weren't working. Otherwise, the cops would be talking with you about now."

There was another pause. "Is that true? The cameras weren't working?"

"So I hear. Did you invest through Devon Wheat?"

"He had a good line. My advisor tried to tell me, but I didn't listen."

"Maybe your check hasn't cleared yet."

"It's been a while."

"Well, good luck." I asked about his weekend.

Stephanie and her little family were already on their way back to Birmingham, he said. Their weekend together had been good. He'd call later, maybe tomorrow.

After he hung up, I realized why he'd called. He was feeling lonely after Stephanie's departure.

Riley was waiting up ahead, sheltered by the corner of the restaurant, watching the last of the little sailboats blend into the coastline.

I caught up with him as I dropped the phone into my bag. "Stephanie's been in Houston for the weekend."

My hand was stiff with cold. He cradled it with his and tucked both into his warm jacket pocket as we walked toward the shore. I had a lump in my throat. I not only felt sorry for Travis, but I also felt guilty for misleading Riley. True, Stephanie had been in Houston, but saying it the way I did implied that the call had been from her. My teeth were chattering by the time we reached the car.

Riley started the engine and turned on the seat heaters. "This wasn't such a good idea, was it? I need better excuses to see you."

"You could just come to the apartment, you know. Everybody else did today." I rubbed my hands together, then rubbed my arms with both hands. "That was Travis on the phone just now. Can you keep a secret?"

He recoiled and stared. "What?"

"Maybe it shouldn't be a secret. Maybe the cops need to know. But I don't want to tell them."

"Tell them what?" he asked again, putting his hand on my shoulder so I'd look at him.

I told him about Travis's investment in the Royale.

He leaned back and relaxed, still holding my shoulder. "A quarter million? Ouch!" He gave me a squeeze. "I was afraid you might be going back to him."

I laughed and shook my head. "That's one thing you don't have to worry about. There's a new man in my life."

"Hmm." He smiled, then took my hand and kissed it. "I hope you'll be very happy."

On the drive home, Riley gave a last-minute signal and turned in at Piggly Wiggly. "Nita asked for some wine. I won't be long."

I got out of the car to go with him and saw Vickie Wiltshire just coming out of the new drugstore.

"Cleo! Long time no see!" she called. "Riley, I hope you've made a decision, sweetheart." She wagged her finger. "Ticktock."

"How are you, Vickie?" He sounded remote.

"I just got Todd's house listed. I'll put it on MLS tonight and there's already another person interested. Don't tell me y'all are hungry again! After that big dinner last night? Whew! I've got enough bread pudding to last a week."

Riley gave her an impatient wave and nudged me forward. "You want anything?"

"I seem to have missed something."

As I was saying the words and going through the automatic door, I almost missed another thing. Mary Montgomery was charging toward the exit, carrying a bag from the deli.

"Hey, Mary!"

She looked up, frowning. "I just came from your apartment."

"A social call?"

Riley gave a wave and went on without me.

Mary snorted, as if the idea of paying me a social call was a ridiculous one. "Chief says you got more information about Wheat."

The woman at the nearest checkout looked up. "Wheat? That guy who got stabbed with knitting needles?"

Mary gave the poor woman one of her stares. "You know anything about it?"

I knew those stares were withering, but the checkout lady seemed unaffected. She shook her head. "I hear it all. Hope you find the guy."

Mary persisted. "You think it's a guy? With knitting needles?"

"Is that right?" She shrugged and scanned a bag of dog food, and I grinned at Montgomery.

She rolled her eyes. "You going home? I'll come by later."

"Bring your food and talk with us while you eat. We'll be there in a minute."

"Hmm," she grunted.

She was on the porch a few minutes later, when Riley and I got there.

I offered to open my bottle of merlot, but Montgomery was on duty. So we sat at my dining table and Mary wolfed down a barbecue sandwich while Riley and I built up our appetites. "You aren't hungry?" she asked him.

"I am hungry. But we're going to dinner in a little while."

"Why didn't you tell me?" She started to pick up her food, but I put out a hand to stop her.

"We aren't invited until five thirty."

Riley looked at his watch. "Actually, I may go earlier. Jim's watching football. Washington's our team."

Montgomery thanked us for the tip on the bicycle. "The kid says he found it in the alley behind the Bistro. Any chance he's telling the truth?"

I said yes. Riley wasn't sure. But we told her some other things we'd learned that day, most of which she already knew, and turned over the new investment invitation. I asked if Prissy had been interviewed.

Montgomery gave an emphatic nod. "Oh, yes."

"You think a woman could strangle a man?" I asked.

Montgomery held her arms out and looked down at her pumpkin-shaped form. "I'm a woman, if you haven't noticed. Think I could strangle somebody?"

There was no doubt.

She hadn't heard about the prowler in the knit shop Thursday night.

"Ann said she hadn't told you about it."

She bristled. "And why not?"

"She thought it wasn't important. Kids, probably, and they didn't take anything. Not even some cash she leaves there."

"What were they doing? Trying to scare her? See, that's what happens when people don't open up about what they know. We could've questioned Prissy about it. Probably cleared it up."

Riley asked, "Did you get any fingerprints from the invitation Ann found?"

"A bunch." She looked at me. "Yours, probably. We need to get your prints for elimination."

"Remember Todd wanted to invest in a Royale, the car mentioned in the invitation."

"Royale as in Royale Court." She frowned. "Was this car at the show?"

"No. Only six or seven were made, eighty years ago."

"And worth millions?" She shook her head. "Ain't no car worth millions. How does that happen?"

"Scarcity and demand," Riley answered, "if economics is anything to go by. *Why* are people willing to pay so much? For that, you'll need a psychologist. Probably something related to toilet training." He told her about Grandfather Barnwell's list of approved investments. "There were about forty options. Blue chips. No exotic automobiles."

Montgomery shrugged. "Well, there was some sense in the gene pool at one time. And Devon Wheat was managing the money? Odd choice for the old man."

Riley agreed. "The kid's immature. His grandfather probably thought Wheat would relate better."

I reminded her that Handleman claimed the particular car cited in the investment invitation didn't exist. "Wikipedia disagrees."

"But the scam's real," Riley said. "There's always somebody willing to take your money, and Todd would've been easy prey."

His phone rang as I was seeing Montgomery off. He stayed inside talking for a minute, then followed us out to the porch and told Mary good-bye.

"That was Jim," Riley said. "You want to go over now?"

"Football? I guess not."

He left, and I went next door to talk with Ann.

"I was just thinking about heating some soup. You hungry?"

"Starving, but I'm going to dinner soon. Fix something for yourself if you want to."

She waved me to the couch and I asked about Evie.

"She's got a cold, but it's not flu. I told her to stay home a day or two. I hope you've got something to tell me."

"I'm working on it. I want to know what happened Thursday night. What makes you think someone went into the knit shop?"

"There's no *think* about it, honey. Somebody was there." She went back to her chair. "First of all, the lock's not commercial quality. A credit card can open it. I figured there's no point installing dead bolts on a knit shop. Anyway, if somebody wants in, they don't have to break the glass. And this was a polite prowler Thursday night. He even locked up when he left."

"So how do you know he was there?"

She rolled her eyes. "There's no doubt. Somebody went through everything. Special orders, invoices, yarn substitution guides. Laid everything out on the counter, even customers' measurements and design notes."

"But didn't take anything?"

"We're planning this February retreat, with menus and class schedules and supply lists. It's a huge undertaking. If I'd had any idea—well, just say he took it all apart, spread things out everywhere, and left it. If we had anything confidential, I'd be worried. But there's not. No social security numbers, no bank account information. And nothing was taken."

"Not even money, you said."

"We leave thirty dollars in the register every night. That's the change fund for the next day. It was all there. No indication he even touched the register."

"And you know it wasn't Prissy? Maybe she went in late and did some planning for the retreat."

She was shaking her head. "That was my first thought, but Prissy lacks initiative. If the place were on fire, she'd wait to see what I thought about calling the fire department. I asked her anyway, and asked Usher, too. By the way, he came to see Evie this afternoon. He says you gave him courage."

"Really?"

"Did he rave the whole time?"

I shook my head. "No. He seemed better today."

Ann sighed deeply. "Cleo, did Usher murder that man? If he did, I hope you'll give him the strength to admit it."

I didn't know the answer to that question, and I didn't want to tell her his name was still on my list of suspects.

* * * *

Scooping the cat box and walking to the garbage bins was a daily chore. It was only a week since Daylight Savings Time had ended and now it was getting dark by late afternoon. I lifted the lid of the container, dropped the plastic bag into the bin, and let the lid drop back in place with a soft thud.

Todd Barnwell stood a few feet away, watching me. Goose bumps shot up my arms.

"You startled me." I brushed my hands together.

"I saw you coming. Are you going to town?"

"Well, no, I wasn't. Are you looking for a ride?"

He looked taller at such close proximity, but slender and boyish. While he was on my list of possible suspects, he was a bit like Travis—someone I didn't quite take seriously as a bad guy.

He nodded about wanting a ride and jammed his hands into his jeans pockets. "The cops took the bike. I wasn't riding it anyway." He walked beside me, up the sidewalk toward my apartment.

"How did you come to have Devon's bike?"

"Just took it. Like, to bug him. But when I heard he was dead, I was afraid people might think…you know. I was going to put it back, but I had to figure out when, so I wouldn't have to explain stuff. It was just easier to put it in the garage and cover it up. I guess Vickie saw it when she looked at the house. Or Riley, maybe. You didn't turn me in, I know."

"How do you know that?"

He did a full-body shrug with a laugh.

"And do the cops suspect you?" I asked. "Have they interviewed you yet?"

"Yeah, yeah. But I don't know anything."

"You know where you got the bike, and when. That could be pretty important to the investigation."

"That's what they said, and I told them, behind the Bistro, Wednesday night. We went over and over all that."

"Come in and have a 7 Up. How do you think the bike got to the alley?"

He began to get agitated. "That's what they asked and I have no idea. I just found it there. You got a beer?"

I shook my head. "You're not twenty-one. Right now, it's 7 Up or water. Or coffee, tea, or milk. Have you decided about moving? Vickie says she found an apartment in town."

"Okay, 7 Up. Got anything to eat?"

"I can find something."

"Vickie was going to show me the apartment this afternoon but the cops took care of that. She says she's writing up an offer on the house."

"That was fast." I thought about her remark about fast versus high. "Remember, you don't have to accept if the offer's not a good one."

I made two sandwiches, one with peanut butter and jelly, and another with some tuna salad I'd bought at Publix. "You can eat one of these now and take the other one home for later."

I poured a glass of milk and gave him a plate with the two sandwiches, paper napkins, and a plastic bag for any leftovers. "Why don't we sit on the porch? Will you be warm enough?"

"You sound like a mom."

"I am a mom."

I took the love seat and turned on the heron lamp. "I'm trying to understand exactly what happened to Devon Wheat. And I think you can help me."

The milk and one sandwich were half gone. "Why do you care?" He spoke with his mouth full, then chewed and swallowed. "You didn't even know him."

"I've been asked to help clear someone who may be a suspect. I'd like to ask you a couple of questions. Then I'll drive you into town, but you'll have to arrange another way to get home. I've got plans for tonight."

"Riley?"

I nodded. "And Nita and Jim Bergen. Do you know them?"

He started on the second sandwich. "It's kinda cool, hanging out here."

"When was the last time you saw Devon Wheat alive?"

He chewed and swallowed. "He got killed Wednesday night? I saw him the night before. We ate together."

"At the Bistro? What did you have?"

"Why does that matter?"

"It contributes to the big picture. Could take some heat off you."

"Well, I did eat with him. And I always get the same thing, a cheeseburger with sweet potato chips. That's their specialty. I don't remember what he got, maybe some kind of burger with mushrooms, maybe a pizza. And he always had beer. Blue Moon."

"And you talked about your trust fund?"

He sighed. "We always talked about the same thing. Money. How much, when can I get it, what I'm going to do with it. How much I owe him." He laughed.

"Do you know who might've killed him?"

He shook his head. I tried to picture him in a struggle with Devon Wheat. Did he have any muscles? "You went to the Bistro with him often? Did you meet there or go together?"

"I drove Pop's car sometimes or walked. Or caught a ride. He'd stop by after work. Or after his bike ride. He only drove his car if it was, like, raining."

"And he parked the bike in the alley?"

"The alley? Why'd you say that?"

"You said you found his bike in the alley."

He shook his head. "The patio has this wall—you can see through but you can't get out there. If you could, nobody'd pay. You never went to the Bistro? You oughta go. Get Vickie to meet us sometime. Riley can come, too. We could do it tonight."

"Some other time maybe. Tell me this. On a normal night, where did Devon Wheat leave his bike? Not in the alley, you said."

"Chained to a tree out front. Like everybody else."

"But you found his bike in the alley."

"Yeah, after he was dead."

"How'd it get there?"

He shrugged, seemingly frustrated by all the questions. I'd let this be the last one.

"It was there Wednesday night. That weird guy was checking it out. Usher? I thought if he could take it, I could, too, so I rode it home." He laughed. "Maybe Usher left it in the alley. Maybe Usher killed him—did you think about that? I saw you talking to him."

Well, that answered one question, whether anyone would notice if I sat on my porch with a possible murderer. Or maybe it was the murderer who noticed.

He raised the glass and drank the last drop of milk. "I went to Devon's office the next morning and everything was roped off. You were there—is that when you found him?"

I nodded. "I remember seeing you. You wouldn't speak to me."

"Hey, I'd just found out he was dead. There I was with the dead guy's bicycle, cops all over the place. What was I supposed to do?"

"What *did* you do, ride his bike home again?"

"Yeah." He grinned and nodded. "Rode it home and put it in the garage."

"One last question. How do you suppose the bike got to the alley?"

He looked at me from the corner of his eyes. "I probably think the same thing you do. It was, like, a getaway vehicle."

"Can you show me where you found it?"

"Sure. Let's go."

I took the empty plate and several glasses to the sink and got my things.

Nita called as we walked to the garage. "The boys are in Jim's office watching sports, but I barely hear it from the living room. We can sit and talk if you'd like."

There was a long pause after I told her I was driving Todd to the Bistro.

"Cleo...by yourself? Do you think that's wise?"

"No problem. He's going to show me where he found Devon Wheat's bicycle. And I want to see how far that is from Royale Court, so I can visualize things better. I'm trying to help Ann decide what to do." I smiled at Todd, who was listening. "I'll be at your apartment by five thirty."

"Please be careful," Nita said.

"I'll be fine," I assured her.

Chapter 19

As we drove into town, Todd asked, "Exactly where is this apartment Vickie found?"

"All I know is near the amphitheater."

"I've got the address. Can we take a look?"

I agreed to drive past it. "I'm sure it's locked up, but you can see what it looks like."

He took a scrap of pink paper out of his shirt pocket and read off an address on South School Street, which ran straight and level beside the community college and then turned twisty. The house number came up on a mailbox in front of a handsome house, set back from and elevated above a paved parking area. I pulled to the curb beside the mailbox. Lights were on in the main house, which stepped in multiple levels up a heavily wooded slope, unlike most of Fairhope. Beyond the parking area was a separate garage with stairs on the outside and a balcony on the second level.

"Can I afford that?" Todd sounded incredulous.

"You're looking at the garage apartment, aren't you?" I pointed. "Not the house." It did look appealing.

"Very private," he muttered, staring.

"Might be hard to get your furniture upstairs."

He snorted. "What furniture?"

"Whatever you keep from your grandfather's place."

He shook his head. "My style's more modern. Chrome and leather, maybe."

"Well, I'm sure you'll have fun furnishing it. If you get the apartment." I drove to the next wide driveway and turned around. Todd craned his neck for another look as we passed again.

We continued into the downtown area, passed the clock, and circled a block before parking near the Bistro.

Todd looked around. "I thought you'd go to de la Mare."

"Okay."

Daylight was fading. I started up again, circled a different block, and parked down the street from Royale Court.

He vacillated when we got out but finally made a decision. "This way."

We walked to the corner, turned, and entered the dark, deserted alleyway in back of the drugstore.

Back doors to the main-street shops were steel, windowless, and painted to match the buildings. Some had little stoops with a bench or a tiny shed roof, or a stack of wood crates or other cast-off items. All of them had garbage containers, one or more beside every door, heavy-duty plastic carts or small dumpsters sitting tipsy and higgledy-piggledy. The smell of cigarette smoke and dead fish permeated everything, and light was fading rapidly.

A few weedy saplings had sprouted between the pavement and the back walls of buildings, where they'd grown to substantial heights. I looked above eye level and saw a rat perched on a branch, looking back at me with beady little eyes.

"Oh my god."

I backed away fast, hoping it wouldn't jump into my hair or, if it did, that my death would be dignified. "I've seen enough."

Todd picked up a pebble and flipped it into the branches. "They're everywhere back here. Must be hundreds."

The rat ran upward, hopped one branch to another, and finally onto the flat roof. I shivered and pulled my sweater close, and we walked on.

The alley was just wide enough for a small garbage truck to squeeze through.

"It's pretty tight in here," I said. "Do the garbage trucks back out?"

"Naw, the alley goes through behind the fish place." He grinned. "We could've come that way. It's closer, but it stinks."

I looked down the alley, estimating where we'd left the car. The patio, walled off with latticework, was near the point where the alley took a ninety-degree turn.

"Right here," Todd stopped abruptly and gestured to an open area.

A garbage cart and half a dozen wooden pallets were on one side of a graveled space, a battered blue mini dumpster on the other. "This is where the bike was."

The garbage cart was four feet tall and so overfilled that the top stood open. I saw cardboard, hunks of Styrofoam, a few black plastic bags, neatly tied. Loose paper was jammed against the side of the cart.

Todd poked through everything.

"Look at this!" He sounded indignant. "I coulda got fifty bucks for this!"

He pulled out pieces of a Bugatti Royale poster, two feet by three feet before it was ripped apart. He handed the heavy cardstock pieces to me and leaned into the cart to dig again. Finally, he backed away from the container and inspected the buildings beside us.

"What is this place? Reckon they've got more posters?"

I was still holding the ripped one, standing in the center of the alley and keeping watch for rats. The building had no visible identification. I counted the closed steel doors. "It's a green building, two doors from the Bistro."

"Let's go around front and see what it is. Maybe somebody's here."

He set off, retracing our route to the side street.

I handed the poster pieces to him as we walked. "Do you want to keep this? It's no good like it is. What would you do with it anyway?"

He took the pieces from me. "I could sell it online if it was still in one piece. Poster collectors love this stuff."

We walked to Fairhope Avenue. At the middle of the block, green paint identified the office of the Henry George Utopian Tax Colony. Lights were on inside and a plain white pickup was parked out front. Two doors farther on was L'Etoile Bistro, with cars lined up on both sides of the street. Light and music spilled out to the sidewalk.

The Colony office was unlocked. A bell chimed when Todd pulled the door open.

"Anybody here?" he called.

Terry Wozniak was walking around the glass partition, coming toward us.

I was pinging with anxiety, which I attributed to rats and encountering Wozniak unexpectedly. Fortunately, Todd did the talking.

He showed Wozniak the ripped poster and spoke tactfully. "I found this in the garbage out back. I wondered if you got any more. I collect them."

Wozniak looked at the pieces, then at me. "Ms. Mack." He didn't sound particularly friendly.

"Mr. Wozniak. We missed you at the gala last night."

He glanced back at the ripped poster and suddenly lunged, grabbing the pieces from Todd's grip. With quick, savage motions, he gave them another rip and then another. But as he did so, I got a good look at his forearms, visible below rolled shirtsleeves.

White gauze bandages covered both arms but the tape had come loose on his right arm. The rectangular bandage dangled free, revealing deep red scratches on pale skin.

I gasped reflexively and covered my mouth. The lacerations were angry and irregular, and I couldn't avoid thinking of the ferociousness with which they'd been inflicted.

My gaze slid upward and met Wozniak's. As he took a step toward me, I reached back for the door.

"Hold on," he ordered.

The bell chimed.

"Come, Todd." I exited to the sidewalk.

Wozniak followed me. "I need to explain."

"Come on, Todd," I called louder, backing across the sidewalk, almost to the curb as I thought about what the scratches meant. No wonder he'd skipped the final lecture, and the gala.

Todd appeared in the doorway behind Wozniak. "If you find any more, just hang on to them." He was still trying to close the deal on some posters. "I'll check back..."

"Todd!" I yelled as Wozniak whirled and grabbed.

"Hey!"

He dodged past Wozniak and we began to sprint down the sidewalk, with Wozniak in pursuit.

"I can explain," he shouted.

We turned the corner but didn't slow down.

"What was that about?" Todd demanded, looking over his shoulder.

I was puffing as we crossed the entrance to the alley. "He killed Devon Wheat." I plunged on toward de la Mare.

Todd stayed beside me. "How do you know?"

We turned onto de la Mare Street and my car came into view. I finally felt safe slowing down. Not that I had much choice. My pulse was pounding and my voice came out in little gasps.

"Todd, what exactly is a stranglehold? How would you strangle someone with a towel?"

He looked confused. "You want me to show you? Here?" He shook his head.

"Yes, just show me," I panted. We had walked a few feet from the corner, but my car was still some distance ahead. "I know you put the towel around the neck, but doesn't the victim fight back?"

He stepped behind me, hesitated, then stretched one arm across my neck. Suddenly, I was jerked backward. Trapped.

I gasped.

Todd was speaking normally, giving no hint that he was an inch away from inflicting a mortal injury. "You could use a towel, I guess, or just apply pressure with the arms."

His left hand came up, tightening the arm angled across my throat. He took a step back and I staggered and lost my footing.

"I hope nobody's seeing this. They'd think I'm attacking you."

I could make the same mistake. My hands went up, pushing at his arm. Scratching and clawing would have come in another instant. I signaled for release and Todd helped me regain my balance before letting go. We walked on.

When I could speak, I asked, "Did you see Wozniak's arm? It's all scratched up."

He seemed stunned. "I saw bandages. You think Devon fought him? Was there blood under his fingernails?"

I felt a twinge of panic. The o*h-my-god* chorus started softly and synchronized with my steps. Royale Court was just ahead, on the opposite side of the street. I pointed to the filigree arch.

"Let's go in here, where we aren't so exposed. I need to make a call."

I called FPD, got Mary Montgomery for once, and told her what I'd just seen. "The office manager said Wozniak burned himself, but his arm is covered in scratches."

"Where are you now?" she asked calmly.

"Todd and I are in Royale Court. My car's right down the street."

"And Wozniak's still at the Colony office?"

"He was. He followed us at first but gave up."

Todd went to Boudreau's and looked in a window. "They're closed but there's a light in the kitchen. I'll see if anybody's here." He walked through the breezeway and out of sight.

"Stay where you are," Montgomery said. "Someone will be right there."

I disconnected and walked toward the fountain, which splashed and dripped onto potted red impatiens that stood on risers in the lowest pool. I sat on the curved concrete bench and bent forward, rubbing my forehead, my breathing still ragged and the *oh-my-god* chorus drowning out Dixieland that played on the courtyard speakers.

It drowned out Terry Wozniak's footsteps, too. I didn't realize he was there until he stepped in front of me and dropped onto the bench at my side.

His breath came in little gasps. "Where's your friend?"

"Ohh," I groaned softly and stood, looking around. Where had Todd gone?

Wozniak grabbed my wrist and jerked. I sat down abruptly. His sleeves covered his arms now and were buttoned snugly at the wrists.

I lifted my phone but he grabbed and hurled it toward the fountain. "I've got to explain."

Oh-my-god. His eyes looked like that rat in the tree. I forced myself not to slap him away and tried to follow his gush of explanation, a tangled tale about hard work and privation and cheats like Devon Wheat.

I couldn't bear to look at him, but he jerked my arm when I turned away. A low groan of dread blotted out half his words, and I was vaguely aware that the sound was coming from me.

When Todd reappeared in the breezeway beside Boudreau's, I waved him away with my free hand.

"Self-defense," Wozniak babbled. "A madman...I didn't know...do you understand?" He tugged at my arm when I didn't answer immediately.

"Yes," I said. "Yes. Yes."

Oh-my-god, the chorus chanted. His face was just inches away. I turned my head and he slid closer.

"Self-defense," he said again and again, almost sobbing.

A voice boomed behind us. "Hands in the air! Stand up and move apart."

Someone was approaching from Skinny Alley, too. Suddenly, my arms were nearly ripped off my body, wrists tugged together and wrapped with zip ties.

"Don't hurt her," Todd was saying, frantic and wide-eyed, as his hands were trussed up in similar fashion.

"Don't hurt her," Wozniak said, his bright little rat eyes scrambling to watch me while a big cop manhandled him.

"Catch her," someone shouted.

I don't know who caught me, but it was a soft landing.

I've never fainted in my life and didn't then, but the rest of the evening was a bit of a jumble. I distinctly remember going up steep, shiny steps into a brightly lit ambulance, where I was checked over by medical people. I assured them I was fine but I couldn't remember when Riley got there.

Mary Montgomery stood over me at one point, blocking the light and agreeing that I was fine. She handed me my phone. "It was in the flowers. Just a little damp."

"I'll drive," I recall Todd volunteering, but Riley said I'd be going with him.

"You bring her car." He asked for my key fob and passed it to Todd.

"Does he have a license?" I asked, but nobody was listening to me.

Nita and Jim were waiting at my apartment with food, and Nita and Ann insisted I eat a few bites while Todd told them what had happened.

Jim ate without being encouraged. "Have you still got that bread pudding?" He went to the kitchen.

I took a long, hot shower that left me so limp I could barely stand. I was sitting on the side of the bed, telling Stephanie what had happened, when Riley took the phone and told her I was fine, just tired and a little confused. "She won't be alone," he promised her. "I'm sleeping on the couch."

"Take the guest room," I said, and plowed into bed.

Hours later, I got up to go to the bathroom, and when I came out, Riley was waiting, wearing sweatpants and a black T-shirt but no shoes. He tucked me into bed again without disturbing Tinkerbelle and went back to the guest room. But I couldn't get back to sleep. I thought about families—my daughter, and Riley's sons—and relationships, about the difference between administrative positions and social work, with all its strict prohibitions, and about unexpected twists of fate and how abruptly lives could end. And finally, after tossing and turning and changing my mind half a dozen times, I slipped out of bed and went to the guest room, too.

* * * *

I awoke hearing conversation. It was almost seven and Ann and Riley were out on the porch, discussing breakfast. When I'd dressed, we went next door.

Ann's round table was full of food and surrounded by people who showered me with hugs and questions about everything that had happened. Ann bustled about, passing dishes and pouring coffee.

I was starving. I ate while I told them what I remembered of Terry Wozniak's confession, still putting details together as I talked.

"He knew Devon Wheat was buying Royale Court and assumed Wheat was wealthy. So when Wheat told him about the Bugatti Royale, Wozniak insisted on getting in on the deal. Then Handleman came along and said it was all a scam, and Wozniak went back to Wheat to demand his money back."

"How did Wozniak know Royale Court was being sold?" Nita asked. "Even Ann didn't know."

"From the Colony," Usher guessed. "He spent a lot of time there, snooping."

Ann agreed. "Wozniak thinks he's a real estate tycoon."

Nita's eyes narrowed. "Vickie Wiltshire says he fed her a lot of tips."

"Not illegal," Jim said, defending the pretty lady. "She got him some good buys in return." He topped a big stack of Ann's pancakes with whipped cream and berries.

Usher wiped whipped cream from his fingers. "Wozniak asked me where Devon's money came from. I told him I didn't know he had any. I wonder if that broker will tell me how much is in the escrow account."

"I think we'll find that some of it came from the Bugatti scam." I was thinking of Travis's investment. "It might go back where it came from."

"I can assure you of that," Ann said. "Whatever's in escrow goes right back. When Olivia gets here, we'll start all over and decide if we want to sell."

"Just think—a worldwide fraud, right here in Fairhope." Dolly sounded so proud.

I hated to disappoint her. "But it didn't necessarily originate here. Devon Wheat might've been conned himself." I thought about Wozniak. "Self-defense. Wozniak said that several times."

Riley rested his arm across the back of my chair. "I guess Wheat couldn't accept the idea he'd been scammed, and attacked the messenger."

Jim agreed. "When Wheat collapsed, probably with a crushed windpipe, Wozniak dragged him to the bathroom and went back to dig around in the office. I'll bet he gave Wheat cash and thought it was still there. And when he went back to the bathroom..." He snapped his fingers. "Wheat was dead."

Nita covered her eyes.

Riley looked at Ann. "I think Wozniak took that invitation from Wheat's office and accidentally left it in your shop when he stopped to remove the camera."

"Where is the camera?" Usher asked.

"Gone." Jim was emphatic. "You can count on that."

"So Wozniak was the Thursday night prowler." I turned to look at Riley. "Looking for the invitation Ann had already brought home."

Riley nodded. "And that's why he missed most of the final lecture."

The group fell silent, thinking. After a minute, Riley squeezed my shoulder. "You okay?"

Stephanie called and I went out to the porch to talk, telling her I was fine, just having breakfast with friends, and I'd talk with her later. But she started crying, saying they had to go to Boyd's parents' home for Thanksgiving. "We promised last year, Mom. Dad says he'll meet us there and I want you, too."

"We'll talk later," I promised and finally got away. No way was she talking me into a family holiday with Travis. But before I got back to the table, who should call but Travis himself. I went out again.

"You okay?"

I told him the important points and ended with money. "I just heard Wheat has some funds in an escrow account. Maybe you can get your money back."

He sputtered. "I don't give a damn about that, Cleo. Stephanie says Wozniak killed Devon Wheat and tried to choke you!"

"Stephanie is a drama queen. It was Todd who choked me." I smiled, realizing how that sounded. "Wozniak just grabbed my arm and took my phone. But I got it back and I'm fine. Really. Just having breakfast with friends."

"That's good." He sounded confused. "Really good. So...who's got this escrow account?"

He was so predictable. I promised to find out, and prepared to click off.

"Another thing—where's Handleman? Still there?"

"He's leaving today, I think."

"You're at Julwin's? With that sweet little server?"

We were nowhere near Julwin's, but I gave his imagination free rein. "I'll tell her you said hi."

"Do something else for me. Ask Handleman if he's interested in a quick trip to Alsace in April. Tell him to call me."

"What? You're still thinking there's a car? Travis, that's crazy."

He laughed but sounded embarrassed. "Can't hurt to find out. Just give him my number."

I turned my phone off. When I got back inside, Riley stood and held my chair. What a sweet man I'd miraculously found. The song started up in my head, reminding me of my recent encounter in the guest room. My cheeks felt a little warm. I caught Nita's gaze from across the table and smiled at her.

I went to the office a little later, talked with everyone there and, between visitors, began getting my work organized and back on track.

Handleman came to say good-bye and we sat in the lobby to have coffee.

"Wikipedia says there's a seventh Royale," I said.

He smiled and shook his head. "A replica. Not twenty years old. I know a guy who worked on it."

"Travis wants you to go with him to Alsace in April. He said you should call him."

He chuckled. "Yes, we talked already. I'm looking into it. Vickie Wiltshire found a furnished apartment for February. That's usually our coldest month at home."

"Ha! Vickie Wiltshire has an apartment any month you want to come. She'll give up her own place if necessary."

We walked back to Patti's desk and Handleman returned his key.

"How'd you like the guest suite?" she asked. Within seconds she was telling him about how she'd like to redecorate it. She even knew the ideal apartment for him. "It faces east, so there's morning sun and you can use the screened porch in the evening. Unlike Cleo."

Handleman was rapt. There were five little turtles on the driftwood.

When Stewart stopped at my office later, I asked him, "Do you know anything about Patti's turtles?"

He grinned slowly. "That girl's crazy about turtles. And my pond's full of them."

I rolled my eyes and wondered.

Riley met us for lunch in the dining room and said he wanted me to meet someone at five. "Can we come to your apartment?"

"Who is it?" I asked.

"Just let it be a surprise," he said. "Can I borrow your door key?"

And it was a surprise. Riley and Michael Bonderant were waiting when I got home. Bonderant was the decorator who'd done Nita's apartment.

As we shook hands, I told him, "I love what you did for the Bergens."

Bonderant was looking around my apartment and sniffing. "But you obviously hate color. Gray and white and black, everywhere! Even your lingerie."

"You looked at my lingerie?"

He smirked. "Do you have a favorite color?"

"Anything but red. Or yellow. I wear a lot of beige and white in the summer."

"Of course you do. Now, what's your favorite piece in the Bergen apartment?"

"I like a lot of things. The lighting, the painting in the dining room, the tree with twinkle lights. But my favorite thing is that thick rug angled across the living room." I rotated my hands, indicating the angle.

Bonderant smiled like it was a trap. "And what color is that rug?"

I shrugged. "Sort of red but it works there, with all the mahogany and green."

He smirked and looked around a little more, measured the hanger space in my closet, and left.

"What a snob," I said.

Riley pulled me into a hug. "Be kind. He's got a tough job."

"Decorating is a tough job?"

"He's going to do something with Todd's house. See if he can make you like it."

I pulled away. "Todd's house? You're the one who's buying it?" I pictured the dark living room, recalled the musty smell, and shook my head. "No wonder Vickie didn't want you advising Todd. You could've talked him into anything."

"We're going to need a bigger place, Cleo. And for your information, I accepted the listing price without negotiating. You don't need to worry about my ethics. Now, on another topic, what would you think about Thanksgiving in Savannah?"

"Savannah?" I perked up. Now *that* was my idea of a nice surprise. "I love Savannah. We could go to the Johnny Mercer House." I hesitated. "But it's a long drive from here."

"Yes." He sighed and smiled. As if distance were the main attraction.

CPSIA information can be obtained
at www.ICGtesting.com
Printed in the USA
FSHW011950291020
75391FS